Hunter's Moon

Also by Sophie Masson

(Random House Australia)

Moonlight & Ashes
Scarlet in the Snow
The Crystal Heart

Written as Isabelle Merlin

Three Wishes
Pop Princess
Cupid's Arrow
Bright Angel

The Chronicles of El Jisal series

Snow, Fire, Sword
The Curse of Zohreh
The Tyrant's Nephew
The Maharajah's Ghost

Edited by Sophie Masson

The Road to Camelot

Hunter's Moon

Sophie Masson

RANDOM HOUSE AUSTRALIA

A Random House book
Published by Random House Australia Pty Ltd
Level 3, 100 Pacific Highway, North Sydney NSW 2060
www.randomhouse.com.au

Penguin
Random House
RANDOM HOUSE BOOKS

First published by Random House Australia in 2015

Random House Books is part of the Penguin Random House group of companies
whose addresses can be found at global.penguinrandomhouse.com.

National Library of Australia
Cataloguing-in-Publication Entry

Creator: Masson, Sophie, 1959– author
Title: Hunter's moon / Sophie Masson
ISBN: 978 0 85798 603 0 (pbk)
Target audience: For secondary school age
Subjects: Stepmothers – Fiction
         Debutante balls – Fiction
         Young adult fiction
Dewey number: A823.3

Cover image by Elisabeth Ansley / Trevillion Images
Cover design by Christabella Designs
Typeset by Midland Typesetters, Australia
Printed in Australia by Griffin Press, an accredited ISO AS/NZS 14001:2004
Environmental Management System printer

One

A silk dress the pearly colour of autumn mist, inserted with lace delicate as wisps of cloud stitched onto raindrop-sheer gauze. Satin shoes of the same shade to match and then, over the dress, a fine velvet cloak of the silvery shade and sheen of moonlight, with a thin ribbon of the same colour threaded through my jet-black hair. Around my neck, a pearl pendant on a fine silver chain; at my ears two pearl drops; on my finger the silver knot-ring my father Sir Anton Dalmatin and my stepmother Belladonna gave me for my seventeenth birthday, two days earlier. And by my side, Belladonna herself, watching with a smile as I paraded in front of the mirror, hardly able to recognise myself in the clothes she had chosen for me to wear at the Duke's Presentation Ball, which was to be held the following night.

'So, Bianca, what do you think?' she said, putting her golden head on one side. She makes me think of a bird when she does that – a swan, perhaps, with her gliding walk, long neck and white dress light as feathers that drapes around her graceful form. She has not long turned thirty but looks a good deal younger.

'I love it,' I answered. It was true. If I'd had dreams of a dress red as a rose, or blue as a summer sky, those dreams had vanished when the grey silk fell softly around me like a blessing.

'I'm glad,' my stepmother said. A smile sparkled in her cornflower-blue eyes. 'It's such a good colour for you, my darling. Subtle.'

I nodded. Belladonna was right, as usual. My instinct had been for bright colours, but she'd gently made me understand that it wasn't suitable. I must not draw too much attention to myself. The wrong sort of attention, that is.

'All eyes will be on you, of course, at your first big social event. You are the only child of the King of Elegance, after all.'

This was what the *Mirror*, the most popular picture paper in the land, had dubbed my father. Sir Anton Dalmatin was the owner of a string of fashionable department stores called Ladies' Fair. His first store had been right here in Lepmest, the capital of the province of Noricia, but now there were branches all over the empire.

'And elegant is what a young lady should be at all times,' Belladonna had gone on. 'Discreet, elegant, refined.'

She was right. Of course she was right. But I knew what she wasn't saying: that elegance was even more important to me than to most other young ladies for with my black hair, red lips and hazel eyes, I do not have the looks of a Norician aristocrat. My father is tall, blond, grey-eyed; my mother had also been fair, with green eyes. I had the looks of a distant ancestor, or so my father had told me. Her name was Tamara, and she'd lived two hundred years ago. Not much was known about her, but there was a family legend that she was a gypsy girl, who had spellbound my Dalmatin ancestor into marriage with her magic.

Whatever the truth, I had her looks, allied to the pale skin that was my inheritance from my mother, and the tallness that came from my father. Together, those things were less than desirable because they were unusual. And unusual was not something a Dalmatin heiress should be. I had to show I had the breeding, the poise, the effortless elegance of a girl from one of Noricia's finest families.

I'd been brought up at home by a succession of nannies, governesses and tutors, but before Belladonna came, four years ago, I'd paid very little attention to their attempts to teach me how to be a young lady. My father was away a lot on business and did not seem to notice. But Belladonna did, and she took me under her wing straight after her marriage to my father.

I'd learnt a great deal, since then. I knew how I should walk. How I should dress. How I should speak. It did not come naturally, but I loved and admired Belladonna and wanted to do my best for her. People said that a stepmother was nothing like a real mother. Perhaps that is true, but what people didn't consider was that if you hardly remember your mother, then you will have nothing to compare a stepmother to.

My mother died when I was three, and my father grieved for her for ten long years before he met Belladonna. He had not spent much time at home during that period. I think he could not bear to stay long in the house where he and my mother had been happy. It did not occur to him that I might be lonely. And for most of the time I wasn't.

Until Belladonna came, I read a lot and played with my good friends Rafiel and Margy Goran, the son and daughter of the gardener and his wife, the under-cook. Margy was my age, Rafiel three years older. He was a bold, daring, laughing sort of boy and unlike many older brothers, did not treat his younger sister like an annoyance. Or me, his sister's friend. Instead, he devised adventures for us: climbing trees to make miniature houses in the branches, or turning the back garden into an imaginary mythical land, complete with dragons we had to vanquish. Other times, we might play card games – Margy's favourite – or hide-and-seek, a game at which I was particularly good.

All that passed the time. I missed my father sometimes but because he was not around much, I didn't know him well and so I didn't think of it often. Children generally don't think about things they can't change. It was only when Belladonna married my father and came to live with us that I realised I had missed having parents who noticed me.

My father and stepmother had met in Faustina, the imperial capital. Each year, beauties from across the Empire competed for the honour of being the face of Ladies' Fair and for the prizes that came with it: money, fame, endless parties, fine clothes, jewels and at the end, very often, the hand of a smitten suitor. Four years ago, Belladonna had been chosen as Fairest Lady in the annual competition that was run by the Ladies' Fair stores and my father, as usual, was to crown the winner. Until Belladonna, my father had never shown the slightest interest in any of the Fairest Ladies. But with her, he fell in love at first sight.

I could tell right away that Belladonna was different to the other ladies. Any other woman might have jumped at the chance to marry one of the Empire's richest men and pretended instant love, too, but not Belladonna. It took my father weeks to persuade her to consider him for a husband. At first it made me worry that she wasn't truly in love but, after she married my father, Belladonna confided in me that although she had loved my father instantly, she was aware that, coming from a poorer background, people may suspect her of being a gold-digger.

That is one of the things I like about Belladonna: she is her own person. She did not have the usual cocooned life of a society woman before she met my father; she had known tragedy young when first her parents and then her grandmother died. She'd had no money so she'd left her home, the island city-state of Aurisola, to work for a living as a governess. It was only when, while on a rare holiday in Faustina, she'd been spotted by a talent scout in the street, her fate had taken a turn for the better. I admire her greatly for the rare spirit and determination she'd shown through it all. I put a high price on her good opinion. And sometimes the price could be high: she had long ago put an end to my 'unsuitable' friendships with Rafiel and Margy Goran, the servants' children, and corrected my foolish impulses with her watchfulness.

'I was thinking of also wearing my turquoise bracelet,' I said, now a little hesitantly. My father had brought the bracelet back for me from one of his trips, many years ago, and I'd treasured it as a child. 'I thought Father might be pleased to know I wore it.' For that was the only cloud on my horizon that day: Father would be unable to be there to see me being presented to the Duke because he was on urgent business far away in Aurisola.

A slight frown briefly creased Belladonna's forehead. 'It is a pretty thing for a little girl,' she said, 'but you are all grown up now. I think that is what your father would like to hear reported.'

And by that I understood that I had been about to make a faux pas. When would I ever learn what came to her so naturally?

Two

)

That evening, Belladonna hosted a lavish pre-ball event. It was to be a preview of the spring fashions which would shortly make their appearance in Ladies' Fair. Two hundred and fifty of our best and most important customers had been invited. As I had not yet been officially presented, I would be taking a back seat, which suited me just fine, as the thought of having to be the gracious hostess to such a high-society gathering made my mouth go dry.

But I would not have missed it for the world, either. From childhood, I'd been enthralled by fashion shows. My father was the first in the world to realise that such things needed to be more than just a parade of dresses; they also needed a touch of magic – a story, a theme that would make each show special. So we'd had shows inspired by famous poems, legendary beauties, rare flowers or exotic places. There were four shows a year, one for each season, and all were hosted in our central

Lepmest store, with smaller ones held in other branches around the world.

This winter's show, for instance, had been inspired by the remote, mysterious underground world of the Kingdom of Night. My father had overseen the creation of a spectacular backdrop that recreated the salt-crystal pillars of that strange realm. But although the winter show had been the talk of the city for weeks, all Ladies' Fair shows were famous. Each one was written up in newspapers, tourist guides and travel books, and talked of over and over through word of mouth. People flocked to the shows from far and wide – and not only from Noricia, but from countries all around the world. To the shows came great ladies, princesses and queens, merchants' wives and daughters, famous actresses and singers, society ladies of all kinds and even learned professors and celebrated writers.

Before Belladonna had taken over the planning, the shows had been put together by store staff and the theme had been based on Father's ideas. Since Belladonna had come into our lives, the design of the shows had become hers, for her talents did not just lie in her beautiful face and manners: she understood the heart of fashion. She understood what made a dress more than just a piece of fabric, but a kind of magic spell in which you were transformed from ordinary girl to dream princess. It was just like when she'd chosen my dress for the Duke's ball: she had chosen the gown that was truly me. It was as if she knew me better than I knew myself. In the same way, she also understood our customers. She knew exactly how to handle people, from the haughtiest princess to the most nervous merchant's daughter, from the most flamboyant actress to the most formidable professor. Everyone who spoke to her was convinced that she thought they were the most important, delightful, charming customer we had ever had and never did Belladonna betray any impatience, no matter how tiresome or difficult or boring the customers were.

Belladonna had also made two bold changes which had transformed an already popular event into an even more feverishly awaited one. The first of Belladonna's innovations had been to inaugurate a competition for two lucky readers of the *Mirror* to win an invitation to the exclusive show. Thousands upon thousands of hopefuls entered the competition every year, dreaming of rubbing shoulders with the rich and famous at the world's most celebrated fashion event.

The second of Belladonna's innovations made the show even bigger. In the past, the theme of each show had been advertised weeks ahead, in the *Mirror*. Now, the theme was kept a secret until the very night of the show, with intriguing hints being dropped in the *Mirror* so that excitement rose not only among the invited guests, but also among the less-exalted customers and ordinary women who also read the *Mirror*.

The theme was such a secret that not even I knew what it was. Dress rehearsals were held in secret locations; sets and decorations were kept under wraps; and on the afternoon of the show, the store was closed, with all the blinds pulled down, so no-one could peek in and see any of the preparations. Belladonna herself spent most of the afternoon there, supervising last-minute details, and only returned home to dress for the show.

Her gown was new, of course. It was a simple, beautifully cut dark-blue flowing-silk dress with short sleeves made of fine gauze, a dress that perfectly showed off the blue of her eyes and the slenderness of her figure. She wore it with the sapphire earrings Father had given her at Christmas. She looked supremely elegant and I told her so.

'So do you, my sweet,' she said, giving me a light, scented peck on the cheek as we were ushered into the carriage by Drago, the burly, taciturn manservant who'd come with her when she moved to Lepmest. He travelled with Belladonna everywhere she went, as if he were afraid she might be kidnapped.

As we rode in the carriage, I thought about Belladonna's compliment to me. I liked it though I was not sure of the truth of it – my yellow muslin dress, though pretty enough, looked like a little girl's frock beside what Belladonna was wearing. But it did not worry me too much. I was not the one on show and I did not want to be. Tomorrow night's Presentation Ball would be different, and that was more than enough to be nervous about.

We arrived at the store a little after six, only a short while before the guests were due to arrive. Belladonna immediately vanished backstage to speak to the models and the staff but I wandered around the enormous airy space of the store's ground floor, which had been transformed into a stage set for the show. All the usual displays had been cleared away, including the mannequins. A large stage complete with catwalk and black velvet curtains embroidered with the feathered-hat crest of Ladies' Fair had been erected at one end. Hundreds of white velvet-covered chairs had been brought in to face the stage, but because the space was so big, and because the walls were inset with mirrors, it did not feel at all crowded.

The setting and decorations were very simple this year, with everything either black or white. There were black-and-white paper chains cut into the shapes of figures holding hands strung around the room; black-and-white rugs on the polished wooden floors; and several large tall glass vases, half of them black, half of them white, each containing one bunch of white tulips and one bunch of black tulips. The long tables at the far end of the room, where pre-show drinks and snacks would be served and where a small army of waiters was already bustling, were covered with snowy-white cloths on which reposed piles of black plates and fleets of fine white glasses. The small group of musicians – two violinists, a violist and a flautist – were dressed in eighteenth-century black-and-white costume, which included powdered white wigs tied back with black satin ribbons. It was simple yet stunning.

Very soon the guests began to arrive. I was not expected to greet them; that was all up to Belladonna, who stood by the front door and welcomed each person as they came in. I stayed in the background at the programs stand – handing them out was my job – watching the guests arrive, feeling my heart swell with pride and admiration for my stepmother. If my father was the King of Elegance, Belladonna was Queen. But she was a queen who wore her crown lightly. I could not help marvelling at the way she went about the task of making each and every guest feel special and valued.

That included the two nervous young women who were the winners of the *Mirror*'s competition, who arrived with the paper's fashion editor, Miss Sommer Malling, who had become one of Belladonna's close friends. The two winners were a little overdressed in gorgeously beaded and sequinned gowns that were clearly last year's styles but Miss Sommer Malling was, as usual, attired in her trademark plain black evening dress with a black pearl necklace to match. She had never been seen in anything else at such events and it had become part of her legend. For nearly three decades, Miss Malling had been one of the great names at the *Mirror*, making or breaking the reputations of fashion designers, stores and models, and though she had a somewhat fearsome reputation and was at least twenty years older than Belladonna, she had been quickly won over by my stepmother's charms, just like everyone else.

In fact, after Belladonna had been crowned Fairest Lady and my father had declared that there would be no more annual competitions – there couldn't possibly exist a fairer lady in the world – Miss Sommer Malling had written up her approval in the *Mirror*. Every year, after each show, the magazine published a written tribute to Belladonna as Fairest Lady alongside a glamorous portrait of her, especially taken to mark the occasion. This year it had been arranged that the portrait would be taken tomorrow, just before the Presentation Ball – Belladonna would be too preoccupied tonight – and published the following day.

The rush began on the programs, now, as the crowd thickened. Some of the guests, like Sommer Malling, knew who I was and spoke to me in a friendly way. I did notice, too, that others who didn't know me stared at me a little. I thought that perhaps they were wondering where they'd seen me before, but I had no time to feel self-conscious, for I was too busy working. In fact, many of the staff were on duty, ushering people to their seats, taking coats and serving glasses of champagne. I knew many of them by sight and a few by name. Most had been working all day and would work all the long night, without respite. But tomorrow, which was Sunday, the store would be closed and at lunchtime the staff would have their own celebration in the big dining room on the top floor – that was a longstanding tradition after a show.

Soon came the high silvery ringing of the bell that announced the show was about to begin. Those people who were still hovering around the food tables hurried to their seats and the very special guests in the front row – three members of the Faustine imperial family; two Ruvenyan princesses; the wife of the Governor of Ashberg, the Duchess of Almain; several top aristocrats from all over the Faustine Empire; and Duke Ottakar's sister, Lady Helena – sat back in their chairs, smoothing their fine dresses in anticipation. The staff fell back into waiting positions at the far end of the room and I slipped into my allotted seat on the edge of a middle row, just behind the two competition winners, who were sitting straight up like guardsmen on sentry duty.

There was a hush as Belladonna glided up the steps to the stage. Though she was slender and almost slight, she did not need to raise her voice when she spoke. She easily dominated the room with her glamorous presence.

'Your Royal Highnesses,' she began, with a graceful nod to the Ruvenyan princesses. 'Your grace,' she nodded to the Duchess of Almain. 'Lady Helena, ladies and friends. Welcome and thank you for coming. As my husband

Sir Anton Dalmatin is unable to be here tonight, the pleasurable duty of master of ceremonies has fallen on me alone, and so without further ado, I declare this show open.' She pointed towards the lights, which were dimmed on cue, and the musicians began playing a soft, haunting tune that made the palms of my hands prickle with delight and anticipation.

The curtain slowly rose to reveal a scene bathed in soft silvery light. At the back of the stage was a translucent screen on which played patterns of light. In the middle of the stage, side-on, stood a tall gilt mirror which seemed, by an effect of stage trickery, to be beaming out a path of light from each side. A collective gasp came up from the audience as suddenly, from behind the screen – and following the path of light from either side of the mirror – two female figures appeared. One was dressed in white. One in black. If it weren't for their clothing, they would be identical – both were tall, dark-haired, dark-skinned and dark-eyed. They walked towards the mirror in the middle of the stage and as they did so, we could see the detail of their gowns, beautiful full-skirted satin dresses with beading around the bodice.

The models reached the mirror, one on either side of it. And then came a spine-tingling moment: each model reached out a hand to the mirror and as their hands touched the glass, there was a flash of very bright light. When it dimmed, we saw that the two models had become one: a striking, tall, dark-haired, dark-skinned girl wearing a beautiful full-skirted satin evening dress in both black and white.

The effect was so magical, so startling, that for a moment there was complete silence in the room. Then the applause started, and it quickly became deafening as the single model paraded up and down the catwalk. When she reached the back of the stage, she stood still and was joined by what must have been the first two models: one wearing black, the other wearing white. The lights were dimmed again and I saw that the mirror had been replaced by a paneless window which stood side-on. Two figures appeared, one on each side of the window. Both were blonde, blue-eyed and petite, but one was wearing a light, pretty pink day dress, while the other was wearing a blue one. Each wore a big lacy hat on her head. As they reached the window, they each reached up to grab hold of the frame and swing herself through to the opposite side. There was another flash of light and when we stopped being dazzled, we saw that the same girls were standing on either side of the window, but that their clothes had changed from pink and blue to red and green.

There was another mighty round of applause.

'How can they possibly do that?' I heard one of ladies in front of me say to the other.

I shared her amazement. Belladonna and her people had really surpassed themselves this time. There was even more than a hint of the usual magic, here. There was something eerie about it, too, something uncanny. It was beautiful, but it was also strange.

The show went on in this vein for a little while, each scene a variation on the last, and each wildly applauded. I could see Sommer Malling scribbling furiously in her notebook some rows away, and the photographer who was with her was taking photo after photo. There would surely be the best write-up ever on this show!

Sommer Malling's scribblings reminded me that I had brought my own notebook – not for writing but for sketching, for drawing people is one of my favourite things, and I knew there would be so much material for sketches here. Belladonna didn't specifically approve or disapprove of my hobby, but I hadn't told her I was bringing my sketchbook. Would this be another faux pas? Unnoticed, I pulled out my notebook and did a few quick impressions of the people around me: the rapt expressions, the open mouths, the craning heads with their elaborate hairdos, the flurry of muslin and satin and velvet and lace and organza. I looked for Belladonna in the crowd. She usually sat in the second row at these events, but I could not see her for there were too many other heads in the way. I hoped she was feeling pleased with the success of her show. She certainly had a right to be!

I heard one of the ladies in front of me say in a stage whisper, 'I've never seen anything like it, not even in dreams. Have you?'

'Never in my wildest dreams,' agreed the other, happily.

At that moment, the curtain fell. But the show wasn't over, for the curtain rose again and there in the very middle of the stage, bathed in misty light, stood Belladonna in her dark-blue dress. She stood absolutely still, unmoving as a statue, her unblinking gaze directed straight ahead. As the lights grew brighter and she still stood there without moving a muscle, a ripple of unease started to go around the room. What was going on? Why was she not moving or speaking? And then, just as the whispers of puzzled unease started to veer towards mutters of baffled

16

annoyance, something happened which made everyone fall silent at once.

The flautist began to play a strange little tune, and Belladonna *cracked open*.

There was not a single sound from the audience. Everyone was struck with something close to horror, unable to say a word or make a sound. And then, unbelievably, the two halves of the figure swung out and from the centre of what everyone now clearly saw was a hollow shop dummy – but an incredibly well-made and startlingly lifelike dummy – stepped Belladonna, the real Belladonna, in a pure white dress of exactly the same style as the dark-blue one.

She advanced along the stage and onto the catwalk, then stopped and looked out into the audience, smiling. For a moment there was utter silence, and then the applause began, even more enthusiastic than it had been before, if that were possible. Cheers erupted as the other models entered the stage again, parading on the catwalk in ranks behind Belladonna. People stood, cheering and clapping and shouting, forgetting their dignity in their excitement.

Belladonna stopped at the edge of the catwalk with the other models behind her. She bowed and then clicked her fingers. As she did so, a stage assistant swung the two halves of the Belladonna dummy back into place and wheeled the dummy to stand right beside my stepmother, where it stood like a strange, still twin.

'Marvellous!' people shouted, as the music swelled.

Belladonna and the models took one bow and then another.

'Marvellous! Stupendous! Amazing!'

Any unease seemed to have quite disappeared, and the crowd was in great good cheer as Belladonna declared the show closed.

She came down from the stage and was immediately mobbed by eager ladies. There would be many, many orders for our spring fashions placed that night, of that I was sure. I was also sure that it would be a long time before people would cease talking about the amazing spectacle they had witnessed.

But even though I was delighted for Belladonna, for my father and for our business, I could not shake that feeling of icy disbelief that had chilled me when the still figure on the stage had suddenly cracked open. It was clever, very clever. I could see that. But that did not mean I had to like it. I knew I could not tell Belladonna what I felt. I could not say I did not like it because I felt it was wrong to play with such things, that it was tempting fate. If I tried, she would just give me that long cool glance of hers and tell me to stop being a little fool.

Three

The next day dawned grey and drizzly. I woke late, exhausted from the previous night, and discovered that I'd not only missed breakfast but the morning church service, too. Belladonna had already been, come back, and had started on preparations for the day's events: the ball, of course, but also the Ladies' Fair staff lunch which we would both be expected to attend. I hardly had time to do more than gulp down a cold cup of tea before I had to rush back upstairs and get myself ready for the arrival of the small army of hairdressers, beauticians and perfumers who were about to descend on our house.

By eleven o'clock I was duly scrubbed, massaged, perfumed and brushed into suitable form. Belladonna had selected a special outfit for me: a simple dark-green tailored suit made up of a long skirt and a jacket with a nipped-in waist, to be worn with a white blouse. Belladonna's outfit was similar, only hers was a rich amber colour and her blouse was stitched with fine insets of lace.

'Now, this is an occasion when you will have to say something, unlike yesterday,' she said, as we drove through the streets of Lepmest, back to the store.

I looked at her in some dismay, for she hadn't mentioned that before. 'But what do I say?'

'Just thank the staff for their loyalty and service to our company, and tell them to enjoy themselves.' She smiled. 'It will be easy. You'll see. The rest you can leave up to me.'

And so I did. After that first awkward speech, which to my surprise was met with lots of clapping, I hardly had to say or do anything besides smile and look interested when people talked to me. There were about fifty people there, all wearing their Sunday best, all full of good cheer and chatter and much praise for the show last night.

Traditionally, this staff lunch was lavish, and this year was no exception. The food looked and smelt delicious and our guests fell on it with much enjoyment. I would have loved to follow suit, for I was very hungry on account of that missed breakfast, but I'd seen Belladonna's warning glance and so forced myself to only eat very little of the braised asparagus and tomato, crab salad, smoked duck breast with cherries, venison raised pie, exotic fruit, and beautiful little iced cakes that looked like jewels. Belladonna always maintained that a true lady never showed her hunger in front of guests.

Instead of eating, I listened to the conversations around me. A lot of them centred on talk of the Presentation Ball: who would be there, who wouldn't, what everyone would be wearing. After a while, the conversation moved to gossip about past balls. As I listened, I began to feel more and more worried that I would do something wrong at the ball and become the subject of gossip like the poor girls and boys the staff were discussing with such relish: girls who'd tripped over the hems of their dresses; boys who'd tripped over their own feet; people who, from sheer fright, had been tongue-tied when they were supposed to be repeating the oath, who sneezed when the Duke was talking to them, who danced with the wrong person, danced too often with the right one, were too shy or too forward, laughed too much, or laughed too little. It seemed as if there were a thousand and one ways I could make a fool of myself, and a thousand and one pairs of eyes to note it.

I said as much to my stepmother, on the way home. She smiled at my worries and said that all I had to do to avoid gossip was to be discreet at all times.

'Though that does not mean to be stand-offish,' she added, giving me a sideways look. 'You do need to have one or two topics of suitable conversation ready for every occasion, or risk looking as if there are no thoughts in your head.'

It was a gentle rebuke, but it stung.

She saw my expression and patted my hand. 'Don't worry, Bianca. I am certain you will do very well and make us proud. Now, this afternoon I still have many things to do and cannot be disturbed so you must keep to your room until the maid is ready to dress you.'

At home, time ticked on. I tried to read but could not concentrate. I tried to come up with some suitable topics of conversation but found myself yawning. Feeling hungry after the little I'd eaten, I went down to the kitchen and, finding it empty, sneaked a couple of slices of bread and cheese. Back in my room, I tried drawing but found that my pencil kept halting as I daydreamed and worried. Not for the first time, I wished I had a friend of my own age to confide in. My mind wandered to my childhood playmates Rafiel and Margy. We'd been so happy in each other's company and I'd always expected we'd remain friends forever.

But not long after Belladonna had arrived, Margy and Rafiel had left with their parents. Nobody told me why, but I could tell that Belladonna hadn't been impressed by my closeness to servants' children. Although I missed Margy a good deal, strangely, it was Rafiel I missed the most. I wished many times that I could find out where they'd gone but I didn't dare ask questions. So in time I accepted it. As my stepmother had said, it was for the best. Their path in life was very different to mine. They'd understand. But although my head knew what she was saying, my heart did not. I felt the loss of my friends, and that was one of the reasons I was so looking forward to the ball. Surely among all the other young people of good social standing there'd be someone who I might make friends with, someone of whom Belladonna approved.

Evening came at last and I stood downstairs in my ball gown, waiting for Belladonna to come down from her rooms. The *Mirror* photographer had come earlier to take the customary photograph of Belladonna, but nobody else had seen what Belladonna would wear to the ball. As she appeared at the top of the stairs, I couldn't help gasping. Last night's dress had been simply elegant. This one, though, was truly magnificent. It had layers of heavy gleaming-white satin and deep-gold brocade; it was full-skirted, puff-sleeved and low-cut. Belladonna's golden hair, piled on her head in artful curls, was topped by a sparkling diamond tiara. Dangling from her ears were massive diamond-and-gold drops and at her throat she wore another magnificent diamond. Her high-heeled shoes were gold satin; her evening bag was threaded with gold beads. She shone like the sun and beside her I immediately felt like a pale and distant moon.

'Do you like it?' she asked, with a little smile.

I nodded, mutely. She would outshine every other woman at the ball, there was not a shred of doubt of that. Her official portrait in the *Mirror* as the Fairest Lady would be stunning. If only Father could be there to see her, how happy and proud he would be! I wished more than ever that he had not had to leave so suddenly. I did not know exactly what unexpected, urgent business had taken him away – he did not talk of business to me – and if Belladonna knew what had called him away, she kept quiet, too.

'Let's go, then, dear Bianca,' she said brightly, and took my arm.

And so together we went out of the house and down the steps, onto Moonlight Boulevard. Drago bowed deeply as he opened the door of the carriage. Just before I went in after Belladonna, I turned around and saw the house staff crowded around to watch us go. I noticed that some of them looked a little askance at me. Was there something not quite right with my dress? Feeling a little self-conscious with their eyes on my back, I hurriedly stepped into the carriage.

Four

)

Duke Ottakar's palace is on Grand Boulevard, not far from Moonlight Boulevard. By day, its slender white towers and silver roofs, which could be seen from our house, gleamed in the sun. By night, they shone eerily in the white glow of the new gas lamps that had been installed along the driveway – the Duke loves everything that's modern, and had torn out the friendly yellow-light lanterns in favour of these things. For a moment, as I looked out from our carriage window at the palace shining over the tops of all the other houses, I felt a little shiver run down my spine.

'A goose walking over your grave,' Margy used to call that spine-tingling feeling, and though I never really understood that saying, I knew what she meant. It's a feeling that something isn't right, that something is out of place, that something is making you feel uneasy, though you have no idea what it is or why it's making you feel that way. That's how I felt, right at that moment – as though I should not be going to the palace. That something bad

24

was waiting for me there, and that I should turn around and go home.

I'd had moments like that a few times when I was a child. Once, when walking in long grass at my grandfather's country house, the shiver had gone up my spine and I'd stepped back. Looking down, I'd seen that I had only just avoided stepping on a snake. Another time, I'd had the same feeling and backed off an old wooden bridge – just before it had collapsed. Yet another time was when I'd jumped off my beloved pony Bruna, just before a horsefly bite had sent her careering around the field. There had been other, less dramatic moments. My old nurse used to say it was my gypsy ancestor Tamara coming out in me, that I had a kind of 'sight' that preserved me from danger. But I found that as childhood faded, so did the so-called 'sight'. I could not recall the last time I'd had this experience. Certainly not in the four years since I'd turned thirteen.

I hesitated, looking at Belladonna. I opened my mouth to speak – then I shut it again, for what was I going to say? That I wanted to turn back? What reason would I give for not going? And really, I didn't want to turn back. I wanted to go to the ball. I convinced myself that it was just nerves and an overactive imagination, like my foolish thoughts last night about tempting fate. Belladonna would scoff at the very notion of 'sight' and 'tempting fate' – polite society doesn't believe in such nonsense as second sight, witches, shapeshifters and other such things.

Still, I've come to realise that there's a strange gap between what people say they believe and what they really do believe. People in Noricia are very superstitious, and everyone knows these creatures *do* exist. And Aurisola, where Belladonna comes from, has a reputation for magic.

Aurisola. Why *had* my father gone there so suddenly?

'Belladonna, do you know why Father had to go to Aurisola?' I asked.

My stepmother looked at me in surprise. 'Why do you ask?'

'It's just that there is only one small Ladies' Fair shop there and I know he doesn't like travelling long distances. Usually he'd just get his manager to look after things –'

'This wasn't usual,' said Belladonna, interrupting me. 'It was urgent business that only he could attend to.'

'But –'

'If he'd seen fit for you to know what it was, then you would,' she said. 'You have to respect your father's decisions, Bianca.'

I could feel my cheeks flaming. 'Oh, I do, but –'

'Enough!' she snapped, her voice harsh. 'Here we are about to appear before the ruler of the land and all you can think of are things that are none of your business! I'm disappointed in you, Bianca.'

I could feel my face go from red to pale. I stammered, 'I'm . . . I'm sorry. I didn't mean . . . I didn't think . . .'

'No. That's true enough,' said Belladonna, ruefully shaking her head. 'But you must think before you speak, my darling, and keep a guard on your tongue, for you do not know who might be listening.'

Belladonna can be a bit too suspicious of people sometimes. Father says it comes from her having grown up in Aurisola, which as well as having a reputation for magic is also known as a city of intrigues and informers. Everyone there treads very carefully.

I nearly responded to Belladonna's comment that in this case it was only her listening, not unfriendly strangers, but I controlled myself in time.

'I'm sorry. I just wish Father was here to see me being presented to the Duke.'

'And I'm sure he feels the same but he must do his duty – as we all must, dear Bianca,' she said, with an affectionate smile.

At that moment, our coach came to a stop. Mindful of Belladonna's disapproval, I didn't dare pull down the window so I could poke my head out and see what the hold-up was. But as we slowly started up again and drew past the obstruction, I looked through the glass and saw men in the green uniform of the City Police gathered around something on the edge of the road. Something that looked at first like a shapeless bundle – but then I realised that it was a body, clothed in the rags of a beggar, with his face covered by a blanket.

'What are you doing? Draw the curtain,' said Belladonna, sharply.

I did as I was told. With a shiver, I remembered the creepy feeling I'd had earlier. It must be another beggar killing: over the last year or so, the bodies of at least a dozen beggars had turned up in the streets of the city. At first, the police and the newspapers had taken little notice, for usually the deaths of such people were not investigated, let alone reported. But as the death toll mounted, reports had started appearing in the papers and the police had at last swung into action – for it appeared that these were particularly mysterious crimes. All the bodies had been found on the street, in broad daylight, and the victims had not long been dead. The victims' faces all bore a look of frozen terror, and they all had a strange puncture wound at their throats. The investigators had not been able to establish with certainty what had made the wounds, but there was speculation that they were either the mark of fangs, or the mark of some hitherto unknown instrument. The more sensational newspapers reported vampire attacks; the more respectable ones reported sinister scientific experiments. But so far, neither rampaging vampires nor mad scientists had been located, and not a single clue as to who or what might be responsible had been found.

'It's awful, what's happening to those poor people,' I said. 'I wish they could find and stop the horrible criminal who's doing this. Do you think they will ever be found?'

Belladonna frowned. 'For heaven's sake, Bianca, such sordid happenings are hardly a fit topic of conversation, especially for a lady about to be presented to society! I never speculate about such things and you shouldn't, either. The police are doing their job, and no doubt they will find the culprit in time. In any case, it is none of our concern. Those people have nothing to do with us.'

That doesn't mean we shouldn't care, I wanted to say, but knew to hold my tongue. Besides, what did I really know about such things? What did I know of the beggars? What, in fact, did I know about anything except my own little world?

So I was quiet, and soon we arrived at the palace gates and were helped out of the coach by one of the Duke's footmen, splendidly attired in blue and silver, with the griffin crest of the Duchy of Noricia embroidered on his waistcoat. Legend has it that thousands of years ago, a griffin saved the life of the first duke by plucking him, injured, from a battlefield where he was about to be captured by enemy forces. I don't know if the story is true but I liked it very much as a child, and so did Rafiel and Margy. I remember playing the griffin game with them – one of us would be the duke, another the griffin, and the other would be a soldier from the enemy forces. Thinking of that made a lump come into my throat, and I gulped it down quickly. Now was not the time to be nostalgic about childhood. The presentation ritual was the first step to entering adulthood. Now was the time to start behaving like an adult, and to put all childish things behind me – games, geese walking over graves, impertinent questions and useless speculation.

As we walked into the ballroom, filing in behind hundreds of others, the footman on duty called out our names in a solemn voice: 'Lady Dalmatin and Lady Bianca Dalmatin.'

I could feel my heart racing as we made our way towards where the Duke and his sister stood at the far end of the room, hearing the first oath from each young candidate. The room was crowded, a mass of colour and sound and fragrance, but the crowd parted as we drew nearer to the Duke and I could hear sharply indrawn breaths from all around as Belladonna walked with stately grace towards the Duke with me following, trying to match her pace.

'Your grace and Lady Helena, I am honoured to be in your presence,' Belladonna said, as she reached the ducal pair. Standing behind her, I saw her sink to the ground in a beautiful curtsey that looked like the dance of a swan and I saw the Duke's eyes light up with admiration. Even Lady Helena, who had the reputation of being a grim old battleaxe, gave a little smile. Around us, the room had fallen silent as everyone watched.

'Lady Dalmatin,' said the Duke, holding out his hand for her to rise, 'the pleasure is all ours. I have heard from my sister, Lady Helena, about the triumph of your event last night, and offer my congratulations along with hers.'

'Why thank you, your grace,' said Belladonna, softly.

'We are very glad to welcome you and Lady Bianca to the Presentation Ball.' He cleared his throat and then said in a low voice, so that only we heard, 'But before we get down to official business, might I ask if I may claim the first dance with you, Lady Dalmatin?'

Belladonna's eyes met his. I could not read her expression. I know she must have been surprised by this unusual invitation, but she did not show her feelings.

'Of course, your grace,' she murmured. 'That is a great honour, and I gladly accept.'

'Good,' said the Duke, beaming all over his broad plain face, looking rather like the frog who'd unexpectedly been kissed by a princess.

But I had no time to think any further about their exchange, for now was my big moment. As we'd practised so often, Belladonna stepped to one side and motioned me forward.

'Your grace,' she said, 'may I formally present my step-daughter, Lady Bianca Dalmatin, only child of Sir Anton Dalmatin and his late wife, Lady Marianna Dalmatin?'

'You may indeed,' said the Duke, but he gave me only a cursory glance before motioning me closer. As I sank to the floor in a curtsey, as I'd been taught, he took a blue ribbon from his sister Lady Helena's hands and placed it on my left shoulder, saying, quickly, 'By the laws of our land, and the power that is vested in me through those laws, I hereby declare that Lady Bianca Dalmatin, only child of Sir Anton and Lady Marianna Dalmatin and lawful stepdaughter of Lady Belladonna Dalmatin, is ready to take the first step into adult estate and the citizenship of the Duchy of Noricia.'

'Thank ... Thank you, your grace –' I began, but I caught a glance from Belladonna and fell quiet. I wasn't supposed to interrupt.

The Duke gave a tiny frown but continued. 'And so I ask my sister, Lady Helena, to instruct you in what is to follow.'

Lady Helena stepped forward. She looked at me and I felt her sharp grey gaze searching my face. I could not help blushing a little. Was there a spot on my nose? I looked at Belladonna but she just frowned. I could not understand what I had done wrong.

To my relief, Lady Helena spoke. 'Stand up, Lady Bianca,' she said.

I did as I was told, trying not to tremble, trying to pretend that there wasn't a roomful of people staring at me, trying to pretend that Belladonna wasn't still glaring at me as though I'd done something to disgrace myself.

'As you know, there are three steps to come into adult estate,' said the Duke's sister. 'The first is this ball, where you are declared ready by his grace the Duke and swear the first oath; the second is in three days' time when you will attend a citizenship ceremony at the Town Hall and swear the second oath; and the third will be in six days' time, when you will swear the final oath in the Cathedral of St Simeon, and be blessed by the Lord Cardinal and all the archbishops. It is compulsory to attend each of these ceremonies and failure to attend will result in you not entering into the full citizenship and protection of the laws of Noricia. Do you understand?'

'I do, my lady,' I breathed.

'And do you profess yourself ready, willing and able to perform these tasks?'

'I do, my lady.'

'Do you swear the first oath, to honour your country in every word?'

'I do, my lady.'

'Good.' She gave a little smile, took the blue ribbon from my left shoulder, and placed it on my right. 'You have taken the first step, Lady Bianca. Well done.'

'Thank you, my lady,' I whispered. Then, turning to Duke Ottakar, I whispered my thanks to him, too. 'Thank you, your grace.' I could feel my legs trembling, my heart pounding. I only hoped I did not look as overwhelmed as I felt.

'Very well,' said the Duke, impatiently, his eyes still on Belladonna.

Taking my cue, I walked away, following Belladonna who was heading towards a group of her friends. A wave of people came between us, though, and I lost her halfway there. I was looking around in panic, thinking that I knew nobody there, when I cannoned straight into a red-haired, round-faced girl in a green dress. 'Sorry – so sorry,' I stammered, trying to recover my composure.

The girl gave me a darting smile. 'It's fine. Normal to feel nervous, you know. I thought I was going to faint.'

'You've already been presented?'

'I was the third in the line. My mother was determined I'd be presented early – she didn't trust me to remember what I was meant to do if we had to wait too long.' She grinned. 'I was sure all those gawking snobs could hear my teeth chattering. I thought I should whistle a tune or something, just to really give them something to talk about.'

I laughed. 'You wouldn't dare!'

'No, I'm the most terrible coward there ever was.' She gave me another of those darting smiles. 'Are you hungry?'

I looked at her. 'Actually,' I whispered, 'I am ravenous, but don't tell anyone!'

'I won't if you don't tell anyone I plan to eat a whole plate of meringues and cream,' she retorted, making me laugh again.

'I promise it will remain our secret,' I said.

To my relief, no-one attempted to waylay us as we scurried off to the refreshment room and piled plates high with everything we could find. After we'd taken a piece of everything we wanted, we went looking for a quiet, private room where we could devour our food in peace. We found a little antechamber with a table and chairs which did us very well. By that time, my new friend had learnt my name and I hers.

'Emilia Sophia Jemans, in full,' she declared, rather indistinctly through a mouthful of meringue. 'Not "Lady", like you – I'm just a merchant's daughter.'

'You could say that my father's a merchant, too –'
I began, but she shook her head.

'No, he is in quite a different league to us,' she said.
'My father's a wool merchant – a good one – but no-one
would call him the King of Elegance! Jemans' Wool –
that's us.'

'Oh,' I said, lamely. 'I'm . . . I'm sure I've heard of it.'
Belladonna had told me that even when you had never
heard of something, it was best not to display ignorance.

Emilia giggled. 'I'm sure you have. Anyway, never mind
about dull business. Tell me about yourself. Do you have
brothers? Sisters? I have two of each, all older, married,
and tiresomely sensible, too. Are you sensible?'

I stared at her. 'I . . . I'm not sure.'

'Then you probably aren't. Which is a good thing,
because sensible people never have adventures. And I plan
to have lots. Don't you?'

'Er . . .'

'I plan to travel the world visiting strange and exotic
places, write about them and become a really famous
travel writer. You have to have lots of adventures if you
want to become a famous travel writer. Don't you agree?'

I smiled. 'Yes. I suppose I do.'

'Come on – have another meringue,' she said, pushing
an extra one on my plate. 'You know, when I was little,
I wanted to be a lion tamer, and I even practised it –'

I was a little dazed by this sudden turn in the conversation. 'How?' I said faintly.

'With the household cat, of course,' she said, grinning.
'But he didn't really get into his role as a lion, so I decided
I'd be a train driver instead.'

'A train driver?' I repeated.

'That didn't last long, because I soon discovered that train drivers have to follow the same route all the time – they can't take the train somewhere different, just for a change.'

'No, I can imagine that might be a bit puzzling for passengers,' I said. I was really enjoying myself and liking Emilia more by the minute. 'What did you decide on after that?'

'To be a magician,' she said promptly. 'But then I worked out that if you have no natural magical talent – and I don't – then you have to sit for years alone in dingy rooms learning lots of boring spells before you can get good at it. So I concluded that I'd leave that to people who like being alone in dingy rooms.'

'A fair conclusion,' I said, mock-solemnly, popping a tiny savoury pie into my mouth.

'Yes. And that's when I decided on my present ambition – to be a famous travel writer! But enough from me,' Emilia declared. 'What about you? What's your dream?'

'My dream?' I looked at her. A funny fluttering begun in my heart. 'I . . . I don't have one.'

'That can't be so,' she said, stopping her chewing to look at me, curiously. 'Everyone has a dream. Some people's dreams are more like nightmares, though – nightmares for other people, that is, if those dreams are about power over others . . .

'Come on, Bianca,' she went on, when I just stared at her. 'People dream of many things – adventure, like me, or love, or power, or fame, or riches, or endless fun, or lots of children, or great talent, or, a pantry full of food, or . . . look, all kinds of things! What do you dream of?'

I swallowed. 'I don't know.'

'I don't believe it! If a feya came to you right now and said she'd grant you the dearest wish of your heart, what would you say? Come on,' she persisted, when I still sat silent. 'Pretend I'm the feya.'

'What?'

She put on a mysterious, dreamy voice. 'I'm Nellia, the feya of the mountain spring, who grants wishes to all who come to her. Bianca Dalmatin, you have come to me with the dearest wish of your heart, and I will grant it as soon as you speak it. But you must speak it aloud –'

'Don't,' I said, getting up.

'Don't what?' She looked bewildered.

My hands were prickling; my throat felt tight. I did not want to explain to Emilia how I felt, as though icy water was trickling through my veins. All I could say was, 'You shouldn't joke about those sorts of things.'

'What sorts of things?'

'The feya – Nellia – she's real, not just a story, and if you speak her name you might –' I broke off, for someone had just come into the room. It was Belladonna, and she did not look very pleased.

Five

'Bianca, I've been looking for you –' she began. Then she caught sight of the remains of our feast on the table and frowned. 'What is this?'

'We were hungry,' I said, uncertainly. 'We ... I remembered what you said about eating too much in front of others, so I thought we'd –'

'Hide away,' finished Belladonna for me. She raised an eyebrow, sighed, then gave a little smile. 'Very well. I don't always remember you are still a growing girl.' She looked at Emilia, who was uncharacteristically silent. Her cheeks were almost as red as her hair.

'This is my friend Miss Emilia Jemans,' I said, shooting Emilia a comforting glance. 'She has been very kind and helpful.'

'In tracking down the best of the meringues, I see,' said Belladonna, her smile wider, and to my surprise, she picked one up and popped it into her mouth. 'Mmm. Perfect.' She looked at Emilia. 'So, Miss Jemans, you have been looking after Bianca, and I thank you for that.'

'Oh, it's . . . it's . . . it's nothing . . . I mean, it's a great pleasure, Lady Dalmatin,' gabbled Emilia, trying to drop to a curtsey but almost falling over her feet as she did so, her cheeks glowing even more scarlet.

Belladonna nodded. 'But now I'm going to have to take Bianca away from your kind company, for she really must not skulk away and hide like a wallflower. For her own wellbeing, she must be seen to be mixing with the very best of society. Wouldn't you agree, Miss Jemans?'

'Oh yes, of course,' said poor Emilia in some confusion, clearly not sure if Belladonna meant to ask her opinion or insult her.

I don't know if it was the misery in her face or the sting of Belladonna's words, but I found myself saying, 'I'm not skulking, and I am mixing with the society I prefer – so there is really no need to be concerned about my wellbeing, Lady Mother.'

As soon as the words left my mouth, I wished them unsaid. But it was too late. Belladonna's eyes glittered and her lips were set in a thin line as she said, 'You will kindly accompany me now, Bianca. Good evening to you, Miss Jemans.'

There was nothing I could do but send a glance of apology to Emilia, who sat down with her shoulders slumped and mouth downturned, and follow Belladonna. My rash words had almost certainly cost me this chance of friendship, for I knew Belladonna would not easily forget my impertinence.

Once we were out in the corridor, out of earshot, I expected her to round on me and give me a dressing-down. But she did nothing of the sort. Instead, she looked at me and gave a little sigh.

'You are your own worst enemy, my poor Bianca,' she said. 'When are you going to realise that you have responsibilities?'

I swallowed, thrown off by her sincerity. 'I . . . I do realise.'

'Really? Then what was that little tantrum about? And that nonsense I overheard you saying just as I arrived?'

I couldn't meet her eyes. Turning my head away, I began, 'It wasn't . . .' but I couldn't finish.

She sighed again. 'People in our position have to be careful. We can't just make friends with any stray cat. You understand that, don't you?'

I muttered, 'Emilia isn't a stray cat.'

'For heaven's sake, Bianca, stop this foolishness!' She halted, then gave me a smile. 'Come, now, this is a special day. You need to dance. To be seen. Not to hide away.' She took my arm. 'There. Let us go back into the ballroom together.'

But the moment we stepped back into the ballroom, Belladonna was claimed by friends and admirers and I was left to my own devices once more. I did not dare to leave the room again but I was too shy to speak to anyone – even more so because I was aware of sidelong glances being cast at me. To avoid the glances, I sat down on a chair against the wall and pretended that I was tired.

To tell the truth, I did feel tired. A heavy feeling had settled along my limbs and my head felt full of thick mist.

I did not want to think about what had just happened, or about my own strange reaction to Emilia's breezy questions. I did not understand it and it made me feel uneasy. Why couldn't I tell Emilia that my dream was to be like Belladonna? Why couldn't I say that I wished I was like my stepmother, who was so at ease in her own skin, so much herself, so much admired and loved by others? Beside her shining presence, I was a pale distant moon hidden behind mist. A superstitious child, frightened of shadows, who knew nothing of the world.

What did it mean, that I couldn't tell Emilia my dream? That I was ashamed of what was in my heart? That I was afraid Emilia would laugh at me? Emilia was not beautiful like Belladonna. She was not rich and famous, she was not sophisticated. But she was still so much herself. We could have been friends. And now . . .

'May I have the pleasure of this dance with the loveliest lady at the ball?'

Startled, I looked up to see a tall young man of about my own age. Dressed in sober grey and white, he had a sharp-featured, handsome face with unusual colouring: olive skin, light-brown hair and amber-coloured eyes. I must have been staring for he smiled and repeated his question, making me blush and stammer, 'Oh . . . I'm sorry . . . I . . . I'm a bit . . . tired, and I . . .'

'Please dance with me,' he said, quietly. Our eyes met. Something gripped inside my chest. I was not used to the attentions of young men. And he was handsome. And kind. I knew I was not the loveliest lady at the ball, but it was nice of him to say so, so I found myself getting up, taking his hand, and following him onto the dance floor.

He danced supremely well, and very soon I forgot all about being tired and despondent, for dancing is something I love dearly.

As we danced, we talked a little, too. He told me his name was Lucian Montresor and that he came from a manor in the mountains.

'You wouldn't have heard of it,' he said, smiling. 'Hardly anyone has. It's nowhere near the mountain resorts, no train goes there, and it's about a day's ride from the nearest station.'

'Oh,' I said, 'that does sound remote!'

As the words left my mouth, I realised they sounded a bit banal but he quickly covered any embarrassment I might have felt by saying, 'It is, but you know what? It's home. And I love it. The city – it's pleasant for a visit, but it's not really for me.' He looked at me. 'But you'd feel differently, of course.'

Our eyes met again and I felt once more that gripping feeling in the chest as I answered, 'I've always lived in Lepmest. It does not mean I would not like to see other places.'

'Perhaps one day I could show you the mountains,' he said. 'Have you heard of Nellia's Spring?'

A little shiver rippled down my spine. 'Yes,' I managed to answer.

'Our place is quite close to there,' he said. 'It is a pretty, peaceful spot, perfect for a picnic.'

'So I've heard,' I said, my scalp prickling with a mixture of awe and unease. Legend had it that to speak Nellia's name could bring unforeseen consequences. That's what I had been about to tell Emilia when Belladonna had interrupted us. Could it be confirmation that something was coming?

Don't be a fool, I told myself. Don't believe stories meant for children. It's just coincidence, that's all.

'Then when the weather is warmer,' he said, smiling, 'we should think of it. What do you say?'

My heart pounded. 'Why not?' I answered, trying to match his light tone.

And then the music stopped, and before I could step away from the dance floor, another young man asked me to dance. I would have said no and hovered to see if Lucian would ask me to dance again, but then I saw that Lucian was already taking the hand of another girl and I knew I had to play my part. Belladonna had told me that it was not done to dance too much with the same person because it made people talk. There were several reporters and photographers here tonight, of course, so I had to be careful not to attract the wrong sort of attention.

So I agreed to dance with the other young man, Alfons, who was pleasant enough, but nothing like Lucian. After that, I danced with another, and another, as for some reason I had become very popular, but all the while, I was hoping that Lucian might ask me again. He did not, though, and I saw him briefly just once after that: to my dismay, Belladonna had buttonholed him. She looked none too friendly, and I hoped she wasn't warning him off me, like she'd put off Emilia. I looked for him when the musicians and dancers took a break but I could not find him. He seemed to have vanished into thin air.

It was Emilia who gave me a clue as to what might have happened. I saw her at the back of the room, on the very chair I'd been sitting on when Lucian had asked me to dance. I looked cautiously around for Belladonna. She was busy with friends, so I hurried over to Emilia and sat down next to her.

'I'm sorry about before,' I said.

She looked at me. 'It's all right. I understand.'

'I'd like us to be friends. Is that . . . Is that still possible?'

Her face lit up. 'Of course. But –'

'But even though I love and admire her, my stepmother isn't right about everything,' I finished, neatly.

Emilia smiled. 'I don't think anyone's right about everything, do you?'

'No. Not even us,' I joked.

She grinned. 'Speak for yourself!' She sighed. 'One thing I do know little about, though, is dancing. Me – I have two left feet, and both of those seem to tread on my poor partner's toes! But I saw you dance – and you're as light on your feet as an angel!'

'Only when I'm accompanied by another pair of light feet,' I said.

She gave me a mischievous sideways glance. 'Oh yes, like those of Lucian Montresor? He's very handsome!' A pause. 'It's a pity about the curse.'

I stared at her. 'What?'

'There's a curse on his family, they say.'

'Nonsense,' I retorted.

'It's true! My grandmother comes from that region and she said that everyone knows the story there. You see, a long time ago one of the Montresor ancestors killed a witch. As she lay dying, she cursed him and his descendants. My grandmother says that some go mad, some

43

go bad, but each Montresor is dangerous in one way or the other.'

'Nonsense,' I repeated, trying to ignore the tingling of my scalp and the prickling of my hands. Such a thing might well explain Belladonna's manner towards him . . . But then I rallied. 'If that were true, why would Lucian have been invited to the Presentation Ball? The Duke wouldn't risk bringing someone dangerous into his palace among so many other people.'

'He can hardly *not* invite the Montresors,' said Emilia. 'They might not be rich but they are one of the most ancient and most proud families in the land. In fact, at one time they could very well have become the rulers of Noricia themselves. It would be an insult if the Duke did not invite a Montresor to take the oath at the Presentation Ball.'

'That's silly. I do believe you're making all this up, Emilia.'

'I am not!' she answered indignantly.

'I've just never heard of such a thing,' I said.

She folded her arms and looked at me. 'That doesn't mean it's untrue, does it?'

I looked at her. 'No, but how do you know it is?'

'Because my grandmother said so,' she said, simply. Her mouth was set in a firm line. 'She never lies.'

I saw that it was pointless arguing any further so I quickly turned the talk to other matters. I'd almost lost her friendship once. I did not want to risk losing it a second time.

Belladonna and I left the ball soon after midnight. She hadn't seen me talking to Emilia. I felt a little uneasy keeping our friendship secret from my stepmother, but it seemed to be the only way.

But I could not keep my dance with Lucian a secret, of course. Belladonna had seen me whirling around the room with him. I waited for her to say that I should keep away from him, but instead she said, 'Well, that went quite well.' She shot me a glance. 'Despite some problems with making the right choices.'

I coloured, knowing she was referring to Emilia, and to Lucian. Though my heart rebelled, I muttered, 'I'm . . . I'm sorry.'

She smiled. 'Don't be. You'll do better next time.'

'Thank . . . Thank you,' I murmured.

'You needn't thank me. You're my daughter, aren't you?' She patted my hand. 'Soon you'll be an adult, and you'll be able to take your place in the world.'

'Mmm,' I said, but I couldn't keep my attention on what she was saying. My mind kept conjuring up a vision of riding with Lucian among beautiful mountain meadows covered in scented flowers; of picnicking with him by the side of a lovely mountain spring. And I knew that tonight a different dream had entered my heart. I didn't want to be like Belladonna anymore. I just wanted to see Lucian again. No matter what Belladonna or Emilia or anyone said.

Six

It took me a long time to go to sleep that night. I kept turning over all the scenes from the ball in my mind. The night had been such a momentous, magical thing: it had brought me a new friend and a new dream. The future stretched before me, bright and promising. I hadn't realised before how discontented I'd been, how lonely and cramped I'd felt. It made me feel a little ashamed, to realise just how far and how deep that feeling went. After all, I had little to complain about. I had a comfortable, peaceful life. I wanted for nothing and my father and stepmother loved me.

But the feeling was still there: what I had was not enough and I knew that now, both in my heart and my mind. I had missed sharing confidences with a friend. And I had craved for something surprising and wonderful to happen. Those things had come into my life, now, and I realised my longing for them had been so deep that it had been hidden from even myself. It was as if, in discovering what I had been missing, I had found my true self. It was as if before, I'd been a statue. An image from the fashion show – of the Belladonna dummy cracking open and the real Belladonna stepping out from the hollow shell – suddenly came into my mind. Yes, that was it. That was what I had been. A shop dummy – stiff, hollow, trying to be what I wasn't. Now the real me could step out at last.

Things would be different now, and I couldn't help making all kinds of plans. When at last I dropped off to sleep, it was into a deep, restful sleep and I woke late, feeling refreshed and happier than I'd ever been. I was ready to start the first day of my new life.

I came into the breakfast room in a cheerful mood. There was a delicious cold spread out on the sideboard, and no-one but I was there to enjoy it. Belladonna must either have breakfasted early, or still be sleeping in. I was just finishing a tasty plate of smoked salmon, boiled eggs and cheese washed down with cherry juice, when Bella-donna's maid Siggy came in. She looked as if she'd been crying. Her eyes were red-rimmed.

'Oh, Miss Bianca, there you are! You are to go and see my lady at once. Something . . . Something bad has happened.'

I started up from the chair. 'What is it, Siggy? Is it Bella-donna? Is she sick?'

'No, it's not my lady, Miss. It's your father. It's Sir Anton. My lady's just received a telegram.' She gulped. 'He's . . . He's been taken ill. You must go up to my lady. Quickly, now.'

I did not wait to be told twice but set off at a sprint through the room, into the hall and up the stairs, holding up my skirts so that I was able to take them two at a time. Reaching Belladonna's room on the second floor, the maid panting after me, I knocked on the door and, without even waiting for an answer, burst in.

My stepmother was sitting at her dressing table. She was still in her nightclothes – a white silk dressing-gown over a pale pink lace nightgown, with satin slippers to match – and her long blonde hair was hanging loose down her back.

She turned to look at me. I saw she was holding a telegram, and that her eyes were as red-rimmed as Siggy's.

'Bianca, my dear . . .' she said. 'Oh, my dear . . .'

I fell to my knees beside her. 'Please, dearest Lady Mother . . . Please tell me . . . Is Father . . . Is he . . .'

I could not say the word, but she saw it in my eyes.

'No, sweet,' she said, stroking my hair, 'he's not dead. Thank God he is not gone from us. But he is . . .' She swallowed, then went on more strongly. 'He is very ill.'

'But where . . . Where is he? What's wrong . . . What . . .' My voice kept getting louder and louder. I was shouting, I knew that, but I could not help it.

'He's in Aurisola, still.'

'But how . . . What . . .'

Without answering, she handed me the telegram.

Sir Anton taken gravely ill last night. Delirious, in great pain. Asking for his daughter to come. Doctors doing best but fear worst.
   HR

HR. That was Hans Reinart, Father's assistant, who'd travelled with him.

'I must go there!' I said, jumping up. 'I must go there at once!'

I was gasping for breath and tears were running down my cheeks. Utter terror filled me at the thought of losing my father. He was a loving, kind, warm man and I could not bear the thought he might be taken from me.

'Belladonna, I must get a train to Aurisola at once!'

'Of course you must go, but not by train,' she said, 'for that will take too long – three days at the least, for there is no direct line there. You'll have to go by the fastest and most direct route and that is by steamer. You'll have to go to Mormest and take the steamer from there. It's only an overnight journey, then.'

'But Mormest is a long way by coach!'

'It is, and so what I'm suggesting is you go there on horseback. Drago knows a shortcut through the forest. You will ride with him – he knows the forest path and he's well armed. You'll be at Mormest in less than two hours if you take the fastest horses.' She was very pale and there were tears in her eyes. 'I . . . I would come with you, but your father . . . He did not ask for me.'

In my terror, I had not thought of that. How it must hurt, that a husband should ask for his daughter but not his wife!

'I'm . . . I'm sorry . . .' I whispered.

'It's all right. It is only natural. You are his daughter, flesh of his flesh. And he needs me more here. For I'm sure that . . . that he will recover.' Her lips trembled. 'The doctors – in Aurisola – they are the very best. They are, Bianca. The best in the world. Really.'

Impulsively, I flung my arms around her.

'It is only because he is delirious. He must be delirious. Otherwise he would want you there. I know it. You have been the best, most loving wife. The kindest mother. I'm so, so grateful to have you as a mother.'

She turned her head away but not before I saw the shine of tears on her cheek.

'Thank you, Bianca,' she said, softly. 'I hoped . . . I really hoped that . . .' She didn't finish her sentence but, taking a deep breath, began to speak of preparations for my journey. 'We must get you ready. Siggy, go and tell Drago he is to saddle our two fastest horses at once. Then come back and help Lady Bianca pack.'

Siggy nodded and set off at a trot.

Belladonna stood up. 'I'll get word to our banker to come at once. You'll need a good amount of money for the journey.'

'Thank you,' I said, through a lump in my throat. 'I . . . I just don't know what I'd do if . . .'

'Don't. We must be strong. Go and start your packing, Bianca,' she said, touching my shoulder gently.

As I left the room, a crumpled magazine that had been lying on the floor near the dressing table caught my eye. It was the *Mirror*, and I could just make out the beginning of the headline: 'Fairest Lady makes her entrance.' Usually I enjoyed gazing at the beautiful photo of Belladonna and the tribute article the *Mirror* published but today I didn't even bother to look twice. The ball felt like a distant, irrelevant memory.

Drago and I set out less than fifteen minutes later. I had taken only a small light bag as I did not want to burden the horses and make them run slowly and besides,

Belladonna had given me more than enough money to buy whatever I might need when I got to Aurisola.

As we left the city outskirts far behind and took the forest path, I was grateful for the fact that Drago wasn't a talker even at the best of times. At the worst of times, like now, his silence was much more welcome than any ham-fisted attempt at comfort. I did not want him to speak aloud, even in comfort, and mention the terrible fear that gripped my mind like an iron band: the fear that we would be too late and that I would never see my father again in this life. I knew Belladonna had sent a telegram to Aurisola just as we left, so that Father would know I was on my way. I hoped – oh, I hoped and prayed so much – that the message that I was on my way would help him hang on. What really scared me was that Father was a fit and healthy man who'd hardly ever had a day's sickness in his life. Whatever illness it was that had struck him down so suddenly had to be something very bad. Would that mean that it would carry him off quickly, too?

We entered the forest. It was very quiet under the trees, but not a sinister quiet. Riding with Drago, I felt completely safe. It was peaceful, with the light filtering green-gold through the spring leaves. There were stories of wild beasts of the forest – bears and wolves and lynx – but Drago had been a huntsman in his youth and although in our peaceful, safe city there'd not been much call on his skills, I knew that in other places he'd saved Belladonna from more than one dangerous situation.

The horses had to go a little slower as we rode deeper into the forest but we were still making good time when suddenly Drago halted and said, 'My lady, this is where we leave the path, for the shortcut to the steamer port takes us this way,' and he pointed into the trees. I nodded and turned my horse to follow Drago's.

At first the way was clear. But soon it grew more difficult. The trees grew closer together and prickly thorn bushes spread in every direction. We had to pick our way much more slowly and I began to be seriously concerned.

'Drago,' I asked, 'how much further is it?'

'Not too far, my lady,' he replied. 'And the way will clear soon. You'll see.'

But it did not. On and on we went for what seemed like forever, further and further into a tangle of wilderness with seemingly no beginning and no end. And the weather was changing – the sunny day turning overcast – so that in the thickness of the forest, it felt later than it really was.

I was getting more and more anxious. How long would it be before we got to Mormest? Would I arrive in time to catch the steamer? Would I arrive too late and have to stay overnight? Would my father not wait for me?

We came to a small clearing. Drago halted. He turned his head to look at me. 'We'll have to stop a moment. I need to take our bearings.'

'Are we lost?' I cried.

'We could be. Best if you dismount too, my lady. Tie your horse to that stump a moment while I have a look.'

I did as I was told and waited anxiously as he took a compass out of his pocket and looked at it, squinted up into the sky, then looked at me. By his expression I knew that what I'd feared was true. We'd gone the wrong way.

'What are we going to do, Drago?'

He didn't reply. He just kept looking at me and all of a sudden I grew nervous.

'What is it, Drago?'

'I'm sorry, my lady,' he said, and in a flash there was a knife in his hand. It was a big hunting knife with a wickedly sharp blade and I knew at once what it was for.

He moved towards me. For a moment all I could do was stare at death coming for me. My body was rooted to the spot, my mind blocked, my pulse not so much racing as almost still. It was as though I was encased in a sheet of ice, incapable of thought, feeling or action.

It was only for a moment, though it felt like an eternity. In the next moment, I flung myself down on my knees in front of him, pleading for my life.

'Anything,' I wept. 'You can have anything! Money, jewels, anything you like – everything you want! My father will give you anything . . .'

He gave me a hard glance and his mouth twisted. 'I do not answer to your father.'

At first I could not take in his meaning. And then I understood. He was not doing this for himself. He was doing this for . . .

'I am truly sorry, Lady Bianca,' he said, almost gently, 'but you must die. And Lady Belladonna Dalmatin wants your heart as proof that you are dead.'

Black horror rose in my throat like toxic smoke. Numbly, I whispered, 'But why, Drago? Why? What have I ever done to deserve this?'

Something flickered in Drago's eyes, something I could not read. He pulled me roughly to my feet, the knife in his other hand, and I thought my last breath had come. But instead of striking me he pushed me away, growling, 'Go. Go now. Never come back. I will kill a deer and take its heart to my lady in place of yours.'

When I did not move – for I stood still in shock and confusion – he shouted, 'Go now, before I change my mind!'

I did not wait to be told a third time. I ran blindly into the trees, away from Drago, tripping over vines, getting scratched by thorns, with my breath whistling in my throat, my head and heart pounding. I took no notice of where I was going. I knew only that I wanted to get as far away from the clearing as possible.

Seven

)

I crashed through the woods till I could run no more and had to stop to draw breath. There was a deep ache in my side and my feet hurt badly, for the soft-soled cream boots I'd been wearing were not meant for a race across rough ground. Looking down at them, I saw that the cream leather was stained with red, and I knew that my feet must be bleeding inside the tightly fitting shoes.

The sight of the blood made my gorge rise and I was sick under a tree, the violent spasms tearing through me like the repeated stab of a knife. When at last the spasms stopped, I sat huddled and trembling on the ground, waves of dizziness washing over me as the horror and terror of what had happened sank in deeper and deeper. I could hardly believe what had happened. My mind fluttered wildly. Could Drago have been lying? But why would he? He was Belladonna's most trusted, most loyal servant.

Belladonna had sent me into the woods to die. If Drago had not inexplicably spared me, I would be lying dead in the clearing right now, my heart cut out. I put a hand over my mouth as the sick threatened to rise up again. Why would she do such a thing? Never had she shown any sign that she hated me. Yet only if you hated someone could you plan to do something so terrible, so cold. All this time, she must have been pretending to love me. All this time, when I thought she wanted the best for me, she must have only thought of the moment when she would be rid of me. But why? And why had Drago spared me? My mind fluttered like a frightened bird in a cage as I tried to make sense of it. But I could not. I was too numb. Too shaky. Too struck to the heart.

After a few moments, I stumbled to my feet. I had to keep going. I had to find shelter before it fell dark and the wild beasts came out. The one thing I did know by then was that Drago had not led us along a shortcut through to Mormest at all, but into some remote part of the forest where there would be few people. Surely, though, no place is truly completely abandoned. Surely I would find someone. Something. A woodcutter's hut. A charcoal burner's camp. A cave. A hollow tree. Anything would do.

I walked and walked, still not feeling my blistered and bleeding feet as the thin soles of my boots wore through even further, not caring that the hem of my skirt was getting ripped and torn and filthy from being pulled through so many brambles and being dragged along the earth as I stumbled and fell.

But as the grey cloudy light began to fade and the shadows thickened and darkened, I still had not found a place in which to hide and when, distantly, from somewhere far behind me, I heard the howl of wolves, I knew I had to stop or risk being hunted down by a hungry pack which would be drawn to me by the sweat of fear and the scent of blood.

Knowing that wolves can't climb, I decided to climb a tree. Though I'd be done for if any bears or lynx came hunting, too, I could only think of one danger at a time. I looked around and saw a tree with low branches that I could get into. I saw that my heavy serge skirt would get in the way, so I took it off and bundled it into a swag. Clad in my petticoat and long johns with my coat over the top, I climbed the tree, grateful that as a child I had climbed lots of trees with Rafiel and Margy. Rafiel had been the best at it, but I came a close second.

The thought of my long-lost friends and those long-ago happy days made my eyes swim with tears so that I nearly lost my grip on the branch. I could not allow my mind to wander. If I were to survive this night, I had to keep my mind clear and focused and not allow myself to be distracted by anything.

It was easier said than done. After I found a fork between two branches, which would serve as a resting place for the night, and wedged myself as comfortably as I could within it, the bundled skirt acting as a cushion, I could not prevent my thoughts from skittering around like terrified mice. I could not stop the waves of nausea that threatened to surge up out of my throat, or the pounding at my temples and the throbbing of my injured feet. I did not dare to take off my boots in case it made the smell of blood stronger, and as the evening advanced and turned into night, I grew colder and colder, stiffer and stiffer, and less and less capable of thinking clearly. Instead, hideous images filled my mind: Belladonna laughing as she held a torn and bloody heart in her hand; Drago staring at me with stony eyes; Belladonna again, stepping out of the dummy on the stage at the Ladies' Fair spring show, but this time with her face and clawed hands covered in blood. Why? Why? I wept, but there was no answer in the air or in my heart or in my foggy thoughts.

Father . . . Father . . . Oh, Father . . . What had happened to him? Was he really sick, far away in Aurisola, or had Belladonna lied about that, too? Could it be possible that she had . . .? No, I told myself. No. He was lying far away, sick but waiting for me. That must be true. She would not have killed my father – I knew that Belladonna really did love him. I remembered her pale, set face as she pointed out that Father had asked for me – for me, not for her. Was that why she hated me? Because my father wanted me by his side, not her? Was she jealous of his love for me? Did she want him all to herself?

My thoughts jumped. How would Belladonna explain away the fact that I had disappeared? And then I realised that she wouldn't need to. I had gone on a journey to Aurisola to see Father. As far as anyone knew, that's where I was. Drago would go back with the horses and he would tell anyone who asked that he'd accompanied me to the steamer at Mormest. As far as anyone was concerned, I was safely on my way to Aurisola. But journeys are danger-ous. Anything can happen. A steamer accident. An attack by bandits. Anything. In due course, Belladonna would 'discover' that I was missing, presumed dead. No-one but Belladonna, with a deer's heart in her hands, and Drago, who let me live, would know the truth.

I was alone, completely alone. And even if I somehow found my way out of this forest alive, where was I to go? I couldn't go home. I'd have to try to get a message to my father. If he lived. Stop it, I told myself. He will live! He must! And so must I. Clasping my hands together, I prayed desperately for his safety, for mine, for all this to be just a terrible nightmare from which I'd awake in my own bed.

The night wore on. The waxing moon rose, silver-white above the trees. It was the time we call 'hunter's moon' in Noricia, the time just before full moon. It was the best time to go on hunting trips, for it was said there was a special magic at this time that gave hunters extra luck. Hunter's moon . . . And I was the prey on which it shone, deep in the dark heart of the forest.

Despite my cramped position and my whirling thoughts, the shock of what had happened had made me exhausted and I was beginning to feel drowsy, my limbs feeling heavier and heavier. I fought against sleep, but my eyes kept drooping. Every time they did, horrible images rose up from under my eyelids and I forced them open again. I do not know how long I continued in this cycle of jagged, nightmare-haunted sleep, my visions of creatures prowling around the tree being interrupted when I jerked awake upon hearing the night sounds of the forest – rustlings and callings and faint howls and snarls. Eventually, I could fight sleep no longer. I fell into a deep black unconscious where neither nightmare nor night rustlings could wake me. I did not wake when my grip loosened and I slid sideways out of my precarious shelter and fell. I did not even wake when I hit the ground, for I fell on a soft deep carpet of dead leaves. I slept and slept and slept.

I slept the sleep of the dead, for to all intents and purposes, that's what I was. My world had ended, and with it the life I had known.

Eight

))

There was red light creeping under my closed eyelids and a delicious savoury smell in my nostrils. I tried to open my eyes but they were stuck down fast. I tried to move but my bruised body wouldn't obey me. I tried to cry out but my voice stuck in my dry throat. Then a stranger's voice, a woman's voice that was quite close, said, 'She's awake. Get some water.'

I heard the sound of footsteps, felt a hand on my forehead and shrank back.

'It's all right,' said the voice. 'You're safe now.'

I didn't feel safe. I couldn't see. Was I blind? I ached all over. I had no idea where I was, only that I was lying on something soft and that there was the smell of fire. I had no idea how I had arrived here. I could remember clambering into the fork of a tree. I could remember nothing after that – but everything else before it. Much too clearly.

I must have moaned or made some sound then because the voice repeated, 'It's all right. Don't be afraid. I will bathe your eyes to get rid of that sticky crust, so you can see. I didn't want to do it while you were asleep in case I woke you.'

In the next moment I felt a warm wet cloth on my eyes, wielded by a gentle hand, and as it worked I could feel my eyelids gradually unsticking. When I opened my eyes, I looked right into the face of an old woman – a face as wrinkled as last year's apples, only not red, but pale – a face which was surmounted by a thatch of white hair. Her eyes were set strangely, with one higher than the other, and the irises of her eyes were green, with a yellow gleam to them.

'There. Is that better?' asked the stranger.

I nodded, mutely.

'Grim has gone to get you some water. You'll be thirsty.'

I nodded again, though I had no idea, of course, who Grim might be. I only knew that my throat was so parched that I could not utter a word.

'There, now,' said the strange woman, as she helped me to sit up with a cushion at my back. She was tall and very thin – almost wispy – and did not look strong at all, but she had a grip like iron and soon had me sitting more or less comfortably. There was a dull throbbing pain in my legs and feet and I felt a little dizzy at first but at least sitting up I could see my surroundings better.

I was lying under a big patchwork quilt on a low bed that had been pulled up close to a big tiled stove. I was not wearing my own clothes. Instead, I was wearing a clean nightgown made of dark-blue flannel. Feeling guilty, I could not help but feel for the jewellery I had been wearing. It was all in a little dish by the side of the bed.

The room I was in looked for all the world like a cave: it was round and without windows, only the walls were not stone but looked like earth – I could even see a small bush growing out of one wall and a pattern of moss on another. A few lamps, throwing golden light and crooked shadows, were placed at intervals around the walls. There was a big table in the centre of the room with chairs and stools of different sizes arranged around it, a bright but shabby rug on the beaten earth floor, bookshelves crammed with untidily arranged volumes, and other shelves crammed with all kinds of things – wooden figures, pine cones, dried flowers and chipped plates and bowls.

The white-haired woman handed me a knitted dressing-gown.

'Here, put this around your shoulders,' she said. 'It'll keep you warm.' Her thin pale lips parted into what must have been intended as a reassuring smile, but which disconcertingly displayed a flash of sharp incisors in her mouth. 'You see, my dear, you're quite safe.'

I swallowed. Where was I? Who was she? But before I could attempt to push the questions past my dry throat, a door at the far end of the room opened and someone came in, carrying a jug and a glass on a tray. This was Grim, I supposed. He was very small – dwarf-like, in fact – and as dark as the woman was pale. He had bright beady eyes and was also very hairy, with a bushy beard and bushy eyebrows and black hairs sprouting out from under his collar. Oddly enough, the only place he didn't have hair was on his round bald head, which had the shine of a billiard ball. As he came closer, I heard a soft tapping and realised he had only one good leg – the other was wooden.

'Water?' he asked. His voice, unlike the woman's rich tones, was thin, even squeaky.

I nodded and he filled the glass and handed it to me. It was full of sparkling clear liquid.

'Drink it slowly,' he said, and I tried to do as I was told even though I was so thirsty it was hard not to gulp it down. It was the best water I'd ever tasted – cool, refreshing, with a faint, very pleasant scent – and like medicine it was balm for my sore throat.

'Thank you,' I croaked.

'You're welcome,' said the white-haired woman.

'I . . . How long have I been here?' It felt as if I had been sleeping for an eternity.

'Only one night – but most of the morning, too,' she said.

Panic seized me as my father's image leaped into my mind, crowding out the horror of what had happened to me.

'I must go at once!' I cried. 'I must go to my father! I must go to Aurisola!'

'Aurisola! You couldn't even go up top in the state you're in,' said Grim, with a dry chuckle.

The woman shot him a cross glance. In a gentle voice she said to me, 'My dear, I'm afraid there can be no question of you going anywhere just now. Your legs aren't broken, thank goodness, but they are badly bruised; your right ankle is sprained and your feet are cut to ribbons. We used Grim's strongest salve for them, but it'll take time for them to heal.'

Dimly I thought, so Grim's a healer. He doesn't look like one. But then, what is a healer meant to look like? Had I not just learnt that looks cannot be trusted? I'd looked into Belladonna's face and seen a kind, loving stepmother. I'd not seen the black heart she hid under those beautiful features.

Swallowing hard, I said, 'But you don't understand! My father – he's ill – very, very ill . . . And he doesn't know . . . He doesn't know what's happened to me.' I felt my chest tighten. 'They'll tell him I'm dead.'

Grim and the woman looked at each other. She said, 'Don't you fret, my dear. We'll see what we can do when the others get back.' There were more people living here? She saw my expression. 'There are seven of us living in this haven. The others are out at work. You'll meet them tonight and then we can talk about it. In the meantime, you will have something to eat and you will rest. Recover a little strength. And then you'll be right.'

I wanted to argue but knew she was right. Only moments ago I had not been able to see. I was in no fit state to travel. Not yet, anyway. So I nodded, trying to keep my voice steady.

'Thank you . . . er . . . Mrs . . . er . . .'

'Just plain "Verakina" will do. And this is Grim,' she said, flashing her sharp-toothed smile. Grim smiled too, showing, in contrast, hardly any teeth at all.

'My . . . My name is Bianca,' I said. I hesitated, uncertain whether to give them my surname or not, and Verakina saw it.

'"Bianca" will do very nicely. Now then, you must be hungry.'

'Yes,' I said, realising all at once that my belly felt painfully empty, especially with that savoury smell tickling my nostrils. 'Yes, I am.'

'Good. There is soup. And bread. I'll bring you a tray.'

'No – please – can I try to sit at the table? I want to try to walk. If . . . If you'll help me.'

'Of course. Grim, get the crutches.'

Grim scuttled away while Verakina lifted the quilt from my legs. I saw then that what she'd told me was true – my legs were covered in purple and green bruises. My right ankle was bandaged and my feet looked swollen and red. I began to think she was right and that I wouldn't be able to walk. But I could not lie here. I had to get up. Whatever it took, I had to walk. I had to heal, and quickly, if I had any chance of getting to Father before he learnt of my supposed death – or died before he heard anything at all. I did not dare to think that I might already be too late.

'Here, let's get these on,' Verakina said, producing a pair of soft sheepskin slippers and slipping them gently onto my sore feet. As soon as they were on, I felt a little better. 'They are coated inside with the balm,' she explained, seeing my expression. 'Another of Grim's inventions.'

Grim came back with the crutches and they both helped me to stand and steadied me on the crutches. I was very glad for their help and for the crutches, too, for though once I was up my feet did not hurt as much as I'd feared, my head was swimming and I felt more than a little unsteady.

Finally seated at the table with a steaming hot bowl of bean soup and a thick slice of fresh bread in front of me, I discovered that at least part of the faintness I had been feeling must have been to do with hunger. I could not stop myself from finishing the soup and bread in a trice and when Verakina proposed I eat more, I did not refuse. It was only then that I found my manners again, and I said, 'This is so delicious. Thank you.'

'Good. I'm glad you like it,' said Verakina, smiling.

I stammered, 'Thank you so very much, for ... for everything. You have been so very kind, taking in a stranger.'

'If an outcast cannot help another, what are we for?' Verakina replied.

Her words struck me deeply. It would not surprise me to know that this strange pair had experienced harsh cruelties. Their curious appearance would be enough for some people to inflict all kinds of miseries upon them. I could believe that this might be the only place they were able to escape to. What did surprise me was that from her words, I knew that they saw me as an outcast, too. It shouldn't have shocked me, though, for indeed, was I not now an outcast?

'How did you find me?' I asked.

'It was the night patrol,' said Grim.

Seeing my puzzled expression, Verakina explained. 'We have a roster. Each night, two of us are on patrol. Last night it was Carlo and Rasmus.'

'Oh.' I had no idea who they were.

'Anyway, they first came across your trail a fair distance from where they finally found you,' said Grim. 'It took them a while, though. Would've been much different if *he'd* been there, of course.'

Surely Grim wasn't referring to himself in the third person . . .

Verakina frowned. 'Well, he wasn't. He can't be everywhere at once!'

Bemused, I asked, 'Who are you talking about?'

'The Prince of Outlaws,' said Verakina, in a hushed, admiring tone.

'Who?'

'Yes, the Prince of Outlaws himself.'

I stared. 'But how . . . How can that be? That was long ago . . .' The Prince of Outlaws was a legendary hero from an old story harking back to a dark time when Noricia was under the thumb of a warlord named Tadeus Melegant, who treated the land like his personal treasure-house and his people like dogs. That is, until there arose a young forest dweller known only as the Prince of Outlaws. He became the leader of the great rebel army that overthrew Melegant. Once peace was restored to Noricia, and a new parliament proclaimed, the Prince of Outlaws vanished, never to be seen again. That was centuries ago, though.

Grim gave a reedy laugh. 'Ach, no, little lady, that one – if he were still alive – he'd be hundreds of years old by now! We speak of the nowadays Prince of Outlaws.'

'But I've never heard of –'

'And have you heard of everything in this world, little lady?' asked Grim, tartly.

I shook my head, awkwardly, colouring as he went on.

'And if you have not heard of a thing, does it mean it must not exist?'

'No,' I said, sadly, for his words had evoked a sudden memory of my conversation with Emilia at the ball. Emilia – and Lucian – whom I might never see again. Oh Lucian, I thought, sadly. We had known each other so briefly. Would he ever think of me? Would he wonder where I had gone? But Belladonna had warned him off, and unlike with Emilia, I hadn't had a chance to explain. A lump formed in my throat again.

Verakina said gently, 'We were all like that at first, my dear. It's the shock, you see. The pain. The confusion. The heartbreak.'

I looked at her. 'You . . . You . . . Something happened to you?'

'To me. To Grim. To all of us, yes. For each of us, the reason we are outcast is different. But for all of us it means loss. Of friends. Of family. Of home. Once, being outcast would have meant a loss of hope, too. A life of loneliness. For me, that's what it was like. For years I wandered alone, chased out of villages, reviled by all . . .'

'But why? Why?' I cried.

She fixed her gleaming eyes on me. 'I am – there is something that – that happens to me, at hunter's moon.' A pause. 'That is why I was not on night patrol, last night, when you were found. I stay inside, always, every time hunter's moon comes around. And Grim – well, he keeps me company. Though he doesn't need to.'

'Oh,' I said, uncertainly, as I remembered a story I'd heard once, long ago, from Rafiel and Margy's mother. Hunter's moon didn't just bring luck to hunters. It also triggered the change in shapeshifters such as werewolves. It was the time when the wolf in them was strongest. Was Verakina a werewolf? Looking at those gleaming eyes and sharp incisors, I couldn't help thinking she probably was. Yesterday the thought would have scared me. Today it only made me a little uneasy.

Seeing my expression, Grim cackled. 'You wonder where you've come, don't you, little lady? Under whose protection you're living? You wonder if you're safe with us.'

'No, no,' I said, blushing and stammering. 'I know I'm safe. I know that you are good and kind. I know that I am very lucky that your friends found me and brought me here. What I do not know is how I can ever repay you . . .' I bit down on my lip, trying to stop myself from bursting into tears.

'By keeping our haven *secret*,' said Grim, quite sternly. I had the impression that he didn't altogether approve of my being here.

'Why in the name of all the angels and saints would she not?' snapped Verakina. 'Now, I don't think that kindling will chop itself, Grim!'

He shot her a sharp glance. 'As if I have to be told,' he grumbled, but slid off his stool and stumped off without another word.

'You mustn't mind Grim,' said Verakina. 'He's a good man, but can be a little crosspatch at times. And his leg plays up every so often, especially at hunter's moon. That's when he lost it, years ago, you see. The flesh one, not the wooden one.'

'Oh. I'm sorry,' I said.

'Why should you be? It wasn't you who set the dogs on him,' she said, making an icy shiver slip down my spine. She spoke of such hideousness so matter-of-factly. Until yesterday, evil of that sort would have seemed like some-thing out of a newspaper report: horrible but far away from me, like the stories of the beggar killings. Today, I knew that I'd been living in a fool's paradise, and the crushing weight of that knowledge was suddenly too much to bear and I wept as I sat there at the table, my head in my hands. Verakina made little soothing noises and patted my shoulder, but did not try to stop me from crying.

It might have been the crying, or perhaps it was simply the shock of all that had happened, but I found myself so tired again that I had to hobble back to bed. I lay there beside the fire of the stove with the patchwork quilt pulled right up under my chin, watching the shadow of the flames on the ceiling, listening to Verakina softly bustling around the room, and the peace of that strange place gradually settled in me so that at last I was able to fall softly into sleep.

Nine

When I woke again, it was to the sound of many voices. Though I did not know it, night was falling outside, and the other haven dwellers had returned home. From my bed by the fire I couldn't see their features properly – and some I could only see from the back – but from the features I could see, I thought that all but Verakina were men.

Verakina must have heard me stir for she came over. 'That was a long sleep,' she said.

'Yes. It was. I feel much better.' And I did, for throughout those blessed hours I had felt no pain, no heartbreak. I had felt nothing but quiet and peace.

'Good.' Her smile was as sharp-toothed as ever but it did not disturb me in the least, now. It was just a part of this kind woman who had taken me in without question. 'Now, do you feel up to meeting everyone?'

I looked over at the table, where I could sense that everyone seated there was carefully not looking at me. 'I . . . I think so,' I murmured.

'Excellent. Now let's get you wrapped up again,' she said, as she helped me with the dressing-gown, produced the slippers and crutches, and smoothed back my hair. 'There, now. You look wonderful, my dear.'

Her words and gestures reminded me of my dear late Babina, my grandmother on my mother's side. Babina had died a year or two after Mother, and I could remember that as a little girl I had been very close to her. She had read books to me, sung songs and played games with me. She had been nothing like Grandmother Dalmatin, Father's formidable mother, who had scared me a little. And although their appearances had nothing in common, it wasn't strange to me that I put Verakina and Babina together in the same thought – the heart has its own reasons and in Verakina's presence, I felt that same sense of unforced sweetness that I had felt in my beloved grandmother.

Six pairs of eyes regarded us coming, or rather five and a half, because one of the people sitting at the table had a black patch over her left eye – I'd been wrong about the others all being men. Despite her short chestnut curls and man's clothes, that one most certainly was a woman, and a young woman at that, a little older than me but not, I thought, by much. With her delicate features and shining hair she would have been very pretty indeed had it not been for that patch and a livid scar that bisected one side of her face, running from under the patch almost to her lip.

I tried not to stare – at her or at the others – but I could not help but look around at my hosts. There was a bony man with a gaunt, smiling face; a big man with a harelip and large blue eyes; a scrawny man with a scarred face and a soft voice; and a tall man with webbed fingers and shining silver hair. All the men including Grim, of course, were a good deal older than the girl and me, and one, the tall silver-haired man, looked to be almost as old as Verakina.

It was she who quickly made the introductions: the girl was Lisbet, the smiley man was Rasmus, the blue-eyed man was Carlo, the silver-haired man was Mattias, and the soft-voiced man was Tofer. They all seemed friendly and even though Lisbet hardly said a word, she flashed me a shy smile. Each of them, it appeared, had their own special work within the haven. Grim, as I'd already learnt, was the healer. Verakina was the cook and main housekeeper, though everyone pitched in to help her with household tasks. Rasmus was the hunter and had brought back two rabbits for dinner. Carlo was the fisherman, and had brought back a clutch of river oysters. Mattias was a woodcutter, and had brought back a pile of new logs. Tofer gathered mushrooms and berries and made baskets and nets. Lisbet, it turned out, was the haven's scout, who travelled hither and thither keeping an eye on what was happening in the woods so that she would be able to warn the group who lived in the haven if danger came close. And she also sometimes brought back goods from outside that the outcasts could not make themselves, such as tea and flour. Today, she had been in one of the forest villages for the arrival of the weekly market barge that brought much-needed basic groceries to the isolated places in these parts.

They did not speak about what had brought them here, only about what they did now. And they did not ask about what had happened to me, though Verakina had clearly told them that my father was ill, for there was already a plan to deliver a message to him in Aurisola.

'Rasmus is going tomorrow to Sarmest, the market town on the other side of the forest, to sell some game,' said Verakina. 'The person there who buys from us is entirely trustworthy. There's a telegraph office in Sarmest and our friend will send a telegram to your father, if you will write the words for it. He will also wait for a reply. How does that sound to you?'

'I'm so grateful,' I said. 'And I hope . . .' I looked at Rasmus. '. . . I hope I'm not putting you . . . putting you at risk in any way . . . attracting undue attention.'

'Not at all,' he said in his deep, slow voice, giving me one of his beautiful smiles. 'I go to market every month, always around this time. People have grown used to seeing me. And as I will not be going to the telegraph office, there will be no undue attention whatsoever.'

Once that was settled, I felt better knowing that there was a plan in place for me to contact my father.

At dinner that night, making a conscious effort to banish thoughts of the dark things that had happened to me, I began to ask the outlaws about their home and the other outcast havens, a topic about which, out of pride, it seemed, they were very happy to expand on.

And so I learnt that there was a network of such havens all over the country, in various remote spots, and that nearly all were underground, sometimes in caves and sometimes, like this one, in man-made shelters hollowed out of the earth itself. Long ago, this haven had been carved out as a wartime shelter but it had been abandoned many decades ago and forgotten until it came into use again for the outcasts. Though the havens themselves were new – the first one had opened just under three years ago – the concept, which originated with the mysterious modern Prince of Outlaws, was built on a long tradition of outcasts seeking shelter in remote locations.

Previously there had been nothing systematic about it, nothing organised – the shelters were haphazardly built and easily discovered, and very often such outcasts had not survived long. These havens were quite different. They were well run, strategically located, and communities were kept small to help members avoid attention. Though they operated independently of each other, each haven kept in touch with the others. Twice a year, at midsummer and midwinter, a Haven Council was held involving all haven members, where matters of mutual interest were discussed. These meetings were always presided over by the man whose idea had brought this extraordinary parallel world into being: the Prince of Outlaws, who was relied upon, loved and revered by all.

When I asked what the prince's name really was, though, each person said they didn't know, for he always came in darkness, and was always masked. By his voice and his manner, they knew he was a young man, but they did not know his true name, or his story, or what had driven him to become their protector. All that mattered to them was that he had given them a home and a full life, when before they'd had neither.

As the evening wore on, they talked, and revealed more and more about themselves and what had brought them here. It was Verakina who started it, for after declaring that she felt I could be trusted, she confirmed what I'd suspected: she was a werewolf. Her story was that she had been attacked by hate-filled neighbours one night on hunter's moon and had been left for dead before being rescued by the Prince.

After that, other tongues were loosened. For all of them, 'up top', as they called it, had been a place of sadness and fear. Two of them – Rasmus and Carlo – had been abandoned children, brought up in cruel orphanages where not a kind word had been spoken to them but where, because of their looks, they'd endured a life of torment both from the staff and their fellow orphans, who laughed at them, reviled them and called them freaks. After leaving the orphanage as soon as they could, they had found the world outside just as harsh, fallen in with bad company, and ended up in prison for a spell.

Mattias, meanwhile, had grown up in a family, but they had been no kinder to him than the orphanage had been to Rasmus and Carlo and Mattias' family had kicked him out of home by the time he'd turned eleven so that he had been forced to beg for a living. Tofer had been accused of a theft he hadn't committed and been beaten so severely that he'd been left scarred for life. As for Grim, he'd been found as a seven-year-old child in a bear's den, unable to speak or walk properly. It had taken years for him to become what the villagers called human and even after that, he'd been shunned by most, and he'd taken to thievery to support himself until the day came when some villagers set the dogs on him and he had lost his leg. Lisbet was the only one who did not even hint at what had happened to her. But I knew just by looking at her pretty but scarred face that it must have been something so dreadful that she could not bear to voice it.

They had trusted me with their stories. Now it was time to trust them with my own. So, haltingly, I told them my full name and my story. It was a strange thing, because although I felt that the terror and heartbreak of Belladonna's betrayal would never leave me, voicing those things aloud helped to lessen the horror a little, just as hearing the others' stories of pain did.

All of the outcasts here in the haven had been lost – and, somehow, all had been found. They'd suffered through hell, but had finally come to their own paradise. They'd made their own family, from people who under-stood what it was like to be outcast. They'd found hope and purpose. They'd formed a new life. And this was the gift of the Prince of Outlaws, who'd found each of them at the moment of their greatest, darkest despair, and brought them into the light. To them, the Prince was more than a man. He was a hero. In fact, some stories they told made it seem as if he had some kind of supernatural power. Grim, who scoffed at the idea that the legendary Prince and their own prince were one and the same, was actually in the minority: his friends clearly felt differently and hinted that the modern Prince of Outlaws was a reincarnation of the ancient one.

'You are under his protection now, too, so you need never be afraid again,' Lisbet told me, giving me a shining blue glance out of her one good eye. I didn't say anything. I was grateful for the Prince's protection but I did not know him. How could I put my trust in appearances again? How could I trust someone so mysterious? None of them even knew who he really was. I also could not help but feel a little afraid of a shadowy figure who was as secret as the night itself, a masked man who never revealed himself, not even to his most loyal friends, whose very existence was a kept secret from the outside world. What was the reason for his secrecy? And was the reason an innocent one or was there something darker behind it?

But if I could not fully trust this shadowy figure, I felt differently about the seven outcasts. They had taken me in, welcomed me into their home, looked after me, accepted me without question. They were even willing to take risks for me – I suspected that, whatever Rasmus had said, there must be some risk to them in organising for my message to be delivered to Father. These people I was certain I could trust. And for the first time since that terrible moment in the clearing with Drago, I felt truly safe.

Ten

The next day, Verakina was the only one of the seven who stayed at home – even Grim left the underground hollow to gather roots and herbs for his potions. But Verakina was very busy, too, bustling about doing household chores and at the same time trying to get me to stay in bed.

'Rest – that's what we need you to do,' she scolded.

'I've rested more than enough,' I muttered. I was impatient to get moving again. The swelling had gone down in my feet and they no longer throbbed. Confined to the bed, how was I to recover enough strength to get to my father?

She looked at me with the same kind but impatient look that Babina used to wear when I was whining. 'As you wish.'

'Can I go exploring? I mean, just in the haven,' I added, quickly. 'Not to snoop or anything, I just want to have a look around.'

'I know you wouldn't snoop,' she said. 'Besides, there are no secrets here. It's a big place though, much bigger than you'd think, so you'll get very tired if you go too far on those crutches. Be careful. Your feet haven't healed yet, whatever it might feel like.'

'I'll be careful,' I promised.

'I'll come and fetch you when it's time for lunch. Now be off with you – and stop interrupting!' said Verakina, flicking a duster at me.

Smiling, I left her to her work and set off slowly on my exploration. I soon found out that Verakina was right. Beyond the big main room which was all that I'd known till now, the haven stretched on and on and on, a veritable rabbit warren of small rooms set along winding corridors that smelt of damp earth.

I opened a few doors, only to close them again when I realised they were people's bedrooms. Soon I came across a set of rooms that were clearly not private: a well-stocked pantry lined with jars of all kinds of preserves, bags of flour and sugar and spices, bottles of oil and vinegar, and boxes full of salted meat and fish; a sewing room where I spied my freshly laundered but torn clothes, set in a pile to be repaired; a storeroom piled with boxes and baskets. Then I discovered the water room. Against a wall was a very large barrel. A pipe ran from the barrel into the wall, and under the tap of the barrel was a china basin. I took a glass from a shelf that housed jugs and glasses and turned the tap. Water tinkled into the glass – the same lightly sparkling, faintly scented water I'd had before – and I drank it down. The water must enter the pipe from the outside, I thought. It must be linked to a spring or a stream, out in the forest.

I went on and discovered a meat storeroom, a very cold place where I didn't linger; a very warm room that, from the look of the many bundles hanging from the ceiling, was used for drying herbs; and a drinks cellar, with wine and beer, cordials and gleaming juices. It was extraordinary: I'd never seen so much food and drink. There was enough, surely, to feed an army or withstand a siege.

The thought made me feel a little uneasy, reminding me yet again of that first Prince of Outlaws, but I tried to push the feeling aside, for of course the people of the haven needed to secure their supplies. Of course they needed to have enough to see them through long forest winters. This was not a sign of some secret conspiracy. The haven network was not a web of rebels and the Prince of Outlaws was not planning a coup. Why would he? There was no war lord laying our land to waste, only pompous Duke Ottakar and his haughty sister who might not be the best rulers Noricia had ever had, but who were perfectly all right in their own dull way.

Oh heavens, I thought, as a memory struck me suddenly. Today I should be presenting myself at Town Hall to take the second oath in front of the Mayor of Lepmest and all his councillors! I would not be there, but Emilia and Lucian would be. If they asked Belladonna where I was – which was unlikely, given that she'd not exactly been friendly towards either of them – she'd tell them that I was missing, that I had vanished on the way to Aurisola. That I was lost forever . . .

It would be a shock, no doubt. I thought – I even hoped – that Lucian might wonder where I was. But they wouldn't suspect anything. Who would, faced with Belladonna's crocodile tears, her supposed anxiety, her supposed grief? They'd be sad. But they'd not ask too many questions. Belladonna would get away with it . . .

No! I told myself fiercely. I will not allow that to happen. Belladonna thinks I'm dead, and that is my one chance. I started to formulate a plan. As soon as Rasmus came back, I would ask – I would beg – for messages to be sent to Emilia and to Lucian. I'd tell them the truth, but that I'm safe. Somehow, together, after I found my father and made sure he was safe and well, we could work out a way to unmask Belladonna.

It was a plan of a sort – a rather weak sort. But the only plan I had, for the moment. And just imagining it made me feel a little more in control of my fate –

My thoughts were interrupted by Verakina bursting into the room. There were two red spots on her cheeks and her eyes glittered. 'There you are. Come at once. Rasmus is back.'

'Already?' We hadn't expected him back till the late afternoon and it was only midday. He'd only been gone four hours.

'Already,' she echoed, and by her tone I knew at once that this was not a good thing.

'What happened? Is he all right?' I panted, trying to keep up with her on my crutches.

'He's all right,' she answered. 'But the message –' She broke off.

'What about it? Verakina, you must tell me!'

'He . . . He didn't send it.'

'Why not?' I cried. 'In heaven's name, what happened?'

She halted and turned to face me and I saw that the glitter in her eyes was the shine of tears.

'I'm sorry, Bianca, my dear. I truly am.'

My heart dropped like a stone and my blood turned to ice. I saw in her eyes what she'd been afraid to tell me.

'No . . .' I whispered. 'No, it can't be . . . It can't be true . . . It can't . . .'

My legs were giving way under me and if Verakina hadn't hurried to my side to prop me up, I would have fallen.

I don't know how I managed to get back to the living room, how I did not scream from the pain that was tearing me apart. But as soon as I saw the expression on Rasmus's gaunt face, I knew the pain was only just beginning. Dumbly, I sat on a chair, my eyes on his face, as he stumbled through his words.

'I . . . had only just got to Sarmest when I happened to catch sight of something at a newspaper stand . . .' He swallowed, and I had to push back a wild impulse to shake him, to tell him to get on with it, and at the same time to tell him to shut up, to stop wringing his hands, to go away and save me from hearing the worst of all news.

He shot a desperate look at Verakina.

She said, gently, 'Come on, Rasmus. Bianca needs to know.'

'Of . . . Of course,' he stammered. 'I don't usually take notice of newspapers, but . . .' He ran a hand nervously through his thinning hair. '. . . It was the name, you see . . . I . . . I would never have known, if it weren't for the name . . .' He broke off and looked at me. 'Angels defend me, but I can't say it. Here.' And he put a hand in his jacket pocket and pulled out a folded sheet of newsprint, obviously an article ripped out from the front page of a newspaper, and handed it to me without a word.

It was dated two days ago. 'Sir Anton Dalmatin Murdered in Poison Plot,' read the headline. And in smaller letters, under that, 'Secretary Arrested, Commits Suicide.'

It was as though the world had stopped. I heard nothing and I saw nothing. Nothing, except for the dreadful words that in a single instant broke my heart.

It has been confirmed that Sir Anton Dalmatin, known throughout the world as the King of Elegance, was poisoned to death in a ghastly plot that was master-minded by his trusted secretary, Hans Reinart.

Sir Anton, who was on a business visit to Aurisola with Reinart, was suddenly taken ill and died after days of agony. It was thought at first that he had succumbed to a particularly virulent form of influenza which had been sweeping the region and had it not been for the suspicions of his widow, Lady Belladonna Dalmatin, he would have been buried as an unfortunate victim of illness. Lady Dalmatin, however, suspected foul play, and in a sensational statement begged the Aurisolan authorities to conduct an autopsy on her husband. When this was performed, the presence of a rare poison called Vertini was at once discovered in his organs. Vertini is made from the concentrated venom of the deadly vertin viper. Vertini leaves a bright green trace in internal organs but leaves no external traces on the victim's body. Had it not been for Lady Dalmatin's suspicions, this crime would never have been discovered.

Suspicion quickly fell on Sir Anton's secretary, Hans Reinart, and when his belongings were searched, a forged will naming him as sole inheritor of the Dalmatin estate was discovered, along with an empty vial containing minute traces of the Vertini poison. Reinart had no expla-nation for how the vial came to be in his possession and was arrested immediately. Before he could be properly questioned, however, he was discovered dead in his cell. It seems that he shot himself using a tiny revolver that he had concealed in his boot. A very short written confession was also found in the cell. It had just five words: 'I killed Sir Anton Dalmatin', and the handwriting matched Reinart's perfectly. Considering the forged will discovered in his possession, it appears that the very large Dalmatin fortune was what motivated Reinart to commit this dreadful crime.

The body of Sir Anton Dalmatin is on its way back to Lepmest, Noricia, where a state funeral will be held in his honour on Thursday.

My skin prickled with cold. I looked up. Rasmus and Verakina were watching me anxiously.

'Bianca, we're so sor–' began Verakina, but I held up a hand to stop her.

I saw Rasmus and Verakina exchanging a worried look. I saw it, but it didn't affect me. My whole body was numb, as if encased in a shroud of ice, the pain of my father's death crushing my heart. I would never see him again. Never hear his voice. Never laugh with him. Nothing . . . Ever again. How could I bear it?

And then, on the heels of the pain and grief, came other things. Rage. Hatred. White-hot, fierce, burning. And I knew it wasn't Reinart.

'The forged will was discovered in his possession . . .' I echoed the article, and my voice seemed to come from very far away. 'She did it,' I continued, and the words came from deep inside me. 'Belladonna – my stepmother – she arranged it all. My father's murder. And Reinart's – she made sure that he would take the blame.

'Two days ago . . .' I went on.

Rasmus and Verakina looked at me in bewilderment.

'Two days ago, this piece is dated,' I repeated. 'What did today's newspaper say?'

When Rasmus didn't answer, I couldn't help but curse. 'Devil take you! Don't tell me you didn't go looking for one!'

He shot me a miserable look. 'Yes, but . . .'

'I need to see it,' I said, fighting to keep my voice steady, to control the dark waves of wild rage sweeping through my body.

'Give it to her, Rasmus,' said Verakina, quietly.

He reached inside his pocket and pulled out not a newspaper but a copy of the *Mirror*. 'Special Edition' was emblazoned across the top.

'Bianca . . .' Rasmus began.

But I wasn't listening. Snatching the magazine from him, I stared at the picture on the front page. It was a candid photograph of me at the Presentation Ball. I was sitting down, looking into the distance. I remembered that moment. It was just before Lucian had asked me to dance.

Underneath the picture, the caption read: 'Tragic Fate of Fairest Lady.'

Something had happened to Belladonna? A savage sort of pleasure flared up inside me. But then, why had my picture been used, not hers?

I turned the page. There was an article with the same title, written by Sommer Malling.

In a tragic twist, it has been revealed that Lady Bianca Dalmatin, only child of murdered businessman Sir Anton Dalmatin, has been missing for nearly two days. Grave fears are held for her safety.

It is known that Lady Bianca had been on her way to Aurisola to see her father, who had sent for her in the final days of his illness, and that she had arrived safely in Mormest in order to catch the steamer to Aurisola. An innkeeper in Mormest testified that she had arrived on horseback, ordered tea, and told him she was going to the steamer office afterwards. The ticket-office clerk confirmed that a young woman matching Lady Bianca's description had indeed bought a ticket for a first-class cabin. 'She hardly spoke a word, and seemed sad,' he said.

The steamer had sailed before news of Sir Anton's death became widely known in Mormest, and so Lady Dalmatin attempted to contact her stepdaughter via the steamer's telegraph service. As Lady Bianca had not been out of her cabin at all during the trip, the message was slipped in under the door but when the ship docked the next morning in Aurisola and was met by the Norician ambassador, who was to escort her to his home, it was discovered that the young woman had vanished. Her light luggage was in the cabin and the telegram inform-ing her of her father's death lay crumpled on the bed, but Lady Bianca herself had disappeared. A thorough search of the vessel for clues of her whereabouts revealed a scarf belonging to Lady Bianca, lying in a corner of the steamer deck. It is feared that, through accident or otherwise, the poor young woman had fallen from the deck into the sea. An inquest will be held into the matter.

In a brief exclusive interview with the Mirror, *Sir Anton Dalmatin's widow, Lady Dalmatin, said that she hoped there would be no ill-informed speculation in the press about her stepdaughter's tragic fate. But it was true that Lady Bianca was fragile, she said. Lady Bianca had been 'absolutely distraught' upon receiving the telegram informing her of her father's illness. 'I begged her to reconsider her decision to go and see her father, for I was afraid she'd arrive too late and feared that this would quite disturb the balance of her mind.'*

Only this week, the Mirror *made the sensational decision to award the title of Fairest Lady to the beautiful young woman Lady Bianca Dalmatin as a worthy successor to Lady Belladonna Dalmatin. It was a decision endorsed by the previously crowned Fairest Lady herself: 'It gives me the greatest pleasure to know that Bianca learnt before leaving for Aurisola that she had been crowned Fairest Lady. I thank you for that, for giving her a bright moment in the darkness.'*

I could hardly hold back my tears of mingled sorrow and admiration as I left my interview with Lady Belladonna Dalmatin. Stoical and dignified in the face of the terrible grief she is facing at the loss of both her husband and her stepdaughter in such terrible circumstances, generous in her words and deeds, Lady Dalmatin once again displays the qualities of heart and spirit that have made her such a beloved figure in our land.

My mouth opened, as if of its own accord, and I heard a scream pierce the silence. One scream, and another, and another. Screams tearing me apart. From a distance,

I heard Verakina and Rasmus begging me to stop, trying to comfort me. But I could not stop, and I would not be comforted.

It wasn't the grotesque revelation that I'd been awarded a crown I'd never sought. It wasn't the memory of a half-seen magazine, discarded on the floor near Belladonna's dressing table. It wasn't the barefaced lies told by Belladonna, the thought of all the people she must have bought off to make the story stick, the thought of all the effort she had gone to in order to construct her sinister conspiracy.

It wasn't any of these things that formed my screams. It was that Belladonna had wanted my heart as proof of my death and that she had gotten what she wanted. She had torn my heart apart as surely as if Drago had cut it from my chest.

Eleven

When my screams stopped at last, I was exhausted. Every muscle ached. Every pore in my skin exuded a cold sweat. I sat with my head in my hands, shaking, only dimly aware of Verakina and Rasmus looking at me, anxiously. Slowly, the shaking stopped and I grew calmer.

I lifted my head. 'I must go.'

They stared at me. My voice felt hardly my own. It was cold, clear, flat.

'I must go to Lepmest at once. From what the paper says, my father's funeral is tomorrow. The Duke and all those who loved and respected my father will be there. At the funeral I will accuse Belladonna. I will tell the world the truth. Have her arrested. She will hang for this.'

'Are you mad?' said Verakina. 'Do you really think that Belladonna has not planned every step of this? She will have informers everywhere. Do you not think that if you put one foot in Lepmest, she will find you?'

'She thinks I'm dead,' I replied, 'so that is my chance.'

'She won't think so for long – when you leave this place, her informers will see you. They will see you, they will tell her, and she will kill you.'

'She has already killed me,' I said, hollowly. 'She has taken everything from me. My father, my home, my hope, my future. I have nothing left to lose.'

'Only your life!' snapped Verakina, fixing her green eyes on me.

'And I will use it well. I will use it to avenge my father,' I said, staring back at her. 'My mind is made up.'

'You must be patient! Not only do you need to wait for your feet to heal, you need to know more, a lot more, before you begin such a dangerous mission,' Verakina implored.

'I've already sent a message to the Prince,' Rasmus put in, eagerly.

'He knows where to go,' added Verakina. 'He knows who to ask for information, who to trust, where the safe houses are. I have asked him to find out as much as he can. He is the only one who can help you.'

I was angry. How dare they pass on my secret, my story, to the Prince of Outlaws? It was not their story to tell, their secret to give. Who was this man, really? How was I to know if he could be trusted?

'I never asked you to do that,' I said, stung.

'You need time. To think things through. To make your plan carefully. Or you will stumble and Belladonna will find you. And then, Bianca, Belladonna will find everyone who helped you. You will draw her to our haven and we will all be in great danger.'

Rasmus looked at me. 'Please, will you give us your word that you will not go until you have spoken to the Prince?'

I looked at Verakina. 'How long will it be until he comes?'

'A day. Two at the most.'

It was true that they had helped me. And I owed them at least the protection of the haven they had worked so hard to create.

'Very well,' I said. 'I give you my word. I will wait until I can speak with your Prince. I will wait to see if he has any information that will help me.'

'Thank you, Bianca. And if there is anything we can do while you wait . . .'

'There is nothing,' I said, adding, quickly, 'thank you.'

'You will tell us if there is, won't you?' said Rasmus, awkwardly.

'I will.' A pause. 'Actually, there is one thing. I . . . I need to be alone, just for a while. To gather my thoughts. To pray for my father's soul . . .'

'Of course,' said Verakina, getting up. 'Come with me.'

I followed her, hobbling on the crutches. I must have been in shock, but I did not feel it. I felt strangely calm. Whatever Verakina and Rasmus suggested, my mind was not confused at all, but absolutely clear. My eyes were dry. I would not weep – I could not weep – for my beloved father. Weeping drains your energies, makes you weak. And I must be strong. I needed to be strong if I were to avenge my father, if I were to make Belladonna pay for what she had done.

Hatred, hot and bright as the midday sun, surged through me again, and I welcomed it, for it would fill me with the strength that I needed. It would turn me from the hunted to the hunter, so I could crush Belladonna without mercy. I pictured Belladonna hanging from the gallows and the image filled my soul with a savage joy. I would not rest until the woman was dead, until she lay lifeless before me. But before her death, I would make sure that she was unmasked, shown for what she was. I would make sure that everything would be ripped from her, just as she'd ripped everything from me.

Everything Belladonna had ever said or done had been a step towards her ultimate goal. Everything had been a lie. She had never cared for me or my father, not one whit. What she had wanted was our deaths, not our love. What she'd wanted was to take everything: my father's money, his business empire that he'd worked so hard to establish, his home, his life, my life, my future.

I remembered thinking, after the ball, that I was becoming myself at last, stepping out from the hollow shell of that which I had been. I'd had dreams of friendship, of love, of a new life. I could see now that they were nothing but the foolish illusions of a little girl who did not see the world for what it truly was. Now I knew. There would be no more dreams, no more illusions. Only the grim determination of revenge. I was no longer the girl of a few days ago, the girl brought up in peace and comfort. I was no longer even the helpless, bewildered girl found by the outcasts in the woods. I was a woman. A woman who understood that the world was a pitiless jungle.

I would take my revenge.

Verakina took me down the corridor, well beyond the area that I'd explored, and stopped before a small curtained archway. Beyond the curtain was a very small room lit by a single golden lamp, with small cushions on the floor facing a niche that had been cut into the earthen wall. In the niche, resting on a blue velvet cloth, was an icon of St Fleur of the Snow, patron saint of the outcast, painted in the traditional fashion, as a sweet-faced beggar girl with flowers growing from the imprint of her bare feet in the snow.

Verakina said, looking at me, 'There is great pain in your heart but I see that you do not wish to speak of it. I see that you do not even cry. I understand why that is, but it will eat you like a cancer if you do not let it out.'

She paused, as if waiting for me to say something, but when I didn't, she went on.

'But even if you cannot speak to us of the pain in your heart, you can tell our dear St Fleur. She will bring you peace if you let her.'

'Yes,' I said, with an effort. I just wanted her to leave and she must have felt that, for she sighed and left the room without another word.

As soon as Verakina had gone, I hobbled to the opposite end of the room and sat with my back to the icon. It wasn't peace I needed, it was justice. And that came from strength. From power.

It was said that the soul of a murdered person could not rest until justice had been done, and that until that happened, they were condemned to wander in the greylands between this life and the afterlife. How could I allow that to go on? And how could I allow Belladonna to live her false life, continuing to deceive those who worshipped her? I could not allow myself to grieve yet. There would be time for that later.

Two things Verakina had said were correct, though. First, that I was not yet strong enough to leave; my feet had not yet healed. Second, that I would need to stop to think clearly and make sure that my revenge would not end in my own death, that Belladonna would not find me and kill me. Both of these things required patience. Belladonna must not know I was still alive. Not until it was too late. She had to think that Drago had killed me, that she was safe. I had to strike precisely when she least expected it, at exactly the right moment. It must be public. I needed solid evidence of her crimes and she had to be accused and arrested in full view of everyone. She had to be shown publicly for the cold-blooded killer and traitor that she was . . .

What evidence might I find? I thought about how I might persuade Drago to testify that he had been ordered to kill me. But it was unlikely he'd agree. Yes, he'd spared my life – but he had told me never to return. If I did, I was certain that he would be my enemy once again. No, I could not go to him . . . The poisoning. How had that been done? Who had carried it out? How had Belladonna lured Father to Aurisola in the first place? Did Belladonna still have family in that city where she had grown up? From what I had been told, her only family, her elderly grand-mother who had brought her up, had long since died, her house had been sold, and Belladonna had cut all ties to her native city well before her marriage to my father. But what did I really know about Belladonna? Only what she'd told us. She clearly still had connections in Aurisola, whatever she'd claimed.

My head hurt. I had too many questions; there were too many gaps in my knowledge.

Someone was coming. I could hear quick footsteps in the passageway outside. Turning to leave, my eyes fell on the icon of St Fleur. The painted dark eyes of the saint gazed sadly at me, making me feel ashamed.

'I'm sorry,' I said. 'I'm sure you can help other people. Just not me.'

Swishing aside the curtain, I stepped back into the passageway and almost ran straight into Lisbet.

'Bianca!' she said. 'I . . . I've only just heard . . .' She stopped abruptly.

I knew what she wanted to say, but I couldn't bring myself to help her. I didn't want comfort or condolences. So I just said, 'It's all right. I feel better now. I . . . St Fleur, she . . .' I couldn't finish either, the lying words sticking in my throat.

'She is the only one I can speak to, as well,' said Lisbet. 'It really helps, doesn't it?'

I nodded, feeling another squirm of shame.

'I know you don't want to speak about it to me, but if ever . . . Well, I'm here if . . .'

'Thank you,' I said, through a lump in my throat, for these were more words than I'd ever heard Lisbet utter at any one time.

'My mother . . . she . . . was killed, too,' she said. 'She . . . tried to . . . to save me when they . . . when they attacked me for being a witch and my eye was . . .' Her voice was shaking. 'If she had not . . . I would be dead . . . She gave her life for me.' A pause. 'For a long time I thought I might as well be, for the only person who'd truly loved me was gone.'

Stricken, I stared at her. I could see the tears shining in her eye. I could feel the tears gathering in my own, and a bitter bile rose in my throat. She was opening her heart to me, but I could not do the same. If I did, I would break down. I would weep for days. I would howl with the pain of loss, with the memories of my father that crowded in on me. I would be fatally weakened. I could not accept the gift she was trying to give me, the gift of mourning.

'I'm sorry,' I said. It sounded stiff, inadequate, and I knew it. I added, rapidly, 'I hope those evil people were punished for what they did to her, and to you.'

Her gaze downcast, she whispered, 'No. They were not.'

'Why not?'

She said, in a low voice, 'Because everyone else agreed with them. I was a witch. I was conspiring against the village. I had put the evil eye on them. That was what they said. That was what everyone believed. Oh, they did not think quite the same thing about my mother. They even regretted her death. And as a token to her memory they decided I would be driven from the village, not hung as they'd intended. But even after that, everyone still believed the right thing had been done to me. So who would punish them?'

'You!' I cried. 'You! In the name of everything that's holy, why didn't *you* try to get redress?'

A faint flush appeared on her cheeks as she said, 'At first I could not. I was broken. And then later . . . I understood that it was not what my mother would have wanted. I understood I had to live, you see. And live well. For her. For the sacrifice she'd made. It is the only way.'

'For you, perhaps,' I managed to say, through the burning bitterness that was threatening to choke me.

'It is the only way,' she repeated. 'The Prince helped me see that.'

'I thought it was St Fleur who helped you,' I said. I hadn't meant it to come out as the sneer that it did.

Lisbet went scarlet. 'It was both,' she said, in a strangled tone, 'and the others – oh, and this haven – so that now I can . . . I can be myself, without fear. Without hate. And you know, since then – since I found my peace – I see my mother. Every night, in my dreams. At first . . . At first, you see, I did not. I could not. She was lost to me.' Her eye lit up; her mouth curved into a smile. 'In this place, I found her again. And I know she will never leave me again.' She put a timid hand on my sleeve. 'If you let it happen, maybe you –'

'It cannot be the same for everyone,' I said, trying not to show how shaken I felt but succeeding only in sounding hostile. I saw her expression and went on. 'You honour me by your words, your trust. But what is your way cannot be mine.'

She looked at me with a sorrowful expression. Then she said, quietly, 'I understand. I will not mention it again. Forgive me.'

Twelve

)

I hardly remember the rest of that day. It went by in a sort of grey blur, and the words and presences of the others were no more than vague shapes at the corners of my perception. They were all very kind, of course. But it was an effort to speak, an effort to eat, and I longed for night to come and to be left in peace. At last that time came, and I was left alone on my bed by the stove, my eyes wide open against the dark, my mind beginning to flesh out a plan.

I could not ask the outcasts for their help. This was their haven; I had no right to ask them to endanger their lives for me. I could not send messages to Emilia or Lucian for help – I had to assume that Belladonna would have spies watching my friends. I had to do this alone, which meant that I'd have to leave here once I had talked to the Prince and seen if he had any information for me and, after that, as soon as I could walk properly.

I would make my way to Sarmest – it couldn't be too far, as Rasmus had been gone no more than four hours that morning, and he'd done a return trip – and from there I would take the coach to the port. I'd take the first steamer to Aurisola, make discreet enquiries there, then return to Lepmest. I'd hole up in the poor outer suburbs of the city, where no-one would know me, where no-one would ever expect me to be, and I'd plan the indictment against Belladonna, in preparation for our final confrontation.

I'd need money, of course. I didn't have any, for Drago had taken what I'd had, but I did have the jewellery I'd been wearing that terrible day. My gold name-day medal; my tiny pearl earrings; my mother's topaz ring. They were valuable. I could pawn them. And I could work, too. I had no real skills apart from drawing and a nice singing voice, but perhaps there was something I could do with that and if not, then I would wash dishes, clean floors – anything. Thousands of people had to do work like that. Surely I could learn.

I clung to these ideas and ran through the broad outline of my plans over and over, so that I would not have space for any other thoughts. I would never see my father again, not in this life, and the knowledge of that was like lead in my belly. But I could not let myself think of that or of how bitterly I would miss him. I could not afford to think of the love we had shared, of happier times, of useless regrets and wishes that things had been different, that I could rewind time to before that evil woman had met him. No. Lisbet's way was not my way and never could be. My father was dead and the girl I'd been had died with him. I would make the guilty pay. I would get justice for my father. I would expose Belladonna for what she was. And then his spirit could be laid to rest. And with these thoughts, I finally fell asleep.

I woke suddenly in the middle of the night, my heart racing. I'd been dreaming that I was in my bedroom, at my home in Lepmest. But it was like a shadow version of my bedroom, strange, silent, dark. In the dream I was not alone. My father was there. But not my living father, a ghost. A sad-eyed, shadowy, restless spirit, begging for release, holding out a trembling hand to me. And in the dream I was paralysed. I could not go to him. I could not speak. I longed to reach my hand out to him but something stopped me. Something jerked me into wakefulness.

When I opened my eyes, I was completely disoriented. Still caught in the dream, I expected to find myself in my bedroom. Instead, I was in the silent dark in a place I did not recognise at first. It took me a moment to remember where I was. In the same instant, I realised I was not alone. There was a figure standing at the foot of the bed. I could not see its face, only that it was a tall, shadowy shape, the same height and powerful build as my father. The figure was utterly silent. I could not hear anything, not even a soft breath.

It really is my father's ghost? my mind whispered, even as the hairs rose on the back of my neck. Strangely, I did not feel in the least afraid. And unlike in the dream, I was not paralysed. I sat up. My stiff lips moved.

'Father,' I murmured, 'Oh Father, dearest Father . . . You have come to me . . . I miss you so, Father . . . I swear I will not rest until you are avenged and Belladonna pays for what she did.'

No answer. My eyes remained on the still figure that did not move but whose sorrowful glance I felt intensely.

'Father, speak to me! Advise me! Please, Father, speak to me . . . Give me a sign! I beg you!'

Still the figure did not reply, but it reached out a shadowy hand and very briefly touched the quilt, just above where my injured ankle rested. For a fleeting instant I felt a tiny shock of cold. But it was so fleeting I did not have time to react before the figure moved back. As I regained my scattered senses and jumped out of bed, crying, 'No! Wait!', it melted away into the deeper shadows and vanished from sight.

Groping desperately for the oil lamp and matches that Verakina had left on the table, I fumbled to light it. When at last I managed to light the lamp there was, of course, nobody there. My father's ghost had disappeared and I was alone.

And now the tears I had been unable to shed that day came flowing out of me in a hot burning flood of grief and despair, the sobs raking my throat like claws of iron. If only he could have stayed a moment more! If only I could have touched him, felt his love and care just once more! If only he could have told me what I must do! If only he had spoken even one word, given one sign!

After a moment, after I had grown quieter, I became aware of something else. My ankle did not hurt anymore, not with the dull ache of today, nor the throbbing pain of yesterday. When I'd jumped up from the bed to go to Father, I'd done so without hesitation, forgetting all about the fact that I was crippled. I unrolled the bandage on my ankle and looked at it in the light of the lamp. The swelling had completely gone down. I touched the ankle, gingerly. It was not tender to the touch. It felt quite normal and I saw that my feet, too, beneath the bandage, had healed.

I sat at the table, prickling with excitement and awe, remembering the tiny shock of cold I'd felt at my father's touch. I had wanted a sign. And my father had given me one: I could walk unaided; he was telling me that what I planned to do was right.

Lisbet had said her mother came to her in dreams, and by that, she knew she'd done the right thing in making the choice she'd made to hide out here and not to avenge her mother's death. She'd implied that if I chose revenge, I would not only lose my peace of mind, I would also lose any chance of reconnecting with my father. But she had been wrong. It must be different for everyone, I had told her, and this proved it was so: my father's ghost had come to me, to tell me that I was on the right path. And that was the only sign I needed, the only peace of mind that meant anything to me. It did not matter if danger was ahead. The only blessing I'd needed had been given to me, this very night.

Thirteen

I did not want to tell anyone what I had seen – this was a special moment I would share only with my father. It was my secret source of strength and resolution, but it did put me in the awkward position of not being able to reveal that my ankle was fully healed, or Verakina would wonder how it had happened so quickly. So I rewrapped my ankle and the next morning used the crutches again to get up and go to breakfast.

Everyone was very kind to me, so kind, almost whispering around me, as though the fact that today would be my father's funeral, a funeral I could not attend, made me so fragile that I might shatter like crystal if their voices had too loud a tone. Fortunately, the calm I felt today looked like the numbness I had felt yesterday, and none of them suspected that the cold stone of fear and grief that had sat so heavily in my chest had turned into the volcanic lava of fierce exhilaration that surged through my veins. I knew I would be strong now, and that my father's ghost had made me so. I did not need the pomp and circumstance of a state funeral to remind me of my duty, a duty that was sacred and intimate to me, in my deepest heart. I felt much closer to my father now than I ever would have done at a graveside.

Once again, most of the others left after breakfast for up top, though this time Grim stayed as well as Verakina. An hour or so later, Lisbet returned, red-cheeked and excited, to tell us that word had come that the Prince was on his way and that he should be here this very day, much earlier than anyone had expected. Verakina immediately began a storm of baking, while Grim scuttled around filling decanters with homemade fruit wine, filling the log chest and sweeping the floors. Lisbet worked to help both Verakina and Grim. I offered to help, too, and after some hemming and hawing from Verakina was given a soft cloth and set to polishing some silver goblets, a silver knife, and a large pewter platter, all of which were apparently only ever used for special occasions such as, clearly, a visit from the Prince.

'Doesn't he come often, then?' I asked, as I sat at the table, polishing away – for the silver had been quite tarnished. 'I thought you said he kept an eye on the havens all the time.'

Verakina raised an eyebrow. 'He is not a landlord checking up on his tenants,' she said, tartly. 'He protects us but does not intrude.'

'But when you get new people coming in ... like me ... surely he'd want to know?'

'We tell him, of course. But it is up to our judgement as to who we take in and who we don't. He does not interfere.

As to seeing him, he is at each Haven Council, of course. And once a year he visits each haven in turn. From time to time he also joins a night patrol. But this is a special visit. It hasn't happened before.'

'It is because of me that he's coming . . . I hope it isn't too much trouble for you,' I said.

Grim shook his head. 'You really don't understand much, little lady, do you?' Ignoring Verakina's glare and Lisbet's embarrassment, he went on. 'How can it be a trouble to us, to welcome the man who saved our lives and gave us a home and a purpose? It is a privilege and an honour. Always.'

'He is wise and kind and generous and brave,' added Lisbet. 'There is nobody like him, not in the whole world.'

In only a few days I had gone from being trusting to being suspicious of all. I wanted to say that the Prince sounded too good to be true. I wanted to say that a man who never showed his face to his friends and never revealed his true name was hiding something. I wanted to say that it was dangerous to give trust so wholeheartedly. But of course I did not say any of those things, for I had promised to stay and wait for him, to listen to any information he may have for me.

As if reading the doubt in my mind, Grim went on. 'We do not question why he does not speak his true name, why he hides his face. He is not some empty-headed society belle craving the world's approval. He is honoured simply by those he has honoured by his deeds. He asks for no further thanks.'

'I am sure you are right,' I said, soothingly. 'You must excuse my ignorance in these matters.'

Suddenly I needed to be out of this dark place under the earth. I turned to Lisbet. 'Is it sunny, up top?'

'Why, yes, it is,' she said, with a puzzled look.

'I'd like to go up, just for a short while. I have been underground for some time and I miss the light of the sun. Perhaps, Grim, you might escort me?'

'Of course!' he said, keen, I think, to make up for our little spat.

The passage to up top was through a door I hadn't opened in my explorations yesterday. It was a simple tunnel that went up and up, ending with a small door that had been cut into the side of a hillock. On the outside, the door was covered with grass so that when it was closed it could not be seen at all, it was so perfectly camouflaged.

Outside it was sunny, just as Lisbet had said, the light filtering green-gold through the young leaves of the trees. The air was mild, pleasant, scented. We walked a little way into a small clearing, with me remembering to hobble carefully.

'A truly beautiful spring day,' Grim said, when we stopped to sit on a moss-covered log in full sunshine.

I nodded. Grim seemed happy to rest in the sun, and I asked him questions about what direction Sarmest was in and other such things. Whereas I had been reluctant to ask the others for help, I felt that Grim would be a bit more eager to see me go and I was right: he'd never really welcomed my presence here; he'd not liked his community disturbed by a stranger. Unlike the others, Grim had a hard core of suspicion and wariness that had never left him and probably never would. I understood that. It was how I'd have felt, had I been in his position. And thinking that made me ask, suddenly, 'Have you never sought revenge for what was done to you, Grim?'

' He gave me a sharp look. 'What makes you think I didn't?'

'Ah. So you did, then?'

He shrugged. 'That is my business.'

'Of course,' I said. But I could tell from his expression that something must have happened. 'Did the Prince advise you against it?'

He gave me a hard stare. 'Why do you want to know?'

'It was just something Lisbet said. About . . . About what happened to her.'

'The Prince never spoke to me about it,' he said, after a moment. 'And why should he? What I did happened before I came to haven.' There was a glint of fierce joy in his eyes. 'I'd made my peace.'

'Oh. I see.'

'Not sure you do,' he said, with an unexpected smile, 'but that's all right. I can see that your path is elsewhere. And you must take it. We must all do what is in us, not what others tell us.'

I looked at him, a little surprised to realise he seemed to understand better than the others. 'That's exactly right,' I said. 'No-one can choose our way for us.'

'Now then,' he said, with one of his mischievous smiles, 'I have chores to complete. Would you like to stay here a while longer, or come back in?'

'Stay here,' I said, at once.

'Very well. But as the door is automatically locked as soon as anyone goes in or out, you will need to signal to us when you want to come back in. Come here.'

He led me back to the hillock. It was impossible to see where the door was, and I watched carefully as Grim pushed aside some pebbles at the base of the hillock. Under them, almost invisible in the soil, was a small dun-coloured metal plate. He rapped on it three times, the first rap followed by a long pause, then a second and third rap, in quick succession.

'That's the signal,' he said. 'Do that and the door will be opened.'

Sure enough, no sooner had the sound of the raps died away when the side of the hillock opened, revealing the doorway. Replacing the pebbles over the plate, he said, 'You got it, then?'

'Yes. Thank you.'

'Good. Make sure you don't wander too far. We don't want to have to go looking for you, you've been trouble enough as it is,' he said, with a crooked grin and, stepping through the doorway, he was gone, the door closing after him and vanishing into the side of the hillock again so smoothly that it was as though I'd dreamed its opening.

Left alone, I breathed a deep sigh of relief. It was good to be above ground, away from the cosy claustrophobia of haven. I went back to the clearing where I'd sat with Grim only this time, instead of sitting on the log, I took off my shoes and put down my crutches – hiding both behind the log just in case – hitched up my skirts, and climbed up a big oak tree I'd noticed while I was sitting with Grim.

From there I thought I might get a view over the tops of the other trees, and so it proved that I could. From the top branches I could see right over the top of a sea of green.

In the direction of north, I caught a shimmer of blue in the distance, which must have been the sea. To the south, closer, a huddle of roofs which must have been the market town of Sarmest. That was useful information: the port and the market town were in different directions. To the east was forest as far as the eye could see, and to the west was more forest and then, beyond that, a ragged range of mountains. The mountains. That was where Lucian lived, I remembered, the sudden thought making a wave of regret wash over me. I'd never see Lucian again. I couldn't risk it. For my sake – and for his . . .

Turning my mind determinedly from such thoughts, I concentrated instead on getting my bearings. I guessed that the west would likely be the direction the Prince was coming from, since he was coming from the mountain havens. I changed the plan I had been forming. I would not head south to Sarmest, but north, towards the sea. Judging from what I could see from the treetop, the port must be further than Sarmest from where we were. If Rasmus had taken roughly two hours to get to Sarmest, then perhaps the port might be three hours away, or a little more. I'd find out.

I was just about to climb down the tree when I heard the crackling of twigs somewhere below. Taking care to stay as still as I could, I peered down between the leaves but could see nothing. I had just persuaded myself that I must have heard a deer or another wild animal when someone came out of the belt of trees beyond the clearing. All I could see from above was that it was a man, tall, broad-shouldered, wearing a brown coat and a tightly fitting dark leather cap that hid all his hair. He was carrying a small pack on his back and walking with a long, easy stride. I could not see his face or any other feature.

My pulse raced. Was it a traveller? If it were, I did not want to give away any hint that there might be a haven of any kind nearby. Was this the Prince? If it were, now was my chance to catch this mysterious figure unawares. It was best I stay put, sit tight, and see what happened.

The man passed my tree without stopping and left the clearing, heading towards the door in the hillock. I waited another moment, then cautiously climbed down the tree, retrieved my shoes and my crutches, and hurried as silently as I could after him. He went a lot faster than I did, though, and by the time I came in sight of the hillock, he'd already disappeared, whether into the haven or passing it by, I still had no idea. Well, there was only one way to find out.

Grim had shown me the spot where the entry plate was hidden. I'd thought I'd noted the spot exactly, but now all I could see were pebbles, scattered all around the foot of the hillock, and I had no real idea of exactly what pebbles he'd brushed aside to uncover the plate. I was on my hands and knees scrabbling through the stony ground to try to find the right spot when a hand fell on my shoulder, and a voice said, 'Allow me.'

Startled, I jumped to my feet and stared at the figure behind me. It was the man from the clearing. He was facing me now, but I still couldn't see his features, for they were completely concealed behind a strange white mask that gave him a ghostly appearance. The eye holes were veiled with a translucent fabric of some sort. I could hardly even distinguish the colour of his eyes. Very few of his features could be seen, for no strand of hair escaped from the leather cap he was wearing and his hands were also gloved in leather. I stared at him, my heart racing. Was it my imagination, or was he as tense as I was?

'Have you been spying on me?' I asked, not intending for it to come it out as sharply as it did.

The man who must be the Prince replied, 'I heard someone following me. I needed to know if that someone was a friend.'

His voice was deep but soft. Something about it nagged at the corner of my mind; sounded familiar. What it was I couldn't quite work out, though, and it made me feel uneasy.

'We weren't expecting you so early,' I said, quickly, to cover my unease.

'Clearly,' he observed, and now there was a smile in his voice. I could feel his gaze on me and I could not help colouring.

He said, gently, 'I hope I haven't frightened you too much.'

What was it about his voice that scratched at the edge of my mind? Something half-recognised, half-remembered, but not quite. And the tenderness in his tone . . . Surely I was imagining it, I thought. How could I remember the voice of someone I'd never met? And why would he feel anything for me, a stranger? I pushed the thought from my mind – it wasn't important, right now, because I had a question, something that was more important than silly feelings of deja vu.

I lied, 'No, you didn't frighten me. But . . .'

'But what?

'I have a question. You know who I am.'

'Of course,' he said, calmly. 'Surely that is not your question?'

'No. I . . . Rasmus told me you . . . you might have information for me. But you've come so quickly . . . And so I wondered –'

'If I'd had time to gather what you hoped for,' he finished. As he spoke, he extracted a small flat parcel from his coat pocket, which he handed to me. 'I am very sorry for what has happened to you and what happened to your father. This is everything I could find.' A pause. 'There is no need for you to go to Aurisola.'

I looked into the veiled eyes of that featureless mask and a strange feeling stirred in me that was nothing to do with the oddness of our situation. Through a lump in my throat, I said, 'Thank you. But I think I must decide that for myself.'

'As you wish,' he said, and though his voice was without inflection, I had the impression that I'd upset him.

'They wanted me to wait till I'd spoken to you,' I said, in a rush, 'before I made my plans. I am glad I have. I will look carefully at the information you have found for me and again, I thank you for your trouble. But please understand that I must make my own way.'

'Of course,' he replied, quietly. 'It is always so.'

His veiled eyes met mine. I felt a strange tingle rippling over me from head to foot. Those eyes – they held me. That voice – so familiar. And the way he had reacted to me – the tension, the tenderness in his voice . . . Could it be . . . Could it be that I knew this man, this man from the mountains? *Could the man before me be Lucian Montresor?*

It was a startling, shocking thought and I knew instinctively that I could not voice it out loud but must do my best to conceal it. For if my suspicions were correct and he was who I thought he was, then he would have known who I was as soon as they told him I'd been found. But he had chosen to stay quiet. He must have his reasons for that, and they must be good reasons. Besides, if he thought I did not recognise him, then I might have a chance of finding out why he lived a double life. And as to what might happen afterwards . . . I did not dare to think of that now. There would be time enough later, once I knew more.

'We had better go in,' I said, trying to keep my voice steady, trying to stop myself from reaching out to him.

'Yes,' he replied equably and, turning away from me to uncover the plate, he signalled us into the haven.

Fourteen

The others were, of course, more than delighted that the Prince had arrived early. As they fussed around, bringing out glasses of mint cordial and plates of freshly made biscuits, they talked nineteen to the dozen, while I watched him closely. He had not breathed a word to them about our conversation, only saying that we'd just met; he had not uttered a sound about the packet he'd given me. He spoke calmly – on haven matters, not on my situation – and in fact seemed to take no further notice of me. That suited me just fine, for I did not want him to read in my eyes what I was thinking.

After a suitable while, I rose from the table, saying I was tired and needed to rest. The others were a little dismayed that I would want to leave the presence of their beloved Prince so quickly, but also a little relieved, I think, for I could sense they wanted to talk to him about me, but were constrained by the fact that I was there. Lisbet offered me the use of her room, for clearly I could not rest in my usual place for this was where they had gathered, and I left the room in a slightly awkward silence, feeling several pairs of eyes on my back and a tingle in my body which told me that the Prince, far from taking no notice, was tensely aware of me.

Reaching Lisbet's room, I closed and bolted the door and, sitting on the bed, took out from my skirt pocket the packet the Prince had given me. In it were several documents – two typed, the other two handwritten – as well as three newspaper clippings. As I began to read, the hair rose on the back of my neck and I forgot all about my suspicions regarding the true identity of the Prince, for what I held in my hands quite eclipsed any thoughts other than those concerning my father and Belladonna.

The first document was a telegram from my father to the manager of the Ladies' Fair store in Aurisola. It was addressed to Guillermo Ghent and dated the very day Father had left for that city. It read 'Need to be certain DS reliable witness. Speak to no-one. Wait for me.'

The next document, also typewritten, was dated the same day, and though it was in Aurisolan, I could read it easily because when Belladonna had first come into our lives, I had applied myself to learning her native tongue to please her. So I soon understood that this was a police report on a body fished out of the canals, noting that the cause of death was strangulation. The victim was recorded as being a certain Dominic Santeria, vagrant, once employed in Signora Gandelfiri's household, no next of kin recorded. 'Gandelfiri' was Belladonna's maiden name! Was Signora Gandelfiri Belladonna's long-dead grandmother? Was Dominic Santeria the 'DS' of Father's telegram? Was he killed to prevent him talking to Father? And if he was, what was the information he had that was so dangerous he'd had to be silenced?

The first handwritten note, which was very short, was in a hand I did not recognise and bore a faint seal that I peered and peered at before deciding it was a smudgy picture of a snake on a pole. This was the standard sign for apothecaries, the more shady kind of chemist. The document itself appeared to be a delivery list for an order which had been placed, but was so cryptic that I could not work out what the words might exactly represent, though it was clear they referred to some kind of chemicals: 'g. cran – 1 g, n. sal – 2 g, v. conc – 1 mL.' Other than this list, there was also a scrawled date, which was about eleven years ago, that is, around seven years before my father had met Belladonna.

Turning from this to the other note, I saw it was in the same hand but undated and a very different kind of note, a few words written in a hectic scrawl: 'It was I who killed her and now I can no longer bear the knowledge I have.'

It ended abruptly, and on the last letter, the 'e' of 'have', was a brown stain that, I thought, my palms prickling, looked for all the world like a bloodstain. With my heart thudding, I turned to reading the newspaper clippings.

The first, dated also around eleven years ago, was about the suicide of an imprisoned man named Adolfus Carlini, underworld apothecary, who had been arrested for the murder by poison of Signora Theobalda Gandelfiri, some weeks before. The report noted that though Carlini had left a handwritten confession note, he had not revealed a motive for the killing. However, the signora's nineteen-year-old adoptive granddaughter Belladonna had testified that he had been a nuisance and that her grandmother had once had to chase him off her property. Belladonna's testimony had been supported by three servants, Drago Lukan, Dominic Santeria and Gabriel Pindari. The Gandelfiri estate would now pass to the Signora's adoptive granddaughter, as she was the only surviving next of kin. However, the article mentioned that the Gandelfiri fortune was nowhere near as considerable as it had once been: after Signora Gandelfiri's death, it had been discovered that she had run into large debt and much of the estate would need to be sold to clear that.

Belladonna. She's done it before, I thought, the chill of it striking deep within me. She's done it before – and in exactly the same way! Only, that time it hadn't resulted in quite what she'd hoped. She must not have known her adoptive grandmother was in such debt; she must have thought she would inherit a considerable fortune.

And then I noticed something else. The article said that Belladonna was the Signora's *adoptive* granddaughter. Belladonna had never told us that. In a way, it made it even more sickening, that a naive, kindly old woman had taken in an unrelated orphan child out of the goodness of her heart – and been rewarded by death.

I picked up the next clipping. This was dated just over four years ago – that is, close to the time Father had met Belladonna. It was from a Faustinian newspaper. It was a very brief account of the tragic death by drowning of a Miss Arabella Talavin:

. . . one of several beautiful aspirants to the crown of Fairest Lady in the annual competition run by the Ladies' Fair department stores. Her friend and fellow candidate, Belladonna Gandelfiri, testified that the young woman had gone walking at night to calm her nerves before the judging day, and that when Miss Talavin had not returned, she raised the alarm. An autopsy has concluded that drowning was the cause of death. It is thought that Miss Talavin lost her footing in the dark, tripped, struck her head on the stone paving of the riverbank promenade, and tumbled unconscious into the river, where she drowned.

That was all the newspaper article said, but it was enough for me. I could see a clear pattern – the coincidental deaths of those who had got in Belladonna's way. Poor Arabella Talavin's 'best friend' had almost certainly caused her death, and my guess would be that it was because she was a serious rival for the Fairest Lady crown, and just 'one of several beautiful aspirants'. With her out of the way, Belladonna's path was clear. Fame, fortune – for the Fairest Lady crown came with a very handsome sum of prize money – and eventually the biggest reward of all, my father's hand in marriage and his fortune, as well.

The last newspaper clipping was very short, and was dated just a day ago, noting the sudden death of Guillermo Ghent from a heart attack, at his home in Aurisola. The article mentioned that he had been the manager of Ladies' Fair in Aurisola and that he had been under a lot of stress since the untimely death of his boss and the disappearance of his boss's daughter.

Another death to add to Belladonna's tally, I thought. Now I understood why the Prince had said I need not go to Aurisola: all the people who may have been of use to me had been killed. All I needed was here, in this slim packet. And yet it would not be enough, for though to me it was glaringly obvious that Belladonna was as guilty as sin, a judge might say that this evidence was all circumstantial. Death had certainly followed along with her, everywhere she went, but as a sentimental *Mirror* reporter might say, she could just be seen as a tragic figure, a sorrowful figure, who had so sadly lost all the people she loved. She certainly wasn't seen as a cold-blooded, ruthless, merciless killer who had arranged for people to be murdered for the sake of her own ambition.

Had she always intended to kill my father and take everything? Perhaps. But at a time of her own choosing. Her hand had been forced by the discovery that my father was investigating her. I will never know when she had planned to kill me, too, but my time was up as soon I had taken the prized title of Fairest Lady away from her.

For now, I knew why my father had gone to Aurisola: Santeria's conscience must have got the better of him, after all those years of silence. He must have contacted Ghent, and Ghent must have contacted my father. Somehow Belladonna – with her network of spies – had found out. And she'd moved, then, with a sure rapidity that showed that this contingency must always have been at the back of her mind. Whoever's had been the actual hand that poisoned my father, she must have had them ready for just such an eventuality.

Armed with this evidence, I now had a much clearer idea of the kind of enemy I was dealing with. I knew now that my friends at the haven had been right and that I must be very careful indeed. Belladonna would be a fearsome enemy, always one step or more ahead of everyone else. To go rashly into my revenge would be to sign my own death warrant. But what the Prince – what Lucian – had brought me was immeasurably precious, for the papers gave me a true understanding of just what kind of enemy I was facing. How had the Prince found these extraordinary documents? How had he known who to ask, who to trust? He is astonishing, I thought, my heart beating a little faster.

At that moment, there came a knock on the door.

'Are you awake, Bianca?' It was Lisbet.

'Yes,' I answered, shoving the documents back into my pocket. I didn't want to show them to my friends here; if they read anything inside the package the Prince had given me, it would put them in danger for I was sure, now, that Belladonna would be ruthless in tracking down and killing anyone who was a threat to herself and the image she has so carefully constructed.

I got up and opened the door.

Lisbet was pale, her face as tense as a bowstring. 'The Prince is about to leave. I thought you might like to say goodbye.'

My heart gave a leap. 'Leaving? Already? Why?' I said, as we hurried back up the passageway.

'Mattias found a dead man by a stream to the north, on the path that leads to the Mormest road. There was a puncture wound on his throat,' she said, and the horror was plain in her voice.

'Like the beggar killings in Lepmest!' I exclaimed. 'Is the Prince afraid the murderer might go after the outcasts now? Was the dead man from the havens?'

'No,' she whispered, 'but there might be people who think *we* killed him.'

I stared at her. 'What? Why?'

'People don't like people like us,' she said, sadly. 'Because we are a little different to them, they think we are capable of anything. Anyway, the Prince will find out who it was. He says that it is part of a larger pattern. He doesn't know who or what is behind it, but he says he's going to find out . . .' She trailed off, then said abruptly, 'The Prince has asked me to guide you to the western edge of the forest tomorrow.'

'Tomorrow?' I echoed.

'Yes. He thinks it is safer for you to go from here now there is this trouble, and he seems to think you are fit to travel and no longer need the crutches.' She looked at me. 'Is that really so?'

'Yes,' I said, a little uncomfortably.

'Oh,' she said, but made no further comment on that, adding instead, 'Verakina wasn't altogether happy with the plan but she had to agree. It is hard to refuse the Prince.'

'I can see that,' I answered, as we reached the living room and its hubbub of raised, agitated voices.

He was at the centre of the crowd, yet somehow still appeared a little apart, and as I came in with Lisbet, I saw his veiled glance shoot rapidly in my direction.

But it was Verakina who said, 'Oh, Bianca, there you are and just in time. Come, come here,' and she motioned me across to his side, and then discreetly went out of the room, with the others following her – some, like Grim, clearly reluctant – so that in a moment the Prince and I were left alone.

'You have read them then,' he said, before I could speak.

I looked at the expressionless white mask, trying to stop my feelings from showing on my face. It was not easy to pretend I had not recognised him, that I was sure I knew who he really was.

'Yes. And I wanted to thank you from the bottom of my heart. What you have brought me – it is extraordinary. However did you find it?'

'I know how to find things,' he said, without missing a beat.

'Things . . . and people?' I asked, not taking my eyes from the white mask.

I could see he was tense and it filled me with a strange gladness. I knew that he, too, was trying to stop himself from reaching out to me. I could feel his longing and it made my heart sing.

After a short silence, he answered. 'As you say.' A pause, then he went on. 'There's something else you need to know. I also had enquiries made in Mormest. The innkeeper and the clerk in the ticket-office both swore you'd been there. And the ship's purser swore, as well.'

'Then they were lying! They were in my stepmother's pay!'

He shook his head. 'My informant told me they were saying the honest truth – or what they thought was the honest truth. They really believed you were there – because they saw someone who pretended to be you, who went under your name. All this person then had to do was to board the steamer dressed as you, go into your cabin, then sneak off the boat before it left for Aurisola. The purser said that you had never left the cabin during the trip and they only noticed your absence when the ship docked in Aurisola. A simple, effective plan.'

My scalp prickled. What he said made a horrible kind of sense. How much simpler it would be to employ someone posing as me than to try to pay off that many people and run the risk of loose tongues! In fact, Belladonna herself might well have pretended to be me. I was sure disguise would be like child's play to her. None of those people in Mormest knew me, and even if they'd seen my photo in the paper, everyone knows that photos don't do their subjects justice, so why should they not believe the impostor was Bianca Dalmatin?

'Dear God,' I said. 'My stepmother – she planned it all so very carefully . . .'

'Yes,' he said, gravely.

'And so I have to be twice as clever and careful as she is if I am to defeat her. But I have right on my side, and I will prevail.'

'That is not always the way of the world,' he said.

'Then I will not go the way of the world,' I said, defiantly. 'Justice must be done and I will do it, no matter what it costs. And nothing and no-one shall stop me. You of all people should understand that.'

'I do,' he said, quietly. 'But as to cost, it may be greater than you think.'

'I don't care. I must do it.'

'Well, then,' he said, quietly, 'I have made some arrangements for you. Tomorrow, Lisbet will guide you out to a village on the western edge of the forest. The village innkeeper, Darian Zymund, is a friend of mine. He will give you new identity papers, money, a coach ticket, and directions to a safe house in Lepmest. From there, it's up to you.'

I stared at him. There was a lump in my throat as I said, 'Then you do not want to change my mind? To ... To persuade me I must not seek justice against that woman?'

'I do not,' he said. 'You must do this. I know that. But if you will heed a word of advice: the deadliest weapon is the most unexpected one, hitting straight to the heart.'

The Prince's veiled eyes gazed directly into mine and for a moment I saw his gloved hands tighten against each other.

'Each person has a weakness, and by that may be undone,' he continued. 'Take care that your own weakness is not turned as a weapon against you. Take very great care . . . I would not want you to be harmed.'

I could not help a little shiver at these words, so like a declaration of love.

'I will,' I said. 'I will be very careful.' I hesitated and then added, in a rush, 'But all this you are doing – it is more than simply not stopping me. You are helping me. Why? Why are you doing all this for me?'

'You have been grievously wronged. You are in danger.'

'So are the beggars of Lepmest,' I hazarded.

'You are right. I have not done enough,' he said. 'I have been trying to protect a little world of safety. Yet that is a selfish thing, for there will always be those who are outside it who will also need protection.'

I was struck to the heart by the sadness in his voice. 'Selfish?' I cried. 'There is no-one in the world more unselfish than you! I know now why you are revered by all who live here, why they speak of you with such respect and love. I do not know why you choose to hide your face, but I do know that you're true and generous. Your heart wears no mask.' I hoped he understood the meaning behind my words, that he understood I knew who he was but respected his need for secrecy.

His voice was low and sad as he replied, 'You do me too much honour. If you knew the truth about me, then –'

'In no way would it alter anything,' I said, warmly.

'You cannot know that.'

'You must believe me when I say nothing – *nothing* – would change that.' I thought of what Emilia had said, about there being a curse on Lucian's family, and was suddenly sure the curse must be the source of his mysterious shame.

He sighed but did not answer. Instead he said, 'One more thing before I go. If you ever need haven again, ask Master Kinberg at the safe house in Lepmest to arrange immediate passage. You are always welcome here.'

'Thank you. I hope I will not need to intrude on my friends here again. Except that . . .' I hesitated, but then plunged on. '. . . I should like to see you again.'

Our eyes met and I caught, deep in the veiled glance, a golden flicker that instantly reminded me of the light in Lucian's amber-coloured eyes, those beautiful eyes I'd looked into on the night of the ball. A thrill went over me, from head to foot. Impulsively, I took a step towards him and held out a hand.

'So might we not say farewell, but only until we meet again?'

But he did not take my hand. Instead, he took a step back.

'I can make no such undertaking. I am sorry.'

'Then if you cannot promise, I will merely hope to see you again,' I said, trying to keep my voice steady, 'and when all this is over – when times are better –'

'They will never be better for me,' he said, in a low, tight voice. 'They can never be.' And abruptly, he turned away and strode out of the room without looking back.

'What did you say to him?' said Grim when the outcasts, who had gone hurrying after him, came back, looking dismayed by his sudden departure.

'Nothing,' I said, 'except words to express my gratitude.'

I looked away so they would not see the tears in my eyes. I was sure the Prince – Lucian – had understood what I was trying to say. I was sure he knew I'd recognised him. I was sure he'd seen what I was feeling and that he felt the same, for the tension I had seen in him was the same longing that had tightened my chest and sent ripples of shivers down my spine. Yet he had turned away. He had gone, and I was left suddenly so bereft that I could have sunk to my knees and howled like a dog.

But the moment passed. I swallowed back the longing because it did no good. I had to be as strong as Lucian was. There could be no looking back.

Fifteen

The atmosphere for the rest of that day in the haven was both tense and dispirited, and the feast food that had been so lovingly prepared for the Prince's coming sat on the tables almost untouched. It was then I realised just how much the killing reported by Mattias had shaken the others. They did not ask me any questions about what the Prince had said to me, or what he'd brought for me, but instead gathered in quiet huddles in conversation in which I was not included. I wished I could do something for them but there was nothing I could do – and nothing I could think of doing – apart from making myself small and quiet for the rest of my time here.

Not that it was difficult to do so – I had so much on my mind. Foremost was the Prince or, rather, Lucian. It was strange how easy and yet how hard it was to think of those two as one and the same. Would we ever see each other again? I did not know and could not even dare to hope it might be so.

The deadliest weapon is the most unexpected one, he'd said. I had to find that weapon to use against Belladonna, the one that would strike right at her weakness, at her heart just as she'd aimed straight at mine. My weakness had been my love for her, my trust in her. Hers was – what? She was a mistress of deception, stealth, ruthlessness. She would not be caught by simple trickery . . . What mattered most to Belladonna? Power? Money? Status? All these things mattered to her, but how could I use them against her? She held them all in the palm of her hand and would be alert to any threat against them. And she loved nobody, cared for nobody except herself. She trusted Drago, but I knew she would not hesitate for one instant to sacrifice him if she had to. Even if I survived long enough to manage to gather an indictment against her, would that be enough? I was sure she would twist everything, make evidence – and witnesses – disappear. She might even find a way to construct a plausible reason for both my reappearance and my accusations, and turn the tables on me. She had a talent for making people believe in her lies, and I had no such gift. I had to find that weakness, that unexpected weapon, and find it fast.

Evening came but I found no answer to my conundrum. In the haven, there was also no real lifting of the general gloom. After dinner, Lisbet and Rasmus made a valiant attempt to lighten the atmosphere by singing snatches of old folk songs. They had lovely voices, both of them, his deep and rich, hers bright and silvery, and the songs were beautiful too, but the trouble was that sometimes beauty can make one feel like crying as much as it can make one joyful.

Because I felt for my friends in their wretchedness, and because I was in desperate need of a distraction, I also made an attempt to make things lighter – by offering to sketch portraits of everyone. To my surprise, not only did that serve to distract them, but also I found that I drew better that night than I'd ever done before.

'Hmm, not bad, though perhaps a touch rushed,' said Grim, critically, when I'd finished his and he was looking at it from all angles.

'Hark at the art critic!' Verakina snorted. 'Don't listen to him, Bianca.'

'I wish I could draw like that,' said Lisbet, wistfully. 'Your drawings look as if they're alive – but they also make us look so much better than we really look.'

I shook my head. 'No, they don't. I have drawn what is really there. You are beautiful, Lisbet, truly beautiful.'

Lisbet went scarlet. 'You are just being kind.'

'No. It is only the truth I tell.'

'My mirror tells me otherwise,' she said, low.

'Then your mirror is a liar and if I were you, I'd send it packing!'

'Now there's a good idea,' said Carlo, with a grin. 'Send all mirrors packing, wherever they are!'

'Excellent idea!' said Tofer, warmly.

'Fair is as fair does,' intoned Rasmus, with a serious air.

'Hark at the philosopher!' laughed Grim.

'And hark at the cynic who, because he thinks he knows everything, ends up knowing nothing,' observed Verakina, tartly.

'Can't anyone say anything around here without being jumped on?' grumbled Grim, but he was smiling, and so were the others, including Mattias, who for the first time that day looked as though he was not thinking about the dead man he'd found that morning.

It was only later, after everyone had gone to bed and I'd settled for the last time in my own bed by the stove, that an idea sparked into unexpected life. Beauty. That was what Belladonna truly cared about. Her own beauty, and the reflection of it in the eyes of everyone. Just as she'd killed my father, she was nearly certainly always planning on killing me. But it was seeing the front page of the *Mirror*, announcing that I had been crowned Fairest Lady in her stead, that had struck her to the heart and forced her hand, in the same way that discovering my father's investigation had precipitated her plot to kill him. That was her fatal weakness, and it would be my unexpected weapon. That was how I would undermine her. She thought I was dead. She thought herself out of danger. Now was not the time to reveal that I was still alive, but what if there was someone out there who was after her crown? Someone unknown to her? Someone she hadn't seen coming? She would be rattled. She would lose her cool. She would make mistakes.

I would create that someone else. I would send a shadow after her. It would be a creature of paper and ink and it would stalk her dreams of beauty. It would burst into the world of the *Mirror* and shatter it into fragments.

Getting up, I lit the lamp and, taking up my pencil again, began sketching the first three scenes of an illustrated story, the kind that is often published in instalments in newspapers and magazines. The story started with a picture of a woman, seen from the back, standing before her mirror. The woman had a crown on her head and in the mirror was reflected a face of rare yet sinister beauty. The face had some resemblance to my stepmother – and yet not quite so much that it was definite. Under that first picture I wrote these words: 'Mirror, mirror, on the wall, who is the fairest of them all?'

The second picture was just of the mirror. I had represented it as a tall gilded thing, topped with a curly carving that mimicked the font used for the *Mirror* magazine masthead: 'You are the fairest, oh Queen, the fairest lady ever seen.'

The third picture was a picture of a crooked crown and on it, a scattering of words made up of what looked like broken jewels: 'Fairest, but for how long?'

I signed the three illustrations with the name Syrena – an Aurisolan name – and a tiny crest, the mermaid symbolising Aurisola, with her trident. It would look as if the artist came from Aurisola, the city at the heart of all my stepmother's dark secrets.

Sitting back, I surveyed my handiwork. The shadowy rival that would haunt my stepmother's dreams and be my advance guard in the attack on her defences had just been born. The *Mirror*'s main rival was the *Ladies' Journal*, and that was where my story would go. Tomorrow, I would begin my campaign.

Sixteen

We set off very early the next morning. Dawn was only just breaking through the forest canopy when Lisbet and I emerged into the chilly air. We were both warmly but plainly dressed: Lisbet in her usual workday costume of serge trousers and a sailor's jersey, me in a plain dark woollen skirt and a matching jacket and coat, clothes that had been rustled up from the bottom of a chest, smelling of mothballs. They were the kind of clothes a respectable but poor young woman would wear – not a beggar, but someone struggling somewhat to make ends meet. But it was more than the clothes that transformed me: my skin had been rubbed with walnut juice to make it darker, my long wavy hair had been cut to the nape of my neck and a powder had been rubbed through it to change its colour from jet black to a kind of dusty brown. The final touch was a pair of steel-rimmed plain-glass spectacles produced from somewhere by Verakina, who declared that now even my best friend would not recognise me.

'It's not her best friend she needs to worry about,' growled Grim, 'it's her worst enemy!'

'That too,' said Verakina, without missing a beat. 'I've washed and patched your other dress as well,' she added. 'I thought you might want to take it with you.' And she handed me a neat brown-paper parcel.

They were so kind that though I was eager to be on my way, I almost asked if I might stay longer, if I might be allowed a little more time to make sure of my own resolve. Almost – but not quite. The uneasy words that hovered in my throat were never said and instead, we exchanged hopeful words of farewell and 'Till next time we meet', though we all knew there was a good chance we would never see each other again.

At first, Lisbet and I walked through the forest in silence, each of us busy with our own thoughts. The path we took was easy to walk on and though at first it was still fairly dark under the trees, we made good progress. I'd not had a lot of sleep the night before, but I did not feel too tired, and every step I took away from the haven made my earlier unease fade into the distance behind me. I'd told Lucian – the Prince – yesterday that I would prevail because right was on my side. I must believe in that with all my heart and I would make it come true. And it did seem as simple as that, on that steadily brightening spring morning, as the rising sun chased away the darkness and the fear.

After about an hour, we stopped for a short rest so that we could eat the snack prepared by Verakina: an omelette wrapped in bread to keep it warm. Washed down with clear spring water from Lisbet's flask, it made a fine breakfast. As we sat, we talked. About simple things: the goodness of the omelette and the bread, the warmth of the sun, the bird calls starting all around us as the sun rose higher in the sky. Lisbet could name every bird, tell what kind of nest they built, what size their eggs were, even what their calls meant.

'When I was little, I used to climb trees just so I could see into the nests,' she said, when I remarked on how good her knowledge was. 'Not to rob them, you understand, but because I wanted to see how they lived. Do you see?'

'I do,' I answered, smiling.

'I made things from feathers and bits of eggshell and twigs that I found. Little decorations. My mother called them my spells, because whenever I hung them in our window, the birds would come calling. Dozens, sometimes many more, wheeling around our cottage. They would settle on our windowsill, on our roof, in our garden, and they would sing, like a great choir. Can you imagine that?'

'Yes,' I said, moved by the extraordinary image she conjured and by the faraway look on her face.

'It was so beautiful, Bianca! Sometimes I thought they were angels come to earth in the shape of a bird, just for us, just to bring us joy. I felt blessed. Truly blessed.' Her face darkened. 'How can people do that, Bianca? How can they look at such a beautiful thing and turn it into something wrong, something wicked?'

'I don't know,' I said, sadly. My mind went back to the moment we had shared in front of the statue of St Fleur: Lisbet had been accused of witchcraft and I understood without being told that this must have been why she'd been accused of being a witch.

'I don't either,' she whispered. 'I would have shared my decorations with them if they'd let me. And I would have told them what the birds speak of: what their calls mean, what they know . . . They know so many things we cannot know: the paths of the sky, the freedom of the air . . . If only they'd listened . . .'

'You told them?' I said, staring at her, the skin of my neck prickling with goosebumps. 'You told them you knew the language of the birds?'

'Yes,' she said. 'I wanted them to understand. But it was I who did not understand. I who would not be warned, who did not listen to my mother when she said that I had been given a great gift by God but that it must always stay a secret between us. How could I believe her, when it was such a joyful thing to have been granted that knowledge? I thought I could teach it to others, so they would be glad, too.' She was silent a moment, then she went on. 'Now . . . Now all I hear in the calls of the birds is the same as what everyone else hears. Nothing more.'

There was a lump in my throat as I said, 'You mean . . . your gift . . . it is gone?'

'Gone. It vanished the day of my mother's death and has never returned. I was punished for my pride and foolishness.' She spoke quietly, in a steady voice, but I could feel the bleak sorrow in it like a cold wind.

'I'm sorry,' I said, gently. 'I did not mean to bring back bad memories for you.'

'Oh no,' she said. 'I have not spoken of those things for such a long time, for fear of the bitterness. But you – you are a friend, and in telling you I have remembered something precious – the feeling of joy the birds used to bring me.' A smile lightened her whole face.

I was so touched that it was hard to keep my voice from breaking as I said, 'When I am in Lepmest, I will light a candle for you at the shrine of St Fleur and pray to her to not only bring back your gift, but to bring you the greatest of happiness with it, forever.'

'Oh, Bianca!' cried Lisbet and, throwing her arms around me, she hugged me tight. 'You are so kind and all I wish is that we will meet again, in better days.'

'And I wish that too,' I said sincerely, hugging her back.

We set off again, then, at an increased pace and with a lighter step. Less than an hour later, we reached the outskirts of the forest and emerged onto a narrow path that led to the village the Prince had told us about. Up until then we had met nobody, but only a short distance along the village path we came across a woodcutter and his son, and then a mushroom gatherer and her daughter. They looked at us a little curiously but greeted us with a cheerful 'Good morning'. It was only when we were past them that I noticed Lisbet was a little pale.

'I'm not used to meeting new people,' she said, seeing my questioning expression, 'that's all.'

But I knew it was more than that and when, a little further along, she told me that the mushroom gatherer – large, with soft features belied by a determined expression – had reminded her in looks of one of the ringleaders of the mob who had turned against her, back in her own village, I understood her reaction.

'It just gave me a little bit of a turn,' she explained. 'Sorry.'

'Don't be,' I said. 'Look, Lisbet, if you would prefer, I am sure I can find my own way now into the village. I'll ask for help at the inn. You do not need to go any further if you do not wish.'

'Oh no,' she said, 'I promised the Prince I would take you to our friend, and that is what I will do. I have been to the village before, just not in a long time.' She gave me a crooked smile. 'Besides, if I turn around now I might bump into that poor harmless woman again!'

She spoke lightly but with an undertone which told me this possibility was not really a joking matter for her. So I smiled back and did not comment and we went on our way.

We reached the village a short while later. It was a reasonably sized village, with about a hundred houses gathered around a church and a small central square. Along the outsides of the square were a few shops: a grocery, a bakery, a smithy. I also saw the inn, which was our destination. It was called The Blue Lion and was a long, low, neat thatched building that looked well cared for. I liked the look of it at once, and also the look of Darian Zymund, the innkeeper, a grey-haired gentle giant of a man with a big moustache. He clearly had met Lisbet before – they were quite easy with each other – and her earlier jumpiness faded quite away.

Just as the Prince had said, Zymund had everything ready.

'I had to make this up in a hurry, so I hope it will do,' he said, handing me a large flat wallet.

In it was a travel document in the name of 'Jana Maria Sebastian'; a rental reference from Mormest, 'which is where you've supposedly been living in the past year,' he explained with a wink; a photograph of an old man and woman, 'Your sainted grandparents who came from here and who brought you up,' he grinned; a ticket for the mail coach to Lepmest and some money.

'When you get to the safe house in Lepmest, there'll be a little more money for you,' he said, and then gave me directions to the house. Lastly, he handed me a shabby carpetbag. 'You can't get on the coach with just that brown-paper parcel or questions might be asked. Put your parcel in the bag. I've taken the liberty of adding in a cloak of my late wife's, just to give it a little weight. I hope you don't mind.'

Mind? How could I possibly mind such extraordinary generosity?

'Oh, this is all wonderful,' I exclaimed. 'Thank you so very much. I should like to pay you for your trouble but . . .'

'It's all been taken care of,' said the innkeeper. 'There is no trouble.'

'But . . .'

'You come from a friend, and that is all I need to know. Now come, both of you, and share some coffee and some bacon sandwiches with me before the coach arrives.'

The bacon was thick cut and tasty, with a deliciously crispy rind. The coffee was hot and strong, and the company was most pleasant. All too soon, the mail coach drew up outside the inn, ringing its bell, and it was time to take my leave from them both, for the coach stopped for no more than a few minutes – just long enough for the driver to swallow a cup of coffee, drop off and pick up letters, and buy a packet of bacon sandwiches from Zymund.

At the last minute, I took the pearl earrings from my pocket and pressed them into Lisbet's hands. 'I'd like you to have these as a token of our friendship, and to thank you for trusting me with your story. Please, take them, for my sake,' I added, when she tried to refuse.

For the second time that day I saw her face light up as she thanked me, shyly but with sparkling eyes.

Hoisting my bag into the coach, I climbed in and found two other passengers in it already: a majestic elderly lady dressed in showy red and blue, and a lanky, big-nosed middle-aged gentleman in a fur-collared coat. The lady and her collection of boxes had taken up most of the room on one bench seat so I sat on the other, next to the gentleman. He seemed shy and only nodded at me before closing his eyes and nodding off to sleep – or perhaps he was only feigning sleep, trying to get a little peace, for as I soon learnt, our fellow passenger was not in the least bit shy.

'Are you going all the way to Lepmest?' the lady demanded to know, as I sank back into my corner of seat.

'Er . . . yes.'

'But I heard you telling the driver you came from Mormest originally?'

She has sharp ears, I thought. 'Er . . . I do, but I . . . I have been visiting relatives here in the village.' To back this up, I showed her the photo of my 'grandparents' that the innkeeper had given me. The lady looked at it without much interest, and nodded.

'I . . . I lost my job in Mormest,' I went on. 'I'm hoping I'll have better luck in Lepmest.' The lies rolled off my tongue.

'Hmm,' she said, eyeing me critically. 'What kind of work have you done?'

'I'm . . . er . . . I've been working in a draper's shop. But my employer got sick and the shop had to close and –'

'Yes, yes,' she said, waving a hand, impatiently, 'I see. Well, there are lots of drapers' shops in Lepmest. You could even try that department store, what's it called again?'

'Ladies' Fair,' I said, quietly, feeling my throat tighten a little as I spoke the words.

'That's the one. They're huge, and they'd be sure to always need staff. Try there first, is my advice.' She said this with the air of conveying a huge favour.

But though I could not help being amused at her haughty tone, the fact was that it wasn't such a bad idea. If I got work at Ladies' Fair – in a very lowly position, well away from Belladonna's sight – I could better keep an eye on what was happening in my enemy's world. I'd be close, but not too close.

I nodded. 'Thank you. That is good advice.'

'But of course,' she said, cheerfully. 'I'm well known for that.'

I heard a quickly suppressed snort beside me, but the woman took no notice and went on.

'In fact, that is precisely the goal of my own trip to Lepmest . . .' She broke off, expectantly. She was clearly angling for a question, so I obliged.

'Oh, what will you be doing in Lepmest?'

'Making sure the right protocols and procedures are followed. You see, my son's daughter is to be engaged. My son is Master Georgy Tomzin. You have probably heard of him. He is a very important man.'

'Oh, yes, Master Tomzin is most well known through-out the land,' I said, lying through my teeth. I had never heard of him.

Preening herself, she answered, 'Yes. I like to think I had some hand in that: he has been brought up properly, in the old customs, not these new ways where anything goes! Anyway, I said to him and my daughter-in-law that it is important everything be done right. And how can it be if I am not there? My son's wife understands nothing of our customs, and my son will not tell her. He may be a lion in business but he is most certainly a mouse at home! It's been like that ever since he married her. Why he ever married a girl from the city when he could have had his pick of girls from home – of good custom and behaviour – beats me! This woman he married, she has no idea! Heavens, she did not even know it can *only* be water from Nellia's Spring that can be used to sprinkle on the engaged couple! Imagine!'

'Nellia's Spring?' I echoed.

'Isn't that what I said?' she snapped. 'Not foreign water called goodness-knows-what-ridiculous-name that she wanted to purchase at great expense from –'

'You are from near Nellia's Spring?' I hurriedly interposed. 'I have heard the lords thereabouts are called Montresor? Is that right?'

'Of course it is,' she said. 'It is Montresor land. As everyone knows. '

'I have heard of the name,' I said, 'but not much else, except that some say they are the rightful rulers of Noricia. Is that true?'

'Of course it is true,' she snapped. 'If there were any justice, it is they who would be in the ducal palace in Lepmest, as the ruling family of Noricia. But the Montresors were done out of their true place by a witch's curse. Every fool should know that.' She shot me a piercing glance.

'But in the city it is true to say they talk all kinds of nonsense about it,' she added. 'They say Hector Montresor killed the witch, and that in her dying breath she cursed him and his descendants. What they do not say is that in those days, the throne of Noricia was to pass to the Montresors, as the duke at that time was ailing, was without descendants, and had anointed Hector Montresor as his heir. What they do not say is that the witch was in the pay of another family, a family that on the duke's death seized the throne of Noricia.' She looked at me. 'The same family that has held the throne since then.'

I stared at her. 'You mean . . . You mean the duke's family arranged to . . .'

'Arranged to dispose permanently of their rivals, yes. But in a much cleverer way than mere killing would have done. For they knew that if it became known the Montresors were cursed, and that any future Montresors would be cursed for generations and generations to come, it would be a more effective way of ending any claim to the throne they might have. No-one in Noricia would want to be ruled by a cursed family. Not ever.'

'But . . . if the family isn't really cursed . . .'

She gave me a pitying look. 'Of course they're cursed! The witch had great powers. The curse is all too real.'

Throughout our conversation, I had noticed the man I had shared a seat with had abandoned his pretence of sleep and was listening as hard as I was.

I said, 'But what exactly *happens* –'

'You really don't know anything, do you, girl?' she said, not unkindly despite the words. 'It is no ordinary curse, for that was no ordinary witch. Ordinary curses are fixed. They always operate in the same way. If you have been cursed to die in a fire, for instance, that's what will happen. If the curse is carried down the generations, then each

143

generation will always die in a fire. But such ordinary curses can be reversed. Not so with the kind of curse that afflicts the Montresors. This is a very rare kind, a quicksilver curse. It changes with each generation, each person. It uses a flaw within each person and turns it into something monstrous. So Hector Montresor, who had a bad temper, was cursed with the werewolf affliction and killed several people; his daughter Maldan, who was a soft, gentle young woman, started having terrible waking nightmares and in a fit of madness walked off a cliff; *her* son Marcus, who was a good hunter, killed his own cousin by mistake, thinking him to be a bear; and so on. It is a most terrible thing, for no-one can predict how or when it will show itself. Sometimes it happens in youth, sometimes much later. There have even been cases when it only happened in old age. But when it does strike, it never goes away, except with death.'

'Goodness me,' said the gentleman, speaking for the first time. He had a slight foreign accent which I couldn't place. 'I have never heard of such a thing.'

'I do not expect that you would have,' said Mistress Tomzin, 'for it is a very rare curse indeed.'

She said this in a tone of great self-satisfaction and I could not help but exchange an amused glance with the gentleman which, unfortunately, she saw.

'Of course, there are those fools who scoff at any such notion,' she said sniffing, 'but then, they are ignorant people who do not know the old ways.'

'Quite, quite,' I said, hurriedly placating her. 'It just seems such a terrible thing, to create such a curse.'

'Of course it is. But that is the way it is,' she said, with a glare at the gentleman, as if daring him to argue.

'This curse,' I said, 'is it still . . . is it still affecting the family?'

'Oh yes. It strikes the family every generation but you never know who it's going to hit.'

'And in this generation?' I asked, holding my breath.

'There is only one child. Lucian Montresor. And so far he has shown no sign of the curse. But . . .' For the first time she hesitated.

'Yes?' I tried not to sound too eager.

'Well, there are rumours. He disappears for days on end. No-one knows where he is. But some say that . . . well, they say that Lucian Montresor suffers the same fate as Hector Montresor. That he is a werewolf.'

Light burst in on my mind. If I'd harboured doubts of the Prince's true identity, I had none now. If Mistress Tomzin was right – if Lucian was a werewolf like his ancestor – it explained so much about his identity as Prince of Outlaws. It explained his strange costume, and the way he made sure that all his skin was covered at the time of hunter's moon, when the wolf-nature is strongest in them, and hardest to resist. Werewolves are rare in Noricia these days. But they still exist, and they are just as feared and hated as in the old days. It was why poor Verakina had been persecuted and almost killed. No wonder Lucian wanted to keep it secret. Even in his own home, his own territory where people knew the sad story of his family, people would be afraid. He must have imagined I'd turn away from him in disgust, too, if I knew. Oh Lucian, I thought, if only I could tell you how I admire and respect you! If only I could tell you that the curse does not alter my feelings for you!

'What's the matter with you, girl?' growled Mistress Tomzin, startling me out of my thoughts. 'You look like you've seen a ghost!' She shot the gentleman a hard glance, as if to imply that it was all his fault.

'It just . . . it seems so . . . so hard on the Montresors. Can't anything be done? Isn't there another witch capable of reversing the spell?'

'Not one,' she said, 'for not even Nellia herself could do anything about it, and her powers are great.'

'You mean, the feya Nellia tried to reverse the spell?'

'Yes. Back in Hector's day. But she couldn't. No, the curse is something the family has always had to live with and always will. That is the way of the world.'

It was an unexpected echo of what the Prince – Lucian – had said, that one mustn't change the way of the world. Again, I responded in the same way.

'Well, then it is high time the world changed.'

She snorted. 'Only the young and silly think the world will change for them. It is you, my dear, who will be changed by the world, not the other way around. Now if you don't mind, I am very tired and wish to have some rest. Too much chatter is most fatiguing.'

And with that, the rude lady closed her eyes and within a few minutes was snoring like a trooper.

'Well, well,' said the lanky gentleman, when she was safely asleep, 'that was quite a story, wasn't it?'

'I do not think it just a story,' I replied.

He smiled. 'Ah, you are so right, for a story is never just a story, is it?'

'Er . . . I suppose so,' I said, hesitantly.

'Do you mind?' he asked, producing a notebook and pencil from his coat pocket and quickly scribbling something. 'Just so I don't forget. I'm a collector of such things,' he added, seeing my puzzlement. 'Observations, stories, customs – I use them in my work. My readers enjoy the local colour.'

'You are a journalist?' I asked.

'No. I'm an author. I am originally from Viklandia, but I travel the world collecting traditional stories as inspiration for my own. I heard that in Noricia the stories are particularly good, and in the mountains, especially.' He looked at me. 'Do you know of any others, my dear?'

'Me?' I thought of all that had happened to me, and wondered what he'd say if he knew. 'Not really. Nothing interesting, that is to say.'

'Oh,' he said, looking a little disappointed. He took a card from his pocket and handed it to me. 'If you think of any, or if you have any friends who know any, here's where I'll be.'

I looked at the card. It had the address of one of Lepmest's best hotels, the Villa Valverd.

'Ask for Dr Nord,' he said. 'That's the name I always travel under, to avoid the nuisances of fame.' And he smiled a rather self-important smile.

I was saved from having to respond with more than a 'Thank you' by the coach coming to a stop. We had arrived in Lepmest.

Seventeen

)

I said farewell to my fellow passengers and quickly made my way through the alleys to the address of the safe house. One of the things my father had taught me was to know my city well – not just the fine areas where our mansion was, but all of it, and he'd accompanied me on many a walk through the less salubrious districts. I wasn't afraid of being recognised because I knew my disguise hid my identity well, but I still could not help scuttling along with my head down, just in case.

I soon found the safe house, which turned out to be a little flat hidden within a tailor's shop, in a narrow alley sandwiched between some tall buildings. The tailor, the man the Prince had called Master Kinberg, was a thin little man with a stooped back, thick glasses and an even thicker Almainian accent. He gave me a quick glance but asked me no questions: he was clearly already well briefed as to my coming.

The flat was hidden from sight of anyone who came into the tailor's workshop because its entrance door was concealed behind some swivelling shelves at the far end of the room. I soon found out that the tailor himself did not live on the premises but in a street a couple of blocks away. He shut up shop early and once he was gone, I had the place completely to myself.

Perhaps he has left early to give me some time to settle into my new surroundings in peace, I thought. But exploring those surroundings didn't take much time. The flat was very small, with only one room. In the room was a bed, a table, a chair, a chest of drawers, and a kitchen corner with a single gas ring to cook on, two or three pots, a tiny sink, and a small cupboard containing two plates, cutlery, a couple of mugs, some pots of jam and dried meat, herbs, tea, rice, sugar and salt. A door at the end opened onto some stairs leading down into a kind of wash area, which included a toilet and a small tub.

The whole thing was very clean and neat, if a little shabby. I wondered how many people had used it before, who they'd been, and what had happened to them. Was it a staging place before admittance to a haven? Or did it fulfill some other function? I did not know and did not really need to know, of course – but it was another extraordinary aspect of that hidden world, the world of the outcasts and the Prince of Outlaws, whose existence I had never suspected before my life had changed.

But I did not spend much time thinking about it, for I had a good deal of work to do. Leaving the flat, I made my first purchase of the day: a pad of blank paper, envelopes, a pen and some ink. Retiring, then, to a busy coffee shop, I made a fair copy of the first instalment of my illustrated story, which I had called 'The Queen and the Magic Mirror:

A Modern Fairytale'. I then wrote a letter in accompaniment, disguising my handwriting and signing it 'Syrena', and addressed the package to the editor of the *Ladies' Journal*, giving my return address as care of the post office closest to the premises of the *Ladies' Journal*. As there were three deliveries a day to the surrounding area, my letter would certainly reach the *Ladies' Journal* before the end of business hours. And then I'd only have to wait. Maybe the editor wouldn't take it, and then my plan would have to change. But I would think of that when the time came.

The first step of my plan complete, I turned my attention to the next: a job at Ladies' Fair, for I needed money and to better keep an eye on how Belladonna was using her new-found queendom. As I trundled through the streets on a tram heading for the city centre and the department store, my skin prickled with nerves and my heart beat fast at the thought of returning to the place that had been the heart of my father's kingdom. Also in my mind was the thought that I'd never gone for a job in my life. I'd never had to. I tried to calm my thoughts by reassuring myself that I knew a good deal about the store. I even had an idea of the kind of work a little country mouse like my alter ego, Jana Maria Sebastian, might be offered: definitely not in any of the front-of-house areas.

Front of house. It was a term Father used to use. It was a term that came from the theatre because, as Father used to say, our store was like a great theatre, with everyone having their role to play.

'Front of house is what the public sees,' he'd say, 'but without what goes on backstage, there would be no theatre.'

He always respected the people who worked behind the scenes – the packers and clerks and typists, the tailors and seamstresses and caterers, the cleaners and messengers and drivers – the dozens, even hundreds of people whose work was not seen by the public but without whom the business would soon grind to a halt. And because he thought I should know how things were run, in the days before Belladonna came into our lives (for she'd soon put a stop to my lessons in business as they were 'not suitable for a young lady'), Father had taken me several times to the back rooms to see how the business worked.

'One day, Bianca, this will be yours,' he'd told me. 'But I want you to understand that a great store like ours does not just belong to one person, or even to a single family. It belongs to all of the people who work here. You must never ever forget that. Everyone has their part to play. True success rests on the shoulders of all of us.' And he'd looked at me and smiled and said, 'Remember that and you won't go wrong, my darling girl.'

The words were so clear in my memory that it was as though he were actually speaking them in my ear. I felt as though if I turned my head slightly, I'd see him there on the tram seat next to me, smiling his sweet smile. My eyes filled with tears but through the wave of grief, I felt stronger. Suddenly, I did not feel nervous anymore. Father was with me. He was keeping watch over me. He would help me. I have no reason to be afraid, I thought, for he will guide my words, my steps, my plans, in the place that had been his kingdom and his creation.

And so, armed with new confidence, I got off at the stop outside Ladies' Fair. There it was, the graceful building my father had built which, as a child, I had thought looked like a palace. It was four storeys high, took up half a city block, and was built of light-coloured stone with decorated cupola roofs and huge windows with stained-glass inserts and gilt carvings. Through the windows at ground level I could see, as usual, all the latest fashions. But I saw as well that something had changed. In the central window there was a fine oil portrait of my father, framed by mourning ribbons of silver and black. In the portrait he was smiling, and though the sight of it brought the prickle of tears to my eyes, it also somehow made me even more confident in the knowledge that he was there with me. 'I love you, Father, and I won't let you down,' I murmured, looking into his painted eyes.

Beside his portrait was a smaller portrait of me, but it was less prominently displayed. The strange manner of my supposed death – the suspicion of suicide – must make people uncomfortable. It would suit Belladonna well. She'd managed to make my disappearance seem both sad and shameful and the portrait, which I'd never seen before but which must have been painted from a photograph, was not a good picture of me and somehow managed to convey a sort of strangeness about me. It doesn't matter, I told myself, it's nothing. But the rush of rage through my veins told me otherwise. It was a small thing but a telling one: not content with killing me, Belladonna has set out to stain my memory as well. Whereas she would laud her late husband to the skies for as long as it worked to her advantage, she needed to destroy my image and memory since I was a rival both for my father's kingdom of Ladies' Fair, and for the title of Fairest Lady. In time, people would be glad that my death left my stepmother in charge of my father's legacy, for she was clearly so much better suited to it than I.

I took a deep breath. Enough of these profitless thoughts! Turning away determinedly from the front of the store, I made my way to the side entrance used by staff and tradesmen and almost immediately happened upon a glass display case in the hallway which held in-house job notices. Two jobs were available right now. One was for a typist; one was for a messenger delivering parcels. Though I wasn't very fast, I could use a typewriter, and knowing that it was men who were usually employed as messengers, it seemed as if the typist job was the one I would go for.

Rehearsing my spiel in my head, I went up the stairs to the recruitment offices. In the past, I had been introduced to three or four of the people there and I could only hope they'd not see through my disguise or recognise my voice. But I did not have to worry – there was not a hint of recognition from anyone. I did notice, however, that there was a subdued air about the offices. Quite a few people were wearing black armbands and an edition of the *Lepmest Daily News*, with a front page featuring a large photograph from my father's funeral yesterday, showed just how much the workers at Ladies' Fair respected my father. Still, despite the sense of understated sorrow, it was clear that my father's motto, 'The show must go on,' had been very much absorbed by the staff, who went about their business with a quiet efficiency. He would have been proud of them, I thought.

'I've come in response to the job advertisement,' I said to Miss Geldpen, the whip-thin lady in charge of the typing pool. 'I've been working as a clerk in a draper's shop in Mormest and I –'

'Stop right there,' she said, looking up from the files she'd been studying when I came in. 'I'm afraid the job has just been filled.'

Crestfallen, I babbled, 'Oh ... I ... I ... Is there no other similar ... I mean ... I was so ... so eager to work for you ... I have heard that despite the recent sad happenings, this is still the best workplace in Lepmest, and I did so hope ...'

She nodded, looking pleased. 'You heard correctly, my dear. This is a good place to work. We all pull together, just as our dear Sir Anton would have wanted. Unfortunately, I have no further jobs available in my section. But you may leave your details at the front desk and if something comes up, we'll be sure to let you know.'

'Thank you,' I said sadly.

I was getting up to leave when she said, 'Wait a moment. You might also ask Master Philipi; he's still looking for a messenger, and I happen to know it's for light jobs only, so all right for you. If you're not afraid of a bit of running around, that is.'

'Oh no, not at all,' I said, fervently. 'I'm happy to do whatever is required.'

'Good. Tell him Miss Geldpen recommended you,' she said.

'Thank you. Thank you so much,' I said, and she flashed me a smile.

'I was once young and eager like you. Good luck, my dear.' And so saying, she turned back to her files once more.

Master Philipi was as large and nervy as Miss Geldpen was small and calm, and he hardly even stopped to ask my name before saying, 'I need someone straightaway,

I mean this instant, not in an hour, not tomorrow. Last-minute order. Can you do that?'

'Absolutely. Of course. I can start whenever you like,' I said, overjoyed.

'Good. I like right now.' He scribbled on a piece of paper, folded it, and handed it to me. 'Take this down to dispatch and tell them you've come for the Eglantine perfume parcel.'

'Certainly, sir.'

For the first time he seemed to look at me properly, and what he saw didn't seem to be to his satisfaction, for he said, 'But that won't do. Won't do at all for you to go out like that. Here,' he called to someone outside the office, 'take this girl to uniforms right now. And don't linger there,' he said, turning back to me. 'Time is of the essence, the parcel was delayed once already and the customer won't be pleased if she doesn't get it within the hour.'

I did as I was told and was given a uniform – a jacket in blue and white with the store's motif embroidered on the top pocket in dark blue thread, a plain blue skirt and a blue felt hat – and thus newly attired headed down to dispatch where on production of Master Philipi's note I was handed a small parcel wrapped in magnificent white silk paper, tied up with silver lace ribbons. They gave me an address, which was several blocks away and, like Master Philipi, repeated to me that time was of the essence.

Instead of walking there, I caught a cab. They had not given me any money for that, so I'd have to use what little left I had, but I reasoned that because this was my first job, it was very important that I work to impress from the start.

I was outside the address in just under five minutes, about a quarter of the time it would have taken me to go on foot. There had been no name on the parcel dispatch note, just the name of the house – Willow Lodge – and the address, so that when the maid answered the front door, I said, 'I have a parcel here for the lady of the house. Special delivery from Ladies' Fair.'

'Oh! Right! The perfume Mistress Jemans was waiting for! At last!' said the maid, in a rush, and as I wondered why I felt as if there was something familiar about what she'd said, a voice called out from another room, 'Is that Mama's parcel, Horatia? She will be so pleased!'

In the next instant, a young woman with red hair came bursting into the hall. It was Emilia.

I could not help taking a step back, and nearly dropped the precious parcel.

'Watch out!' cried Emilia, rushing towards me. 'If that breaks, Mama will be livid!'

'I'm . . . I'm sorry,' I mumbled, holding it out to her, trying to hide the shock I felt at seeing her again. 'I must have tripped on something.'

'Don't worry, anyone can be clumsy sometimes!' Emilia had not really looked at me, only at the parcel. 'Thanks so much for getting it here so quickly. Mama was so worried because my aunt is such a pernickety sort and we know she only likes Eglantine, and she's coming over, and it was unexpected, so we had to find her a gift all in a hurry. Perfume always goes down well, Mama says. But it had to be the right one! And I nearly forgot to order it!' As she spoke, she tore open the parcel, the silk paper in tatters on the floor, the ribbon flung off pell-mell to reveal an elegant silver cardboard box. 'Just checking it is the right one, before you go, just in case,' she added, opening the box and pulling out a lovely flask in the shape of a stemmed rose, filled with a pale pink liquid. 'Perfect!' Unstopping it, she smelt it. 'Phew! Bit strong for me, but that's what she wants. All good!' She beamed at me. 'Thanks again, you've saved our skins!'

At that moment, someone else came into the hall – an older and slightly larger version of Emilia, with the same shade of red hair.

'Mama!' cried Emilia, brandishing the flask. 'It's come, and so fast, too!'

'Wonderful,' said the woman who must be Emilia's mother. Turning to the maid, who was hovering at the end of the hall, she said, 'Horatia, please go and ask Cook to get some tea and cake ready for this young lady to thank her for such promptness.'

'No, I mean, no, thank you very much,' I gabbled. 'It is very kind of you but I really need to get back to the store. I have another errand to run, and –'

'Well, then, let me at least give you this,' Mistress Jemans said, rummaging in her pocket and bringing out a silver coin, which she handed to me with a smile.

'There's no need –' I began, but then Emilia interrupted me, with a puzzled frown.

'Wait a moment. Have we met before somewhere?'

'No ... No ... I hardly think that would be likely,' I managed to say. 'I've only arrived from Mormest this week.'

'Mormest! I don't know anyone in Mormest. Are you sure you're from Mormest?'

'Emilia!' broke in her mother, before I could gather my scattered wits. 'What is the matter with you, asking such questions? Apologise at once.'

Emilia went scarlet. 'Sorry. So sorry. That was rude of me. Sorry.'

All her bounciness had gone so suddenly that you could see it had been a desperate, almost manic attempt to keep up her spirits.

'It's no problem,' I said, through the lump in my throat. 'Don't mention it.'

'I'm not usually like this –' she began, then with a little cry, she turned on her heel and flung herself out of the hall as impetuously as she'd rushed in.

'Is she . . . Is Miss Jemans . . . I didn't mean to upset her . . .' I stammered to Emilia's mother, my heart as heavy as lead.

'It wasn't your fault,' said Mistress Jemans, gently. 'It's just that, you see, you're from Ladies' Fair – and from Mormest – that was the last place anyone really spoke to that poor girl – to Lady Bianca Dalmatin – before she disappeared. My daughter had met her at the Presentation Ball, just the day before she disappeared. When she heard of Lady Bianca's death . . . It was a great shock to her.'

It took every bit of energy I had not to go after Emilia and tell her that it was all right, that I was alive and well, even though her instincts that something wasn't right were correct. But I knew I could not. It was too dangerous. For me and for her. If I were to bring Belladonna down, no-one could know that I was still alive. No-one.

'Oh. I am sorry,' I said, because she seemed to expect a response. 'I . . . heard about it, of course . . .'

'My daughter feels things intensely, more than most people,' sighed Mistress Jemans. 'She didn't know poor Sir Anton Dalmatin and she hadn't known his daughter for very long, but you know how friendship is. Emilia liked her very much. She has a soft heart.' Her tone changed. 'I must say, I am very impressed that even in the midst of such sad and turbulent times, Ladies' Fair continues to give such excellent service. It speaks highly of Sir Anton's widow that she has been able to keep the ship on its course without a hitch. Please convey my gratitude to your employers.'

'I will. Of course,' I muttered and, not trusting myself to say any more, I took my leave.

Out in the street, I walked blindly for a short while, feeling quite shaken from my encounter with Emilia. Like her mother had said, we hardly knew each other, but it seems that she had felt the same as I had at the ball: that we would be friends. An instant sympathy had sprung up between us, as instant as the attraction that had sprung up between the Prince and I – only different in type, of course. It touched me that she thought of me still, even though she had been told that I had died.

As I walked I felt calmer, more capable of assessing what had just happened. Fate had led me into a strange situation, but in so doing had done something very useful for me: showed that my disguise was good enough to pass muster. It felt like a step in the right direction, a sign that fate was in my favour.

But on the way back to the store, I called into the great cathedral. Inside, I knew, was the humble shrine of St Fleur of the Snow. With the silver coin Emilia's mother had given me, I bought three candles and lit them: for Lisbet, as I had promised; for my father, in his memory; and for Emilia, so she might stay safe.

Eighteen

☽

The rest of the day passed without incident. That evening, after I finished work, I made my way by tram to the cemetery which was my father's last resting place, in the Dalmatin family vault. At least he has been laid to rest beside my mother, I thought, as I stood at a discreet distance from the vault, tears trickling down my face as I said a prayer for him. Strangely, I felt less close to him at the cemetery than I had that morning in the tram, when I heard his loving voice in my head. His body might be there, in that forbidding monument of marble and gilt, but his spirit was with me, by my side.

By seven o'clock I was back in the safe house, cooking a simple meal of stew made from the dried meat and herbs, with rice. I spent the rest of the evening drawing some new panels of the next instalment of 'The Queen and the Magic Mirror'. Once again, my pencil flew over the page as I drew a panel showing a portrait of a black-haired girl dressed all in white, with the caption: 'But the Queen had a rival in her beauty. Her name was Snow White because her innocence was white as the winter snow.' In the next panel I showed the Queen in a beautiful dress, and Snow White before her, handing her a cloak. 'Snow White was a lady-in-waiting to the Queen but no-one noticed her because beside the dazzling Queen she only cast a pale light. The Queen reigned supreme, her mirror told her so.' In the last panel I drew the mirror reflecting a ball scene with a flurry of skirts, dancers and twirls and these words: 'And then came the day that everything changed . . .'

There were only three panels, but I worked on them for hours, making them perfect. I saw as I worked that the portrait I had drawn of Snow White bore more than a passing resemblance to the portrait of me I'd seen in the display window of Ladies' Fair. There was a curious comfort in it, for it took away the sting of rage and pain I'd felt then – taking something terrible she'd made and using her own work against her. It too would be a weapon against Belladonna, just as the name 'Snow White' would awaken echoes of my own name, 'Bianca', which means, 'the white one'. Signing the panels with a flourished 'Syrena', I made a fair copy and when at last I went to bed, well after midnight, I felt almost triumphant.

It may have been a feeling of beginner's luck, but from the start I was convinced the *Ladies' Journal* would take my work. When I called into the post office the next morning before work and discovered that there was a letter waiting for me, I wasn't altogether surprised, but I was still delighted to read the picture editor's words: 'You have very good timing, as we were looking to start a new picture story. An excellent beginning – good illustrations – we will publish it in Monday's edition. Please send more; we can publish one set every two days.' There was no mention of payment but I did not care about that.

I posted the next instalment. Despite the fact that my creation was not for my own pleasure, I could not help feeling glad that my story had been liked, and would soon appear in print on Monday, in two days' time, and for a few giddy moments I even half-forgot about the serious purpose behind my work. But I soon sobered up. Once upon a time, such giddiness would have been excusable. Now, such dreams were part of a past which had died with my father. There could be no happily ever after for me, not until my stepmother had been punished for her crimes.

That day passed in a flurry of delivery jobs. I kept my eyes and ears open in the store's office for mention of my stepmother but learnt nothing very startling. I did not want to ask too many searching questions yet, for I was afraid that such curiosity might reach the wrong ears, so contented myself with a bland question or two about the store itself. I made friends with another of the messengers, a lad called Jeremie who was a couple of years younger than me but who looked even younger than that because of his small, skinny frame.

But there was nothing childish about his shrewdness. Over a snatched cup of coffee that afternoon he told me, 'We all worried that Lady Dalmatin would want to make changes now she's in charge, but it seems that so far she's content to leave it to the managers Sir Anton Dalmatin had appointed. But for how long, some say.'

'And what do you say?'

He shrugged. 'I don't think anyone knows what Lady Dalmatin will do. She's a deep one.'

'I got that impression, from what everyone said,' I observed, cautiously. 'How well is she liked here?'

'A lot of people love her,' he replied.

I heard the reserve in his voice. 'And you?'

'It is not my place to like or dislike her,' he said, and from the tone in his voice I knew that he did dislike her. 'All I can say is that I miss Sir Anton. He was a great man.'

I could only nod, for his simple words had brought a bitter lump of grief to my throat, and I had to turn away so that he could not see the prickle of tears in my eyes.

On my way home to the safe house that evening, I passed a newsstand and bought that day's edition of the *Mirror*. This one featured four pages of photographic tribute to what the headline dubbed 'A Beautiful Love Story', featuring pictures of my father and Belladonna – at their wedding and at various social events. In every photograph, my father was smiling, but seeing his face so happy like that was like a stab to my heart. He had so trustingly welcomed that snake into our home, and he had been happy because he had been so much in love with her. How dreadful it must have been for him when first he suspected that his Belladonna may not be who she pretended to be . . . How he must have struggled against suspicion, wanting to give her every chance, hoping against hope that it was all a mistake. From the telegram in the package that the Prince had given me, I knew that my father had known the truth, at the end. He knew what black heart beat beneath that beautiful breast, what evil genius lit those lovely eyes. It hurt to think that such bitter knowledge must have filled my father's last conscious hours . . .

The second-last photograph, titled 'Sad Goodbyes', showed Belladonna in an elegant black velvet dress and hat with a black veil, placing white roses onto my father's coffin. By her side were Duke Ottakar, stiff in his braided bemedalled dress uniform, and his sister, Lady Helena, dignified in black brocade. Behind them stood the cream of Lepmest society, looking grave and solemn, and behind them again was a mass of other people. My father had been a popular man. He had touched the lives and hearts of so many people. I wiped away a tear from my eye and looked at the last photograph.

The final photograph showed Belladonna at the Lepmest Ladies' Fair store with staff members all around her. She was at a desk, with piles of ledgers surrounding her, and was looking into the distance. The caption read: 'The grieving widow dries her tears and sets to work in honour of her beloved husband's memory.'

It nearly made me retch. There sat the usurper, the queen of lies, her crocodile tears quickly dry, digging her vicious claws into my father's legacy. Anger at the fatuous fools at the *Mirror* for only seeing a 'grieving widow' welled up inside me – until I remembered that even I, her stepdaughter, had never seen Belladonna for who she truly was until that night in the forest with Drago.

There were no photos of me, of course. It must have been for the same reason that the Ladies' Fair store had not wanted to focus too much on my death: they would have thought they were sparing my memory, avoiding the scandal that was attached to suicide. Again, I could see just how perfectly it worked with Belladonna's plans: no inconvenient questions would be asked, my existence would be brushed from people's consciousness.

I didn't care. I didn't care about this gutter rag, I told myself, as I flung the paper across the room. But I did care, and that night I was unable to work on my cartoon, I felt so angry.

The next day was Sunday, the only day the store was closed. It was raining heavily and I spent most of the day indoors, working on the third instalment of 'The Queen and the Magic Mirror'.

'The day of the ball was the day everything changed,' read the caption under the first panel, which was of the Queen looking into her mirror again. And curling like black smoke out of the mirror, I wrote: 'You are no longer the fairest, oh Queen, no longer the fairest to be seen. Another has taken your place, another is fairer of face.'

The Queen's furious face – teeth bared, eyes flashing, claws out – filled the next panel, along with these words, rendered in jagged, shouting script: 'Mirror, mirror, who is she? An evil witch she must surely be!?' And coming from the mirror: 'Not a witch, but Snow White, and her beauty is real, and right.'

The final panel showed the Queen drawing the curtain across the magic mirror. She is turned towards the reader so that we can see her face, which is cruel and filled with a wicked light. The caption read: 'She will pay, she will pay with her life, for her beating bloody heart I will hold in my hand this very night!'

If Belladonna hadn't guessed earlier, this instalment of 'The Queen and the Magic Mirror' would make her know for certain that the mysterious Syrena knew her secret. I couldn't wait for the first instalment of my story to appear in tomorrow's paper, but I knew, too, that the next thing I needed to consider would be to somehow make sure that Belladonna saw it . . .

On Monday morning, after posting this instalment, I went to the newsstand on my way to work. 'Sorry, young lady, today's edition of the *Ladies' Journal* has been delayed a little,' said the friendly newspaper seller, when I asked after it. He saw my crestfallen expression. 'It'll be out this afternoon,' he continued. 'Don't you fret, young lady. You'll soon get your fill of society gossip.'

I gave him a weak smile and hurried away. But I couldn't help worrying. The editors would by now have received the second instalment of my story, too. Had they understood the real meaning behind my story and panicked and changed their minds? Even though my original plan had been to frighten Belladonna into doing something rash, I had become more and more excited thinking that other people reading the story might make the connection to the real-life Queen, Belladonna. I didn't just want to catch her out, I wanted to expose her. What if Belladonna had somehow learnt of 'The Queen and the Magic Mirror' and made the *Ladies' Journal* pull it? Or was I fretting over nothing and it wasn't even the picture-story page that had been holding up the printing?

All through the morning at work I worried, and by the afternoon I'd bitten my nails down to the quick. Jeremie, seeing my turmoil, asked me if I was ill. When I said I was fine, he told me I'd better be careful, that Master Philipi was kind but he didn't like his staff to be distracted in work hours and made sure to keep a sharp eye on such things. I knew Jeremie was right to warn me to be careful, so I tried hard not to think about the *Ladies' Journal* and to give all my attention to my work. But in the afternoon, I ran to the nearest newsstand to buy a copy.

Hiding in the staff bathroom, I leafed through the paper feverishly. There it was! It was in the mid-section of the paper, prominently displayed, in bold type. As soon as I saw it, my heart beat faster. The editors had changed their minds and decided to devote almost the whole page to my story – not only had they printed the first instalment, they had printed the second one as well! And, underneath 'The Queen and the Magic Mirror', they'd added a subtitle that hinted that there was more to the story than met the eye: 'Exciting New Story Mirrors the News'.

My pulse raced; my ears rang with excitement. The editors had clearly guessed that this was a story with a key. There was no need for me to think up a plan to force it on Belladonna's attention; the whole of Lepmest would be talking about it! The trap was sprung. I only had to wait, wait for Belladonna to panic, to do something rash, and then to catch her in the act and expose her.

I went to bed feeling pretty pleased with myself, sure that now I had my prey within reach. She'd go berserk when she read the story. She'd know exactly what it referred to. She would know that there was someone in Lepmest who knew what she had done to me and, because of the Aurisolan name I'd picked to sign the artwork and the Aurisolan crest I'd drawn beside Syrena's name, she would know that that someone knew the truth of her past. Would Belladonna go to the *Ladies' Journal*, make a scene, and demand to know who the mysterious Syrena was? Or would she try to ignore it but inwardly, the first tendril of unease would creep into her heart . . .?

I did not work on another instalment that night. With any luck, the journal would print the third one in their next edition in two days' time, and I wanted to leave a little time for it to be digested, for readers to start wondering, to start asking themselves questions about Snow White and the Queen, before I drew the fourth instalment. I wanted Belladonna to slowly roast on the hook of suspicion, of fear, of panic. I wanted my weapon of paper and printers' ink to do its deadly work, to make her feel so unsafe she started to make mistakes. I would wait for her to be tried in the court of public opinion, wait for her reputation to be torn to shreds. And then I'd go in for the kill. I'd reveal myself to the world, and reveal the truth about the real Belladonna.

But despite going early to bed, I found it hard to sleep. And it wasn't just thoughts of exposing Belladonna that kept me awake, but softer ones, those I desperately tried to banish. I'd told myself so many times that I must not think about Lucian, or wonder what he was doing. But in the dark reaches of the night, I kept playing over and over in my head that final scene with him at the haven and my longing to see him again was like a sharp thorn under my skin.

Nineteen

☾

I rushed to the newsstand again the next morning to see if the *Mirror* had made any official comment on my story in the *Ladies' Journal*. There was nothing, not even a mention. It was a little disappointing, but not too much, because I hadn't genuinely expected them to want to draw attention to something that showed them in such a bad light, as the eager slave of the Queen.

But if the *Mirror* kept a dignified silence, I soon found out that many others did not. At work, the gossip around the tea-break table was of the strange story in the *Ladies' Journal*, which quite a few of the staff, especially the women, seemed to have read. Opinion was divided as to its merits. Some had enjoyed it and debated its true meaning, others thought it was nonsense – 'It's just a story, after all,' said a typist, shrugging.

But the general opinion was uneasy.

'Even if it's supposed to be a story, it is a bit too close to real life,' said a young woman from the hat department.

'Really?' I asked, innocently. 'In what way?'

The woman looked to one of her friends. 'Well, Lady Belladonna Dalmatin's always had the title of Fairest Lady,' someone said. 'Until –'

'Until that story in the *Mirror* – the title was passed on to Lady Bianca, her stepdaughter,' put in her friend.

'It is in very bad taste to bring that up again,' said the hat woman, 'and so soon after all those tragic happenings, too.'

'I bet the *Mirror* will sue,' laughed Jeremie.

'It looks like the writer is from Aurisola,' I hazarded. 'Isn't that where Lady Belladonna Dalmatin comes from?'

A few people nodded.

'I wonder if it's someone who knew her there?' said another typist.

Miss Geldpen frowned at her. 'Best to leave such speculations alone,' she said. 'Now back to work, everyone.'

The seed of doubt has been planted, I thought, as I went back to my duties. Here and everywhere else. Soon the whole city would be buzzing with rumours. It was a wonderful first strike against the woman I hated, and I wished that I could share my triumph with someone. With the Prince, preferably . . . But of course I could not.

The rest of the day passed in a blur, for though my body was kept very busy with deliveries, my mind was buzzing with thoughts of my success and what might follow it. I was so exhausted by the time work was finished that though I'd intended writing another instalment of the story once I was back at the safe house, I just could not stay awake. That night, I had all kinds of strange dreams and when I awoke the next day, my head was full of weird, ominous images. I passed the newsstand again on the way to work, but as the *Ladies' Journal* published the second instalment of 'The Queen and the Magic Mirror' at the same time as the first, I didn't bother to check today's edition for my work would not be inside. For a couple more days, there would be no news on that front.

The morning passed slowly, but then I got a delivery job that made me feel as though fate was handing me an occasion to do some investigation, for what I had to do was deliver to the *Mirror* offices a packet of photographs of our new range of hats.

'Take a cab, Jana, you look exhausted,' said Master Philipi who, despite his eagle-eyed fussiness, was a kind man.

I arrived much more quickly than I would have done walking, and when I turned up at the *Mirror* offices, I was just in time to see someone else arrive there, a visitor at whose sight all my confident cockiness about my small triumph vanished like smoke.

No, it wasn't my stepmother. It was Drago. Thank God he did not see me, for his vehicle had arrived instants before mine. He had just stepped out of it when I saw him, and I shrank back into the cab until he had passed through the *Mirror*'s double doors, out of sight. My head was pounding, my palms prickling, my heart racing. Fear invaded every part of me. The terror of that moment in the forest, when Drago had turned on me and told me what he'd been sent to do, crept through my pores, paralysing me. If he recognised me – and for that frightened moment I was convinced he would look right at me and see through my disguise – he would come after me and kill me. He'd spared my life once, but he wouldn't again, I was sure of that. He couldn't afford to let me live a second time. He'd told me never to return, and I had. He'd have to kill me or risk Belladonna finding out he'd not done it in the first place.

'Hey, little lady! Isn't this where you wanted to go?' came the irritated voice of the cab driver, breaking into my thoughts.

I almost told him I'd made a mistake and asked him to drive on somewhere else, but there was the delivery I had to make. And, further, how could I ever believe I'd achieve my ultimate goal if I fell at the first real hurdle?

Controlling myself with an effort, I said, 'Yes, it is. Sorry.'

Hurriedly paying the fare and a tip on top, I walked into the *Mirror* offices with my head down, thinking that if the worst came to the worst and I happened to cross Drago in there, all he'd see in a quick glance was a Ladies' Fair messenger in a silly hat. And that would hardly be an unusual sight around here.

But despite my reassuring thoughts, it was with a furiously beating heart that I delivered the packet of photographs to the girl at the front desk.

'Hey, wait for your receipt,' she called after me, as I attempted to scuttle away.

I had to go back and wait for her to write it out slowly, all the time mortally afraid that Drago would reappear. But he didn't and so I got out safely.

Forcing myself to walk calmly to the end of the block, I halted for a moment in a side street, out of sight of the main road but still with a clear view of it. I was trying to get my breath and my steadiness back, for much to my disgust I was trembling from head to foot. It was then I happened to look back into the main road – and saw Drago walking straight towards me!

I can't describe the feeling that seized me then. I do not believe there is a word for it. I didn't think; all I did was act. Running down the street, I came to a narrow alley and dived down it. At the end of the alley was a door and I ran towards it, thinking I might open it and hide on the other side. But it was locked and though I hammered on it, nobody answered. Heart beating wildly, I raced back down the alley and was about to go back into the side street when I saw Drago turning to come down the alley!

Had he seen me? I had no idea, but now I was trapped. Terrified, I made for the only hiding place I could see – a large box full of scrap metal, which was obviously awaiting the scrap-metal merchant's cart. I couldn't get into it, for it was too tall, so I squeezed behind it, ducking down as far as I could. There I squatted, uncomfortably, my ears buzzing from the wild beating of my heart, my head filled with thoughts that it was a silly place to hide, for Drago would be certain to find me in a trice as soon as he started looking. But there was nothing else I could do.

Instants later, I heard the ringing of boots on cobbles. The footsteps – firm, unhurried, relentless – got closer and closer and, crouching down further, I bit down on my lip so hard that I could feel the blood come. Now he was here, right in front of the scrap-metal box . . . I felt oddly calm, almost disconnected from my body, from my mind, from fear itself. In a moment he would find me; in a moment he would kill me. But even that hardly seemed to register in my mind anymore.

And then the footsteps went past me. Past the box. They did not even pause, but kept going, down the alley.

Then came the sound, quiet in reality, but loud in my painfully tuned ears, of a key turning in a lock. In the next moment came two more sounds: the scrape of a metal door opening, and then the scrape of a metal door closing.

Stunned, I could not react at first, for my mind was quite blank. Then thoughts came rushing in: he has gone in through that door I had beaten on but could not open; he hasn't seen me, he hasn't been looking for me, he doesn't know I am here! Now I can go, run away, and never look back! I can stick with my plan – go back to Ladies' Fair and see if I can find out any information through my job there. It will be safer that way.

I was about to do exactly as my disordered thoughts urged me to when something held me back. Questions. What was Drago doing here? Where did that door lead? And I knew, whatever he was doing here, whatever this place was, that it had something to do with Belladonna, the mistress to whom he had dedicated a lifetime of loyalty.

I had to find out what that was.

The calm, strong part of me pushed aside the fear I felt. And so I climbed out of my hiding place and hurried down the alley to the door. I stood and listened for a moment. Not a sound. I tried the handle. It turned in my hand. Very quietly, I opened the door. I saw stairs leading down into darkness. The hair rose on the back of my neck and I almost turned back. But in an instant I had recovered my courage and, very, very quietly, closed the door behind me, taking off my shoes so that my stockinged feet would make no sound.

I was in total darkness as, clinging to the wall, I began to grope my way down the stairs.

Twenty

Down, down the stairs I went. It was very quiet, except for the beating of my own heart. It was madness, I knew, to go down into that place. Every step I took brought me closer to discovery for if Drago should suddenly start back up the stairs, then I was lost.

But he didn't come, and so I kept walking almost despite myself, my throat thick with fear, my skin crawling, but determined to know what was down there. After walking down a little further, I came to the bottom to find . . . nothing. The stairs ended at some kind of landing. Reaching out, I could feel damp stone walls, very close together. It was some kind of small, square room – and there was no obvious exit, for I walked around the whole space, feeling the walls, and found no door, no window . . . nothing.

My head was spinning. Where had Drago gone, then? He had come down the stairs. He hadn't gone back up. He wasn't a magician! He couldn't walk through walls, surely.

Yet the fact was that somehow he'd disappeared from this place, because there was no other place the stairs led to.

Struck by a sudden thought, I felt along the bricks of the walls a second time, this time pressing each one. A third brick, then a fourth. I had almost given up the idea when, on the ninth attempt, a panel sprung open and, peering inside, I saw that it opened onto an elevator. The hair rose on the back of my neck and I thought, again, that I should turn back. But I'd gone too far to stop now, so I stepped into the elevator and pressed the button that was marked by a downwards arrow. At once, the elevator started moving down, so rapidly it felt as though we were plunging, freefall, down a bottomless well.

The elevator stopped. The doors opened. I stepped out and found myself standing at the end of a very long passageway, which had no features except rough stone walls, a damp floor, and dull lamps lighting the way. I began to inch my way along the passageway, going as softly as I possibly could, keeping in the shadows as much as I could, and looking always for places where I might duck out of sight if anyone came. I saw that every so often there were sections where the stone stuck out enough to provide a very small possibility of concealment, and felt a little safer.

The passageway turned left, and I followed it. A little further along I came to a door, set in the wall. I tried the handle. It was unlocked. I opened it. And stepped into a strange, strange world.

It was brighter in here. I was in a large cavernous space, with a second door at the end, opposite from where I stood. It was lit by a few gas lamps here and there. This place must once have been some sort of warehouse or workshop,

I thought, for there were bits of rusty-looking machinery and other odds and ends lying around. Against one wall, close to the door where I stood, was a tall, wide wooden cupboard. Across the room from that, at the far end to me, was a row of ten cages, about the size you'd need for a large dog to stand upright. Most of the cages were empty but in four of them there crouched still, huddled shapes. My first thought was that they were animals – but then it occurred to me that they seemed to take up more space than any animal I'd seen. Were they people? I couldn't be sure from where I stood.

I was about to go over to have a closer look at whatever was imprisoned there when suddenly there came a sound that was midway between a low whistle and a buzz, with an eerie, mechanical quality to it. It came from outside the room, from behind the second door. At the sound, the huddled shapes in the cages began to stir and to shift, and a feeling of unease and fear filled the air. I knew that I must hide. Hurrying over to the cupboard, I opened the door as softly as I could. It smelt stale and musty and there were strange stains on the floor but it was empty, and it was my only option. Pulling the door shut behind me, I put my eye to the keyhole.

I was just in time, for at that moment the door down the end of the room opened and Drago came out. He was carrying a bag and he headed straight to the cages. Kneeling down, he took a blanket out of the bag, laid it down on the floor near the cages, then took out some other things I couldn't see properly, as his back was to me.

He straightened up and I heard the creak of a key and the scrape of a bolt as a cage was unlocked and Drago dragged something – no, I could see what the shapes were, now – dragged *somebody* out of the cage. I could not see the person's face, only a vague outline of their shape from behind. From their clothes, scrappy, dirty and old as they were, I thought that it was likely to be a small man, or a boy.

The person was limp as a rag, not struggling. It was as though he were drugged, or so weak he could not even try to fight. The three remaining people in the cages were still again, frozen like statues, as Drago placed his unmoving victim on the blanket. Then Drago raised his arm and I saw something silver flash in the air – not a knife, but some kind of two-pronged needle – as he brought the weapon down, plunging it deep into his victim's neck.

Realisation hit me like a punch to the belly. Drago was the beggar killer!

An unearthly scream of terror and grief came from the cages and filled the air as the poor beggarman arched his back, convulsing wildly. I heard the muffled drumming of his heels on the blanket, and felt rather than saw the agony contorting his face, turning it into a frozen mask of horror. And then came a smell. A thin, strange smell, something I had never come across before. All I could say for sure was that it wasn't the smell of blood. There was no blood, not that I could see . . .

It was all over in an instant, yet it seemed like an eternity. Soon, all spasms ceased and Drago, who had been squatting motionless over the body of his victim, waiting patiently for the death throes to end, moved away, dragging the body wrapped in the blanket away from the cages and towards the second door. In the next moment, he passed through the doorway.

Now was my chance. I had to get away at once.

But my heart stopped me. My head told me to go, but my heart told me that I needed to stay and *do* something. What I had just seen was so terrible that I could not just run away. Knowing, now, that Drago was the beggar killer, I knew I had to find out more. But on no account must I alert him or his prisoners, or I was lost, too. And so I crept out of the cupboard and, ducking and weaving behind the bits of machinery, made my way to the door through which Drago had passed. What was he doing inside? I reached the door and began to inch it open, but just as I did, one of the prisoners lifted her head and looked straight at me. I saw a pair of frightened, wide grey eyes, set in a pitifully thin face under skeins of tangled fair hair. And I felt as though my blood had turned to ice.

For I knew that gaze. I knew it, from the past. The terrified girl crouched in the corner of the cage staring right at me was none other than my childhood friend Margy.

But she didn't recognise me. I could see that. And I had a feeling it wasn't because I was disguised in my glasses and my uniform. Her wide eyes were empty of any recognition; all that was there was fear. Fear had turned her mind, clouded her memory, emptied it of anything except the knowledge that she was going to die here in this terrible place.

Never. Never! My mind filled up with heat. Suddenly, I didn't care about finding out more than I knew already. I didn't care what Drago was doing, beyond that door. I hardly even cared about my own safety. I only cared fiercely that nothing like what had happened to that poor man would happen to Margy. I had to get her out.

I ran over to the cages and tried to open one but the doors were locked, bolted. I could not get them open without the key. So I had to get the key. And that was in Drago's possession.

I must have been a little mad, I think. How else can I explain what I did next? I snatched up a rusty iron bar, swung open the door and, when I came upon Drago in the next room, kneeling over the body with his back to me, I hit him on the back of the head as hard as I could.

He fell like a log, toppling forward onto the blanket-wrapped body of his victim. The glass bottle he'd been holding, which contained a small amount of clear liquid, shattered as he fell, and the liquid spilled out onto the floor. As it did so, there was a hissing sound, and the liquid turned into a kind of silver mist before vanishing and leaving behind only for a moment a faint smell – the same strange one as I had smelt before.

I had no idea what the liquid – or the smell – was. All I could see was that Drago had been somehow extracting the liquid from the victim's body using that same strange two-pronged needle, but made of a faintly phosphorescent material that looked terrifying. This was the same thing he'd used to kill the poor beggar. It lay on the floor near the shattered bottle and I made no attempt to pick it up. It turned my stomach, but I had no time to speculate what exactly it was, for more urgent matters filled my mind.

Drago lay very still. Had I killed him or was he just unconscious? As evil as he was, the thought that I might have killed a man filled me with horror. Either way, I wasn't going to take the chance of hanging around to see. Rummaging frantically through his pockets, I quickly found a bunch of keys and was about to leave when it struck me that I should tie him up – for if he came to,

I might be able to stop him from escaping before I could alert the police.

The bag he'd brought in was propped against a wall. I searched through it, hoping for a rope or wire or other kind of tie, but to no avail. The rest of the room was empty, but after it was another room, and in that was a long shelf filled with an odd assortment of things – small, empty bottles, some stone jars, also empty, blankets stacked up in neat rows, empty flour sacks – and yes, a coil of rope. I was about to pick it up when I noticed that at the far end of this room was a curtained alcove. Seized by an instinct I could not explain, I hurried over to see what was behind the curtain.

I don't know what I was expecting, exactly, but it certainly wasn't the sight that greeted my eyes and made me freeze on the spot, breath whistling in my throat. For there, unnaturally still, glaring straight at me out of icy blue eyes, stood Belladonna.

I wanted to run but I couldn't. Her gaze was so sharp, so hard, so glittering, that it fixed me to the spot like a butterfly stuck down by the sharp edge of a pin. But she did not move towards me, to grab me, to kill me. Not one tremor. Not one blink. Not one . . .

And then, with a spasm of mingled relief and unease, I realised that this wasn't my stepmother. Or at least, it wasn't the living, breathing Belladonna. This was the dummy replica of Belladonna, the one that had been unveiled at the Ladies' Fair spring fashion show.

At that moment, there came that eerie sound again, a half-whistle, half-buzz, and now I saw that it came from the waxen Belladonna and that it was vibrating, ever so slightly. The paralysis that had frozen me evaporated as I took to my heels, not understanding what I'd just seen and heard but not really wanting to, either. Some devilry was afoot, I knew that, but what it meant, I had no idea.

Grabbing the coil of rope on the way back through the room, I tied Drago up as best I could. I could see his chest slightly rising and falling, so knew he wasn't dead. But as I rolled him carefully off his victim's body, a sudden, sickening thought struck me. Margy was in one of the cages, but I hadn't seen her brother, my friend Rafiel, there. Could this dead man be Rafiel? With a feeling of dread, I slowly folded back the corner of the blanket to uncover the victim's face . . . and looked on the pale dead face of a stranger, a small, thin young man with red hair and blue eyes that were open in a look of utter terror. As much as I felt for this young man, the biggest thing I felt was relief, overwhelming relief that this poor young man was not Rafiel. Saying a rapid prayer, I gently closed his eyes and folded the blanket back over his face, for there was nothing I could do for him now.

I went back to the cages, my fingers slipping with cold sweat as I fumbled with the keys. I managed to unlock the three cages that held prisoners and, pulling open the bolts, flung open the doors.

'Come on!' I yelled. 'We don't have much time!'

Out scrambled the first prisoner, a wiry, tough-looking woman of around thirty-five, and then the second prisoner, a young man in his early twenties, pitifully thin and small, like the poor soul who had just been murdered by Drago. But Margy didn't move. She crouched in a corner of her cage, trembling like a leaf, shrinking away from me when I tried to touch her so that in the end, it was the beggarwoman who, by dint of soft words, managed to coax her out.

'Quickly!' I called, as I raced to the elevator, the others stumbling after me. Poor Margy had to be led in by the beggarwoman.

We reached the small dark landing, and I whispered, 'Stay close, there's still a way to go.'

The others nodded, except for Margy. She was holding onto the beggarwoman's hand with a tight grip, but her eyes were wide and blank as ever. Remembering the bright, lively girl she'd been when I knew her, I felt a sharp pang.

'You'll be safe now, Margy, I promise,' I said. 'I swear it on my life.'

Her gaze flicked up at me, but she said nothing.

The beggarwoman touched Margy's shoulder gently and said, 'She hasn't spoken since we were taken. I fear the poor girl's mind is quite gone.'

I swallowed. 'She can be healed. I know a place where she can be healed.'

I hurried down the passageway to the lift, the others following on my heels. We got there and went up the stairs without incident, emerging into the alley, which was quite deserted. Ushering everyone out, I locked the door behind us, using a key from the set I had stolen from Drago. I wanted to make certain that when Drago awoke – and, given the crack on the head I'd given him, I doubted that would be soon – even if he managed to free himself, he'd be locked in.

'Come on,' I said, as we stood outside the door for a moment, adjusting our eyes to the light. 'We'll go to the City Police first and then I can . . .'

'No,' broke in the beggarwoman. 'Not the police.'

'But I have to tell . . .'

'*You* might have to,' she said, firmly, 'but *we* don't. Or they'll come after us.'

Confused for a moment, I began, 'No, the police have been trying to . . .'

'I'm not talking about the police,' she said. 'I'm talking about *them*. Those *devils*.' A tremor shook her, and she looked up and down the alley. 'If we go to the police, *they'll* know. They can find out anything.'

'I don't have much choice. If we don't go to the police, I can't think of another way to stop them,' I said, quietly. 'Is that what you want?'

'What we want is to be safe, as far away from Lepmest as possible,' she answered, fixing me with a steely glare.

'And I *can* take you somewhere safe, far away.'

'Who are you?' she said. 'Why are you doing this?'

I hesitated, then plunged in with, 'My name is Snow White, and I work for the Prince.' The words had come unbidden to my lips.

She blinked. 'What?'

'The Prince of Outlaws. You've heard of him?'

She nodded. 'I've heard rumours. I thought it was just wishful thinking.'

'No. He's real. They're real. The havens.'

'I see.' She didn't look convinced.

'We'll go to a safe house first, and then I'll arrange safe passage to haven.' I looked at her. 'Do you trust me?'

She looked me in the eyes for a long moment. Then she nodded. She held out a hand. 'My name's Tollie.' She jerked her head towards the young man. 'He's Hugo.' She nodded towards Margy. 'And you know her.' It was a statement, not a question.

'Yes. I'll explain later. Come on.'

Twenty-One

Master Kinberg was alone, hard at work in his tailor's shop. Casting a quick, wary glance over the three beggars who hovered in a corner of his workshop like ragged shadows, he told me in a low voice that he could make arrangements for them to go to haven that very night but that meanwhile, we would have to wait in the safe house and not show our faces at all. When I asked if I could leave the others there while I went to the nearest police station, he shook his head firmly and to my surprise repeated what Tollie had said.

'The police are not to be trusted; there is much corruption in their ranks. I will go now and get a message to the Prince. He knows who can be trusted within the police, and he will deal with it much more quickly and effectively than you or I could.'

And with that I had to be content, though inwardly I chafed at being treated as though I was as helpless as the people I'd rescued.

Not that Tollie and Hugo looked nearly as helpless any longer. I made some food for them and they wolfed it all down in a trice. But not Margy. She sat bolt upright on the floor, not looking at anyone, not saying anything, refusing to eat.

'You said you knew her,' said Tollie, swallowing the last mouthful of the stew and rice.

'Yes,' I said, quietly. 'She was one of my childhood friends. Margy and her brother Rafiel. But they and their parents ... they ... they left our neighbourhood. I ... I lost touch with them years ago.'

She looked at me. 'I see.'

Her tone was impassive, but I felt a squirm of shame. 'I ... I was only a child ... I had no way of finding out where –'

'Then you don't know,' she said. 'You don't know what happened.'

I shook my head.

'Margy ... when she first fell in with us, we didn't know her story. It was only later that we learnt that her whole family was dead. A house fire ...'

A clenching pain gripped my chest. I whispered, 'No ... No ...' My gut twisted as I remembered Margy's beautiful mother and her father, a gentle giant of a man. And Rafiel ... teasing, patient, kind, clever Rafiel. 'They can't all be gone ... They can't be ...'

'I'm afraid they are,' said Tollie. 'And Margy blamed herself for it.'

'She was unhappy in that place where they were living,' broke in Hugo. 'It was a miserable spot, and she missed her old home, and her old friends, no doubt, too ...'

Here he looked at me, and a great pang of sadness went through me.

'I missed her, too,' I cried. 'I missed Margy and I missed Rafiel. I so wished that they hadn't been made to leave . . .'

'Margy decided to run away,' said Tollie, ignoring my outburst. 'That night, she wasn't in her room, as she should have been. She had crept out of the window, into the streets, planning to somehow make her way back to where she used to live. But she changed her mind and went back to her family, for the streets were dark and she was scared and she missed her brother and her mother and her father. But when she got home, the fire brigade was at her house – too late, too, for the fire was fierce and had already burned everything – and everyone – to cinders . . .'

'Dear God,' I whispered, stricken with horror.

'A kind stranger found her wandering aimlessly through the streets the next morning – speechless, like she is now. They took her to an orphanage. She stayed there a year and got better but then she ran away again. Eventually she found her way to us. She's been with us for the past fifteen months or so and until the time we were snatched, we all thought she was doing just fine – she would speak to us and though she never said much, she wasn't like she is now.' Her mouth twisted a little. 'She was good for us. She brought in good money, begging. It was her smile, you know. It's so lovely . . .'

'Yes,' I said sadly, looking across at the still figure of Margy crouched on the floor, and remembering old times. 'Whenever I was cranky or out of sorts, her smile made me feel like the sun had come out – it made me feel better . . .' She had often smiled at her brother, I thought. She adored him. Followed him around everywhere. A sharp pain gripped my heart again as I thought of Rafiel. Gone, and in such a dreadful way . . . I could hardly bear thinking about it.

'Yes,' said Tollie, softly. 'That smile of hers – it was beautiful. But in a way, it was her undoing. And ours.'

'What do you mean?' I asked, the breath catching in my throat.

'We'd done all we could *not* to draw their attention,' she said, 'but in the end it was her smile that did it. We were on a street corner, begging, and he . . .'

'Wait a moment,' I said. 'You knew about these killings. Why did you stay in Lepmest, then?'

'But we weren't in Lepmest,' she said, staring at me. 'We were in Mormest. Of course we knew about the killings here, and we'd made ourselves scarce. There'd been no abductions in Mormest. We thought we were safe there. Until that day . . .'

'What happened?'

'It was a few days ago – a little under a week, I think,' she said. 'We were, as I said, on a street corner – me, Hugo, Margy and poor Simeon and Tomas, God rest their souls,' she added, and I knew she must be referring to the man Drago had killed in front of our eyes, and another, who must have been killed earlier. 'A man came up to us and gave us money and then Margy smiled at him and he smiled back and asked if we wanted to earn some really good money . . . It had been a hard few weeks, the pickings were small, and Margy would only go with him if we went, too, and we figured that there were five of us against one of him, so it would be all right – especially because straight

188

after that he took us to an inn and bought us a square meal and a cup of wine ... and besides, there was something about him that made us feel safe.'

'Drago made you feel safe? I mean, the man who ... who killed Simeon and Tomas?' I added, when she looked puzzled.

'No. Not him. This was another man, younger. Brown eyes. Brown hair. Small moustache. Kind voice.'

'Oh.' The description did not evoke any echoes in me. 'Would you know him again if you saw him?'

'I'd know him anywhere,' she said, grimly.

'The man today, the one who killed –'

'We only saw him later, when we woke up in a coach, gagged and trussed up like chickens.' Her mouth twisted. 'The wine – it had been drugged. We were taken in the coach to that place where you found us. We never saw the other man again. He – the man today – he was the one there, most days. He brought us food, drink, blankets. It might seem strange to say this, for he killed our friends, but he did not treat us cruelly. It was as if he just saw it as ... as a job.'

'We thought at first we might be able to move him to mercy,' put in Hugo, 'so we tried. But nothing worked. It was strange, too, because Margy wouldn't help at all. She didn't try to move him with her smile – she wouldn't even look at him. Every time he was in that place, she kept her head down and she trembled like a leaf.'

Because she'd recognised Drago, I thought, uneasily. She'd recognised him from the past, remembered my step-mother's taciturn servant, and known that whatever was going on, my stepmother must be involved. The only good thing I could think that came of it was that with her face down, Drago wouldn't have recognised her, or else he'd have told Belladonna and Margy would have been killed right away.

'Was anyone else taken there?' I asked. 'Besides those two men, I mean?'

I saw the quick glance that passed between Tollie and Hugo. 'We heard a woman's voice, once,' said Tollie. 'But we didn't see her. That man – he blindfolded us at first.' She paused. 'We got the feeling she was in charge.'

I nodded without speaking. It could only have been Belladonna.

'And we also got the feeling that she was there more than once,' added Hugo. 'Only, aside from that first time, she wasn't *really* there. There would be a strange sound – a kind of whistle – it was as if it were some form of communication, from her to him. As if it were a signal to do something. We heard the whistling right before Tomas was killed. And Simeon . . . Simeon is the poor one who you saw killed.'

So the dummy was used as some sort of telegraph machine, in a manner of speaking. It was an intensely creepy idea, and I could not imagine how exactly it might work.

'But also, other times we would hear the whistling and the man would leave right away,' added Tollie, 'as if it were a summons.'

I thought back to the whistles I had heard earlier: the first must have been to command Drago to take his next victim. But there had been a second one: Belladonna must have been trying to summon Drago, just before we'd left. If she didn't hear back from him soon, would she go and see what the problem was? Perhaps not, had this happened a few days earlier. She would have sent one of those in her employ. But things had changed since then. I was willing to bet she would have seen 'Syrena's' story of 'The Queen and the Magic Mirror' and would have been growing more and more suspicious, more and more on edge. Would this be the slip-up I had been waiting for? What if, instead of sending a minion, she went herself to see what the problem was, to see why Drago hadn't answered her summons? What if she did go, and I was able to trap her in that place along with Drago? She would be caught red-handed! She would not be able to talk her way out of that so easily!

'I must go out,' I said, getting up. 'You'll be all right here. Don't go anywhere until Master Kinberg comes back.'

'Where are you going?' said Tollie, her eyes narrowing. 'You heard what I said – what *he* said – about the police . . .'

'I'm not going to the police. I'm going to get evidence.'

They stared at me.

'You're going back *there*?' whispered Hugo.

I could see the terror on his face and I knew that they would try to talk me out of it – especially if they knew I was planning to wait and trap the powerful woman they'd heard of.

'I'm going to take photographs of the crime scene,' I said, improvising quickly. I didn't want to give them a chance to talk me out of it. And it actually wasn't a bad idea. If I could get hold of a camera, I would be able to take some photographs while I waited for Belladonna. 'It's the only way I can think of to preserve the evidence for sure, and in a way that doesn't drag you into it. I just don't want them to have a chance to get away with it. Do you?'

'No,' they chorused, and then Hugo said, 'But Master Kinberg said that the Prince would . . .'

'I can't wait for the Prince to investigate,' I said. 'By that time, Belladonna or the police who are in her pay would have disposed of all the evidence, and then all that would be left would be you as witnesses, and even if you do agree to speak, who's going to believe the word of a beggar over that of a high-born society lady?'

It was harsh but it was also the truth, and they knew it. I was sure they could tell, too, that for me, this was personal. They did not remark on it, but only nodded gravely.

'Wait here for Master Kinberg,' I went on. 'He won't be too much longer, I imagine. You'll be in haven before the night is out. And when you see the Prince, tell him . . .' I paused. What I was about to do was, perhaps, the riskiest thing I had done yet. Would I ever see the Prince again?

'Yes? Tell him what?' asked Tollie, giving me a shrewd glance.

'Tell him I know he'll be able to take care of my friend Margy,' I said, quietly, 'and give him my warmest greetings.'

I left them there and went away swiftly, before I could change my mind, for I realised my weakness, the longing that would sap at my purpose if I let it. If I'd gone to the haven with the others I'd have seen the Prince again, and part of me wanted that so much. But another part – the stronger, the righteous, the honourable part – knew I must push my feelings aside until I had fulfilled the mission I had vowed to complete.

On the way to the alley, I made a detour to a funny little shop that my father had taken me to once, long ago. It was a shabby, ramshackle affair, but like an Aladdin's cave for a child, as it sold toys and novelties of all sorts. Father had bought me a little camera there, for my ninth birthday. It hadn't been a professional's camera, with glass negatives and levers and buttons, but it had a little box with a pinhole lens and thin cellophane paper for the negatives which Father helped me to develop in some special fluid. It was a child's toy, but it would be cheap and it would take basic photographs. I could only hope they still stocked such things.

I was lucky – the store did still sell those toy cameras. Armed with my weapon of sorts I set off again.

Shortly after, I reached the alley. I looked up and down the street, but could see no sign that anyone had been there since I had left with Tollie, Hugo and Margy. I still had the keys, so quietly unlocked the door to the 'house of horrors', as I thought of it. I closed it behind me but left it unlocked, in case I needed to make a quick escape, and swiftly went down the stairs and straight into the elevator. As the elevator doors opened then closed and I descended, I felt all my nerves tensing, my heart clenching. What if Belladonna was here already and was lying in wait? What if Drago had awoken and somehow freed himself, and *he* was lying in wait?

I looked out cautiously. Nothing. No-one. The place was deserted. It was silent. The cages stood empty, their doors flung open, as we'd left them. Creeping to the door at the opposite end of the room, I opened it gingerly. Nothing seemed to have changed. Drago lay trussed up, unmoving, and poor Simeon lay dead, under his blanket, while the two-pronged weapon lay gleaming with that faint, evil phosphorescence.

I took photographs of the scene, then a close-up of the weapon. Should I take the weapon with me, too? I wondered. Gingerly, I put my hand close to it, but recoiled as the phosphorescence grew brighter and I felt a stinging pain in my fingers. I'd have to leave it for the investigators to handle, I thought, half-relieved, half-ashamed.

There was, of course, no trace of whatever it was that Drago had drained out of Simeon's body – it had evaporated long ago. I still had no idea what the liquid could be. It was like nothing I'd ever seen before. It wasn't blood, that was clear. But it was also clear that it came from the victims. The newspapers had spoken of vampire attacks. But if my stepmother was a vampire satisfying an unnatural hunger, then she was like no vampire I had ever heard of. She did not carry out the attacks herself, as vampires who enjoyed the blood-lust did. And she did not take blood, as thirsty vampires did – although she did attack at random, as rampaging vampires did . . .

Going into the third room, I took some more photographs – of all the vials and other equipment. I didn't know what much of it was for, but perhaps someone else might.

I couldn't help feeling uneasy as I glanced into the fixed stare of the Belladonna mannequin. There was no sound from it this time, no vibration, but the painted eyes glared in a way that made me feel so uncomfortable that I had to turn away.

I was just returning to the first room, ready to make my way back down the corridor and into the elevator, when I heard a groan behind me. Drago was coming to! I spun around. His eyes weren't open, but he was stirring. Would those ropes hold him, once he was fully awake? I was not at all sure of the strength of the knots I'd tied. The iron bar still lay on the floor where I'd thrown it after hitting him. I picked it up. Should I hit him again? If I hit him hard enough, in the same spot as I had the first time, I would probably kill him. And he would never be able to tell Belladonna what had happened. But instinctively I shrank from it. He was trussed up, helpless. I'd be doing it in cold blood. To do that would be to become just like Belladonna.

No, I had to find some other way. Rushing out through the door, I closed it behind me and scrambled through the bunch of keys, trying to find one that would fit. There didn't seem to be one. I looked around wildly for an object I could use to hold the door closed. The abandoned machinery was mostly too big to lift and was probably bolted to the floor, anyway.

The iron bar! It was still in my hand! I used it to wedge the door handle shut. It would take some time to shift.

I ran down the corridor, went up in the elevator, and sprinted up the stairs. Out in the alley again, I locked the door behind me. I needed, now, a place to hide and wait, in case Belladonna came to investigate why Drago had not answered her summons. I walked down to the end of the alley and looked up and down the side street for a place where I could hide, where I would be able to watch the entrance to the alley and wait for Belladonna.

I glanced up to the end of the street that joined the main road where I had walked that day after visiting the offices of the *Mirror*, and as I did I saw two people stop at the corner, pausing for a moment to talk. It was a man and a woman. The woman was Sommer Malling, the famous journalist. And the man . . . Though he had his back to me, I could see his tall figure, light-brown hair, and the grace of his bearing . . . My God, I thought, astonished and thrilled. It can't be! It surely can't be!

I watched from a distance as the pair finished their conversation, then shook hands in farewell. I watched as Sommer Malling walked back in the direction of the offices of the *Mirror*, while the man crossed the road and walked in the opposite direction. All thoughts of hiding from Belladonna forgotten, I ran up the side street, turned and raced down the main road to catch up to Sommer Malling's companion, my heart racing with hope.

I reached him and tapped him lightly on the shoulder. But before I could say anything, he spun on his heel and grabbed me by the arm. His grip was like iron. His eyes were hard as stones yet with a strange light within them. His nostrils were flaring and for an instant, I felt real fear that his wolf-side would break through, even though it was still light and not hunter's moon anymore, either.

'Lucian,' I said, 'it's me.'

'Who are you?' he said. 'I don't know you.' His voice was huskier than it had been in the haven, as though he'd come down with a cold.

I was hurt, wondering why he did not recognise me. Did I mean so little to him? Had I just been imagining that he felt the same way towards me as I did to him? Then with a jump of the heart, I remembered that I must look very different to when he'd last seen me in the haven – and certainly different from the night of the ball. In relief, I gabbled, 'It's the haircut, and the walnut juice Verakina gave me. Lucian, it's me. It's Bianca Dalmatin.'

'Vera–? Wha–?' He went very pale. Released his grip. Stared at me. Said, in a low voice, 'Bianca? But you were supposed to be dead . . .'

I stared at him. 'But you knew I wasn't! When you saw me in the haven . . .'

'I'm sorry,' he said, shaking his head. 'I just mean – everyone thinks you're dead. It's not safe to –'

I broke in. 'I know; you told me to be careful and keep my head down. But Lucian, here's the thing –'

'Don't,' he said. 'Don't use my name. Not here. You never know if Belladonna's spies might be watching . . .' He looked up and down the street, a little anxiously, and led me into a doorway, so that we would be hidden from anyone walking past.

'Sorry. Of course.'

'What . . . How did you escape? What are you doing here?'

'Didn't Master Kinberg send you a message? He said he was going to.'

He paused for a moment, then shook his head.

'It doesn't matter. The thing is, he's arranging for a passage for three to the haven, and he wanted me to wait too, but I couldn't, because we need evidence, you see?'

He ran a hand through his hair. 'I don't see. You have to understand. I didn't get Master Kinberg's message. I don't have a clue what's happened. Tell me what happened. Tell me everything.'

'Sorry. Of course.' And I told him, very quickly, what had happened, while he stood there looking at me as though he could not quite believe his ears. When I finished, he said, shaking his head, 'My God. You took a huge risk.'

'No more than you do every day.' I met his eyes. 'I know what's at stake for you.' I paused. 'You see, I know what your secret is; I know why you hide behind your mask.'

His face went quite still. 'Do you now?' he said softly, and something in his tone made me feel suddenly that I'd said the wrong thing, said something that he had not wanted to hear.

I said, haltingly, 'Please, just listen. Because I feel that what you do as the . . . as the Prince of Outlaws, saving those people . . . It's even more heroic, because the . . . your . . . affliction . . . it could have turned you into a . . . a creature of darkness – but instead you are of the light.'

Something flickered in his eyes. His body, which had been tense, relaxed slightly and he said, 'You are kind. Much too kind.'

'No! I'm just telling the honest truth. And I'm trying to tell you that I . . . that I think . . . our paths lie together. Not apart.' The last had come in a rush and I could feel my cheeks flaming as I spoke, but I had to say it. I had to tell the Prince how I felt.

Our eyes met for a moment. He said, 'Tonight they do meet, clearly.' There was a note of warning in his voice, which stung me.

Drawing myself up, coolly trying to mask the deep hurt that pierced my heart, I said, 'Yes. I know it's not really your concern, I know that for you, the outcasts come first. But I had hoped we could work together to expose Belladonna –'

'You're wrong,' he said at once. Then he paused, as if he had said something he hadn't meant to say. 'It's very much my concern. You have no idea why I was here in the first place?'

I looked at him, a little startled. I hadn't thought about it really, not until that moment, for I'd been too happy to see him. 'I suppose you're in Lepmest because of the beggar killings and that dead man Mattias found. And you thought the *Mirror* might have some useful information, perhaps?'

He shrugged. 'Hardly. Sommer Malling is the fashion editor after all, not the crime reporter. I thought I might find out something about your stepmother. A secret or something I – we could use.'

'Now that *was* a risk, for Miss Malling is one of my step-mother's closest friends,' I said, lightly, my heart lifting. Up until then, I'd had the uneasy sense that somehow his feelings towards me had changed – or had never existed as I'd thought. But I could see now that it was simply that I had surprised him, popping up unexpectedly like a jack-in-the-box. His words made me understand that he wanted the same thing I did – to make Belladonna pay. It meant so much to me that we wanted the same thing.

'You'd be surprised,' he said, with a crooked smile, 'what people really think about Lady Belladonna Dalmatin, even so-called close friends.'

I returned his smile. 'I'm glad to hear it. Did Miss Malling have a secret to tell?'

'Nothing of importance, unfortunately. Just a touch of common spite. The lady does not exactly have the sweetest nature.' He looked at me and flashed a white-toothed smile. 'Forgive me if I've seemed . . . strange. It was just a . . . a shock, seeing you here. But now I've recovered. And there's no need for the police, Bianca – we'll do it together, just you and me. What do you say?' There was a bright lightness to his voice now, and a warm quality to his glance, which made my pulse race.

'I say I think it's about time we started, then,' I retorted, trying to keep the happiness from showing too plainly in my voice.

Everything was different now. I was no longer alone. Lucian Montresor, Prince of Outlaws, was with me, and together we would take on the world – starting with my wicked stepmother.

Twenty-Two

🌙

'First things first,' said Lucian. 'You are sure that Drago did not see you at any stage?'

'Quite sure.'

'Good. Then we must keep it that way. They must not know that you are still alive. You cannot risk going back to that place, under any circumstances.'

'But we need to wait for Belladonna, to see if she'll come back to see why Drago didn't answer her summons!' I said. 'We have to catch her and we have to make sure Drago doesn't have a chance to get away.'

'Of course. And what I propose is that *I* do that – I will wait at that place while you go to my apartment – my family's apartment, that is, which is nearby – and you can wait in safety for me there.' He gestured towards the camera. 'Plus, if they are to be used as evidence, those photographs will need developing. My father is a keen photographer and there is a small darkroom at the apartment that you can use. I assume you know how to develop photographs?'

I nodded. 'My father taught me.' I was about to leave – we had been standing there a while and I did not want to waste a single more second in case Belladonna came by – but I couldn't help but ask shyly, 'But Lucian, what about your servants?'

His mouth twisted humorously. 'I didn't think you would be afraid of a *scandal* of all things, Bianca.'

I flushed. 'I'm not! It's just . . . It's just that if by any chance they recognise me . . .'

'Florian and Clara, the only staff we have in town, have worked for my family for decades – and their parents before them. They won't ask any questions. Believe me, they are utterly trustworthy.' He drew his signet ring off his finger and gave it to me. 'This will prove to them that you are my friend, to be protected at all times.'

'Do they . . . Do they know you are the Prince of Outlaws?' I could not help asking.

'Nobody knows who does not need to. And you must not tell anyone,' he added quickly, and our eyes met. 'Now, Bianca,' he went on, 'we'd better be on our way. Let's meet again at my apartment.' He gave me directions to the apartment, and I gave him the key to the door in the alley.

Now I knew that the Prince was doing everything he could to help me to expose Belladonna, I felt so much better as the burden of loneliness slipped off my shoulders. I hadn't realised until that moment how great the burden of that had been. This must be what the outcasts felt like, safe in their haven at last, I thought, safe in the knowledge that they were no longer hunted, secure in the feeling that the Prince was protecting them.

We parted, then, and as I headed off, I looked back once and saw him walking towards the alley with a long, loping stride and a kind of wary alertness to the set of his shoulders that reminded me of a hunter on the trail. I was glad to have such a strong person on my side.

It was just as Lucian had said. As soon as the old man Florian saw the ring, the suspicion on his face disappeared, and he ushered me inside. When I explained I needed to use the darkroom, he did not ask any questions, but only led me through the apartment till we came to a door that was screened by a heavy black curtain. Beyond was the darkroom. There was everything in it that a photographer needed. Florian left me there, saying that if I needed anything, I only had to ring the bell.

I got to work at once, carefully extracting the small glass plates from the camera and gently putting them one by one into the developing fluid, then onto photographic paper, then into developing fluid where the images actually appeared. When I was a child, I had never tired of the magic of seeing the images slowly appear, and even now I held my breath as they manifested. There was Drago, lying motionless. There was his victim. There were the cages. One thing that I couldn't see was the two-pronged weapon: the photographs I had taken of that hadn't worked; the negative was black. Similarly, the photos I had taken of the Belladonna dummy had not worked. Why? Are they made of some other-worldly material? Or had I just not taken the photograph properly? But it doesn't matter, I thought. We have enough evidence with the rest of the photos.

After developing, the photographs would have to dry, and that was the part that would take the longest, for they needed to be left in the dark for quite a while. There was no point in hovering over the process – it would get on very well without me. I emerged from the darkroom and was about to ring the bell to summon Florian when I thought that instead I would take the opportunity to explore the apartment and perhaps get to know a little more about Lucian. All I wanted was to feel closer to him. And to perhaps begin to understand how he had become the Prince . . . So I prowled through first a dining room and a drawing room, then a library, where I looked at the pictures on the walls and the books on the shelves.

There were reminders everywhere of the mountains. For example, in the library there was a framed photograph of Nellia's Spring and beside it, a painting of the feya herself. The artist had painted her as small and delicate, with a cloud of silver hair, yet with an unwavering dark gaze that seemed to follow me around the room. It was as though she were watching over not only this room, not only this apartment, but the family itself. Yet I remembered what Mistress Tomzin had said, about Nellia being unable to break the curse that had been put on the Montresors by the witch. What good did it do, having a good fairy to watch over you, if she was unable to protect you from such evil? A profitless notion, I thought, as I turned away from the painting.

A little to my disappointment, there was not a sign of Lucian's other life as the Prince of Outlaws. But then, was that so surprising? He'd said, 'Nobody knows who does not need to.' That must mean even his parents and his servants did not know. It is a shame, I thought, that they would know about the curse – that Lucian was a werewolf, just like the first cursed Montresor, Hector, had been – but not about the honourable way he had chosen to rise above his fate, by reaching out to and protecting all his fellow outcasts in Noricia.

I left the library and headed down the corridor to another room. But I had only just put my hand on the door handle when someone appeared at the end of the corridor. It was a small, old woman with a stern grey bun and a pair of steely eyes.

'Can I help you, Miss?' she asked. Despite the polite words, there was not a hint of deference in her voice, and I flushed.

'I'm . . . I'm just looking for the . . . for the bathroom facilities,' I said, lamely.

'This way then, Miss,' the old woman, who must be Clara, said. I could sense the disapproval emanating from her as I followed her meekly down the corridor. I'd been caught poking around. I knew it; she knew it. Like most old and faithful servants, she was protective of her master's affairs. I wanted to say I wasn't doing any harm, that I would never betray Lucian, that I only wanted to find out more about the man I loved. But of course I said nothing at all.

The bathroom was a pleasant sunny room with a window that faced over the street. I was washing my hands when I happened to glance out the window. It had begun to grow dark but I saw a vehicle drawing up under the streetlights just opposite the house. It was a light cab-like carriage, only it had 'Police' painted on the side. I watched as two men in the black uniforms and balaclavas of the Noricia Special Police stepped out of the vehicle.

The Special Police were deployed only for dealing with the most dangerous of criminals: traitors, spies, terrorists, and the worst kind of murderers. They worked in the shadows, out of the glare of publicity. Many people feared them, for they had extensive powers and could hold you for long periods without trial.

My first feeling was relief: Lucian must have sent them here to interview me about Belladonna's crimes. But then, as the men crossed the road and headed purposefully towards the house, unease began to fill me. Hadn't Lucian said that we shouldn't contact the police? And if, for whatever reason, he had decided to do so anyway, wouldn't they still be at Drago's house of horrors? Why wasn't Lucian with them? And why were they wearing balaclavas if they had just come to interview a witness? They looked more like they were planning to conduct a raid or arrest a criminal . . .

I had begun only a few days ago to learn not to trust appearances, and I must have learnt quickly, for the unease I felt would not leave me. What if Belladonna had caught Lucian in that dreadful room and turned the tables on him? I already knew she had members of the City Police in her pocket – why not members of the Special Police, too? Together they could spin all sorts of stories. Why not have Lucian arrested as the beggar killer? Why not arrest me as his accomplice? Had she tortured him into giving up my whereabouts?

As the men knocked on the door, I made my decision. I had to leave. Now.

I hurried back to the library, which I remembered had a window that faced out to an alley behind the house.

I threw open the window and looked out. There was a steel fire-escape stairway leading down. I swung myself over the window frame and began to climb out, then suddenly remembered the photos, still in the darkroom. I cursed myself for having to leave them, but I had no time to go back – already I heard the sound of loud voices downstairs.

Out in the alley, I didn't waste a moment but ran like the wind. I had to get back to the safe house as quickly as possible and warn Master Kinberg and the beggars that Lucian might be in the hands of our enemies and that they must get away at once.

But when I got to the safe house, I found Master Kinberg, by himself, looking as nervous as his usual phlegmatic features would allow. 'Thank God you're safe! I told the Prince you were a resourceful girl but he –'

'The Prince? He's been here?' I interrupted, relief flooding me as I realised he must have evaded Belladonna's tame police.

'Yes. Briefly. He's sending the beggars to the haven this very night.'

'How?'

'Night coach. From Grand Dome. But he said you must stay here and wait till –'

I didn't wait to hear any more. Ignoring his protests, I hurried away.

Twenty-Three

Grand Dome Station, the central railway station of Lepmest from which not only trains but coaches to all parts of Noricia depart, is the busiest in the entire city. And this time in the early evening is one of the busiest times there, with crowds of long-distance travellers, gawping tourists and homeward-bound city workers bustling in and out of its massive central hall, famous throughout Noricia and beyond for its marble floors, bronze chandeliers and the magnificent stained-glass dome ceiling that gave the station its name.

Something had gone wrong with the ticketing system this evening and there were impatient groups of people shouting for attention, with staff desperately trying to restore order.

I looked around everywhere for Lucian and the beggars but could not see any sign of them in the heaving crowd. Knowing that they'd have to catch the Mormest coach, for it went closest to the haven, I collared a station official and asked him where it was to be found.

Looking at his watch, he said, 'You're going to miss it. It's just about to go.'

I thanked him and hurried away in the direction he'd indicated but by the time I elbowed my way through the crowds to the coach stop, the coach had gone. And Lucian was nowhere to be seen . . .

I had just come back into the central hall to see if I could find him when I caught sight of something that made my blood run cold. A knot of City Police in their green uniforms were pushing through the crowds. Although I was sure none of them had spotted me – I still wasn't even sure that they were looking for me specifically – I panicked. They must be on our trail! Desperately making my way out of the seething mass, I hurried away, expecting that at any moment a heavy hand would come down on my shoulder, and a voice would say –

'Stop!' The voice was so close to my ear that I jumped in fright.

'Don't turn around, Bianca,' said the voice. 'Keep walking.' It was the Prince.

'Stop, now,' he said after a moment, 'but don't turn around. Pretend to be looking for someone.' I did as I was told.

'I'm so glad you are here,' I began, 'but we need to –'

'We need to get away,' he interrupted sharply, so that I flinched.

'How *are* we going to get away?' I cried, and turned so quickly that he was unable to step away, so that he was forced to stare straight into my face for an instant. And I stared back, speechless.

This man was not Lucian! He was dressed in the black uniform of the Special Police, his face hidden by one of those balaclavas, with only a pair of fierce hazel eyes showing. Who he was, how he'd found me here, and what he wanted from me I had no idea, but in that instant my paralysis left me and before the policeman could say another word, I twisted desperately out of his grasp, shoved him aside, and ran. Taken by surprise, he did not react quickly enough, but in an instant, whistles and shouts filled the station as the City Police saw me running and set off after me. In any other place they would have caught me easily, but in the surging crowds, the advantage was less pronounced, and in a short while I had plunged down the stairs towards the station platforms.

The platforms were almost as crowded as the hall above and there were trains waiting at two or three of them, with the usual chaos of passengers and families bidding farewell to each other. I looked up and down, panicked, wondering what to do. I heard the clatter of heavy boots on the stairs and, turning my head, saw a sea of green uniforms heading towards me. I couldn't see the Special Policeman but he must be with them. With a squeak of dismay, I ran down the platform, scattering the crowd as I went. Some people glared at me, others looked bemused, but nobody interfered or tried to stop me. Still, I would have been caught for sure before I reached the end of the platform if it weren't for a very sudden puff of steam from one of the trains which instantly enveloped the station in an impenetrable fog. In the next instant, a soft hand grabbed me and a calming voice said in my ear, 'It's all right. Stay quiet.'

It was a young woman's voice. And though it spoke Norician, it was with a strong accent. She is from Ruvenya, I thought. Or somewhere near there.

The fog still enveloped us in white, and it dawned on me that this was no ordinary mist of steam from the train.

'Come,' said the voice, and I felt a hand in mine, guiding me, leading me on. As I followed the young woman, I realised that I could see beyond the fog as though through a misted mirror. I saw vague shapes agitating beyond the cocoon in which we were moving. Then the shapes became solid and I could see the police running up and down the platform looking for me, but though I stood right there in the centre of it, they did not seem to see me. Looking down at myself, I realised that, in fact, I could not see myself, either – and nor could I see my companion. It was as though the fog clung only to us. We were enveloped in what could only be a cloud of magic. It was the strangest thing, but though I felt a shiver of awe, I was not frightened at all.

After a while, we made our way through the crowds that didn't see us, back up the stairs to the main level of the station, past the green-uniformed policemen who ran around like desperate dogs on a trail that had gone cold. I couldn't see the one in the black uniform, however. Perhaps he'd given up and gone away.

'Here,' said the voice. To my surprise, we had stopped in the station buffet, and my guide was leading me towards a table of people. There was a gaunt old woman with pallid skin that seemed almost grey, and small black eyes; a bearded, very tall and broad young man – almost a giant – holding a baby of around eighteen months on his lap, a little boy with green eyes and honey-blond hair. Alone among the crowds in that station, those people seemed to see us, with the young man raising a hand in greeting and the old woman and the baby both giving me a direct, unblinking stare. The old woman had a presence which was both disturbing and exhilarating, and my heart raced as her black eyes stayed on my face. Strange images filled my mind, images of deep forests and snow storms, a hut on stilts and three enormous cats sitting by a glowing fire . . .

Then she looked away and spoke to my rescuer in a language I could not understand. As my rescuer replied, I watched her taking shape in front of me: black-haired, green-eyed, with a lithe, wild grace in her movements.

She flashed me a smile, her teeth gleaming white and sharp under the buffet lights. For an instant, I caught a glimpse of sharp incisors and thought of Verakina. Was this young woman a werewolf too?

'Don't be afraid,' she said. 'They can't see us. None of them can, until Lady Grandmother wishes it so.'

'How . . . Who . . . who are you?' I stammered.

'I'm Olga of the family Ironheart,' she said, comfortably, motioning me to a seat. 'And over there is my husband Andel.' The tall, bulky man smiled and nodded. 'And our little son Frans-Ivan.' The baby regarded me warily. 'And, of course, Lady Grandmother, who has done us the honour of asking us to accompany her.'

'Oh,' I said. I shot a glance at the old woman. She was looking away, as though she were bored with the conversation and the situation. 'Thank you so much,' I added, suddenly realising I must appear rude and ungrateful.

'I am a total stranger to you. Yet you saved me from great danger.'

'You are most welcome. None of us has ever much liked the police,' said Olga, 'and Lady Grandmother could see that you might need some help.'

'It is so very kind. But forgive me, I forget my manners, I have not even told you my name. It is Bianca . . . and I . . . .' I gulped and couldn't finish, for all at once my legs gave way.

Olga helped me to a chair and made me sit down, and gave me a glass of water. I drank it slowly and began to feel better. I looked at the old woman who, quite unperturbed, had trotted off to have a look at the cake display. Even though she was in full view of the waiters, no-one seemed to notice she was there.

'How do you . . . she . . . how does she . . .' I said to Olga, stumbling over my words because even now I did not quite believe the evidence of my senses that told me that I was somehow kept within a protective spell that hid me and my companions from sight.

Olga smiled. 'I cannot tell you. Not that I won't – I just cannot. It is all Lady Grandmother's doing.'

'She . . . She is a witch?' I ventured. 'An enchantress?'

'Oh no. She is immortal. She is a feya. The most powerful feya in all Ruvenya.'

I stared. 'What?'

'I know what you're thinking,' said her husband, speaking for the first time. 'Feya don't normally travel. Especially not Old B– I mean, Lady Grandmother,' he corrected himself hastily, throwing the apparently oblivious old woman a wary look. 'But this is a special case.'

I felt faint. How could they talk of feya in this blithe, down-to-earth way? How could I take in the fact that one of those legendary immortal beings was actually here in this station buffet, greedily eyeing the rows of cream cakes as though she were an ordinary sweet-toothed grandmother? Nellia, the feya from the mountain spring, was the only feya I really knew anything about and even that was all hearsay. Superstition, Belladonna would have said.

'I . . . What special case?' I asked, trying to cover my unease.

'We are here to track down someone,' said Olga. 'Normally Lady Grandmother would not concern herself with such a thing outside her own domain – but as I say, this is different.'

'Why?' I asked. I didn't want to seem rude, but I was curious. And besides, I still did not think it would be safe for me to leave the station quite yet.

'Because it's personal, for her. It concerns an old enemy,' said Olga. 'A wicked sorcerer named Messir Durant. It's not him we're looking for, by the way,' she added. 'He's dead.' She saw my puzzlement and continued her explanation. 'There's a rumour he may have had an apprentice. From Noricia. And if that's so, we have to find out what their plans are. For if they're anything like Durant, they've got to be stopped. But we don't know for sure yet if the rumour is even true. We've only just arrived.'

'And we still don't know exactly what we're looking for,' grumbled Andel. 'Man, woman, young, old. In the dark, as usual.'

'Hush, Andel,' said his wife, without heat. She took the baby, who'd begun to fret, in her arms and rocked him gently, saying, 'But here we are talking on and on about our concerns, and you . . .'

I stopped listening. I had spotted Lucian, who had come into the station, looking red and out of breath. He looked around wildly, searching for someone in the crowd. Me. I was sure it was me. And then, out of the corner of my eye, I saw the City Police appear. And this time, a short distance behind them, was the black-clad Special Policeman. I saw him freeze as he spotted Lucian.

'Please,' I cried, 'please, help Lucian, the young man over there. He is my friend, and that Special Policeman is going to try to get him too!'

The old woman didn't even turn from her examination of the cakes. 'Please,' I begged Olga, 'you have to help him, he's going to be . . .'

'He's going to be all right,' said Andel, and in the next moment I saw he was right, for the black-clad man had turned and headed for another exit. As for the City Police, they passed right by Lucian without seeing him. The old woman must have made him invisible.

'Thank you,' I said, turning to the old woman. 'Thank you so much.' But all she did was shrug.

'Would you please let Lucian see us? Let him come to me,' I begged.

The old woman shook her head, firmly.

'Please!'

'It's no good,' Olga said, as the old woman stalked off with two cakes in each hand, cakes she'd spirited away from the display case under the very nose of the waiter. 'If she doesn't want to do something, she won't change her mind.'

'But why on earth not? He's my . . . friend. He's worried about me.'

'She sees further than anyone,' said Olga, gently rocking the sleepy child. 'There must be danger abroad. For him. For you. For both of you.'

Lucian looked around him once more. Then he shook his head, as if dazed, and walked out of the station, unchallenged. In less time than it takes to say it, he had vanished from sight.

'Lady Grandmother says you may go now.' Olga's voice made me start.

'If you wish, that is,' corrected Andel. 'Or you could stay with us.'

'Andel, you know that isn't possible,' Olga said, casting a look at the old woman who was now impassively devouring her cakes. There was cream on her chin and crumbs in her hair, and she would have looked a comic sight if it hadn't been for that stony, unblinking black gaze which would make anyone think twice about turning her into a figure of fun.

Andel frowned. 'I don't like to leave you –' he began, but I interrupted him, hastily.

'Thank you, but I need to find my friend as soon as possible, so please don't trouble yourselves on my account. I cannot express my gratitude for all that you have done for me, a stranger.'

'It is no matter, no matter at all,' said Andel, gruffly. 'Stranger or no stranger, we try to help those in trouble.'

'We know what it is like to be hunted,' said Olga, 'and you are no stranger to us anymore.'

'If you do ever need our help again,' said Andel, 'we will be staying at the Wheat Sheaf Inn on the market square. We'll be glad to be of service in whatever way we can,' and here he gave Olga a somewhat defiant look.

Olga countered with a white-toothed smile, saying to me, 'Of course. I add my voice to my husband's – if you are in need of a friend, you must not hesitate one moment to come to us.'

Twenty-Four

Thinking that Lucian might have gone back to the safe house, I headed there, but found it empty and Master Kinberg's shop closed for the night. I intended only to rest for a short while before going out again to search for Lucian, but was so exhausted by the events of the day that it wasn't till early morning that I opened my eyes again. After some thought, I decided I'd go back to Lucian's apartment. After yesterday's visit from the Special Police, I didn't really expect to find Lucian there, but I had a faint hope that the police had not found the photographs or, if they had, I hoped that they may have left them, not knowing of their significance. It was my one last chance at gaining evidence of Belladonna's crimes without having to expose the beggars.

I took out the dress Verakina had washed and patched – the dress I'd been wearing that terrible day when my friends, the outcasts, had found me – put it on, and flung over it the old cloak the innkeeper had given me.

I perched the wire-rimmed glasses on my nose and pulled up the hood of the cloak. Leaving the safe house, I made my way through the streets and approached the apartment cautiously, for I did not know if it was under police surveillance. It was not. Still, I thought it best to be careful, so instead of trying the front door, I got in the back way, through the alley that ran at the back of the house, and back up the steel stairs. Up these I ventured, carefully, till I reached an open window, through which I scrambled.

Once in the house – I was in a kind of box room on the first floor – I listened for any sound. But the house was very quiet. Not a soul stirred. Tiptoeing out, I made my way to the darkroom. By some miracle the photographs were still where I'd left them, and clear as day, too! Thrusting them hastily into my pocket, I was about to leave the way I had come when suddenly I heard voices downstairs. Clara. And Lucian!

Without stopping to think, I sped out of the room and looked over the railing in the void that dropped down to the first floor below. Lucian was in the hall, talking to Clara. I couldn't discern what he was saying, but he looked pale and shaken. I called down to him.

He looked up. 'Bianca!' Breaking away from Clara, in a few long strides he was up the stairs and coming towards me. 'Thank God you're all right. I thought they'd got you!'

'I'm fine. And I'm so glad to see you are safe, too!'

'Where have you been? I was so worried . . .'

'I spent the night at the safe house . . . But before that, I went to the station to find you because Master Kinberg told me you'd taken the beggars to the Grand Dome

Station – but I couldn't see you at first – and then there were the police, and I –'

'You were at the station?' he said, interrupting me. 'But I didn't see you.'

'I was just . . . well, hard to see.'

'You were hiding?'

'Yes.' I wasn't sure why I was reluctant to tell him about the old woman and her spell. 'What about you? I looked for you at the coach stop but couldn't find you. And then I saw you, later . . .'

'I was just checking everyone had got away safely,' he said, 'but when I came back into the station, I saw the police and knew something was up.'

'Did you see that one in the black?' I asked. 'The Special Policeman? He tried to grab me but I got away. It was only then that the City Police caught sight of me.'

He shook his head. 'I didn't see him. But some of those Special Policemen are even worse than the City Police. And I know there would be some working hand-in-glove with Belladonna – I heard she has informers there. But why did you leave here in the first place? That was so risky!'

'I had to leave,' I said, and explained about the police coming. I added, 'Why did they come, do you think?'

'I don't know,' he said, 'but they must suspect me, for some reason.' He looked quite pale. Taking my hand, he said, very seriously, 'You need to leave, Bianca. You need to go at once. Far away. Far, far away from here. Forget Belladonna. Forget it all. Run.'

I stared at him, my heart sinking. 'I can't do that, Lucian! You know I can't. She's got to be stopped. She's got to pay for what she's done. I thought you understood that. I thought you felt the same way.'

'I do, but . . .' Lucian paused, as if he were thinking hard about what he was about to say. When he continued, he spoke his words quickly, desperately, as if he were afraid that had he spoken any slower, he would hold the words back. 'Bianca, there are things that are more important: your safety. I want you to be safe. Far away. It's over for now – the beggar killings, I mean. You should go, Bianca, while you can.'

'How do you know that?' I burst out. How could this be the Prince I knew? How could the Prince, who would do anything to protect his friends the outcasts, ask me to abandon my own mission?

'I went to that place, like you told me to,' he said. 'Bianca – there was no crime scene there. Everything you told me you'd seen – it was gone. There was nothing! No cages, no strange implements, no body, no dummy, no Drago.'

It was what I had feared. Belladonna had acted quickly and erased the evidence of her crimes. 'It doesn't matter,' I said. 'She's not going to stop. She'll start again some-where else. She'll hide whatever she's doing better this time. Whatever she's been doing – whatever ghastly exper-iment it is – she's only been interrupted, not stopped. How can we be safe? How can any of us be safe, while she is free and at large? We must bring her down, Lucian, we must!'

'I'm not sure this is the right time,' he muttered.

I could not understand this reluctance, his excuses. Wasn't this was the Prince of Outlaws, a man who risked his life every day to help poor souls in mortal danger? What was wrong with him?

I took the photographs from my pocket. 'She might have cleaned the crime scene. But I have these. We can use them as proof.'

He looked at them, then at me. He said, quietly, 'These could just as easily be used against us, Bianca. Can't you see that? Even if they believe us, that this is the real work behind the "vampire" attacks, Belladonna could say *we* were the captors of those poor people. She could say this is evidence that *we* were the criminals.'

I looked at the photos and saw at once that he was right. How had I not seen that before?

'But . . . But she's already told one version of the story; she can't change it now!'

'You've seen what she can do – she'll manage it somehow.'

In that moment I made my decision. It was time to reveal myself.

'Well, we still have a great advantage,' I said, 'and that's me. She doesn't know I'm alive. We can take her by surprise if we go – not to the police, because clearly we can't trust them – but to the Duke himself, and tell him everything.'

He sighed. 'And what if the Duke believes her, and not you?'

'You forget – he thinks I'm dead, too. He believed her lying story about me, that I had committed suicide. When he sees I'm alive and well, he'll know Belladonna lied. And when I tell him that Belladonna was behind the beggar killings, and that there is something even bigger behind it all, then everything will be unravelled! I am the living proof of her crimes, can't you see?'

He gave me a long look. 'So you are,' he said. 'But for God's sake, Bianca! What's she going to do when she sees you alive?'

'What can she do, once the Duke himself knows what she's done? She'll be arrested on the spot. This won't be like the ambush in the forest she had planned for me. This will be right out in the open, in front of witnesses, in front of the Duke. She can't touch me. Not there.'

'I wouldn't be so sure,' he said. 'Bianca, you don't know what you're up against!'

'I understand that as the Prince of Outlaws, you do not want to be unmasked,' I said, containing the dismay I felt at his reluctance. 'But for me, there can be no more running. No more hiding. I cannot bear for this wicked woman to continue unpunished, for her crimes to remain a secret for one more moment. I owe that to my father's memory, and to the memory of all those she's wronged, to all those who have paid for having loved and trusted her, and to all those innocents who have suffered at her hands.' I drew myself up. 'If you don't want to come with me, that is your choice. But I am going to the Duke, no matter what you say to try to persuade me otherwise.' And so saying, I turned on my heel and made for the door, my heart pounding with the bitter knowledge that once again I was alone.

I had just reached the door when I heard his footsteps behind me.

'Perhaps, after all, you are right,' said Lucian, 'and there is only one way to find out. So let's go find the Duke.' And he gave me a smile which made my heart lift.

Twenty-Five

The Duke had only met me once, at the Presentation Ball. And even though he could not have failed to see my photographs in the paper, after my supposed drowning, I was afraid he might not recognise me. I was of the opinion that we should announce at once to the chamberlain who I was, but Lucian was of another opinion.

'Better if it comes as a surprise,' he said, 'because otherwise he might think it is someone playing a trick, and refuse to see you.'

So we did as he said. Lucian, being high-born, had excuse enough to visit the Duke, and to the chamberlain he introduced me as his cousin. On his suggestion, I kept the glasses on, so my identity would only be revealed at the last moment.

'The Duke is in an important meeting,' the chamberlain told us, 'so you will have to wait. In the antechamber, if you will.' He had shown no particular curiosity about us at all. Of course, the Duke saw several visitors every day. Why would he think we were anything out of the ordinary?

We'd been waiting in the antechamber for quite a few minutes, neither of us saying very much, when a door opened down the corridor and the Duke's sister came out. She did not look to be in a good mood. Her face was red, her mouth twisted. She swept past without looking at us, muttering fiercely beneath her breath. I couldn't hear the words, only the tone, but it was enough. She'd just had some kind of quarrel with her brother. It would not be likely that he would be in a good mood either . . .

The door opened again and someone else came out. The Duke. I was about to jump up and go towards him when he turned back towards the door of the room he had just left and said, in a loud, carrying voice, 'Come, dear lady. We will walk together.'

My breath froze in my throat, for who should come out of the doorway but Belladonna! The real Belladonna: living, breathing, smiling as the Duke took her hand.

This was the last thing I would have imagined and yet it should have been plain all along. Belladonna was a widow now; the Duke had always had an eye for the ladies. All she had to do was put herself in his way and he would become easy prey. Was that why the Duke's sister had looked so angry? Had she, for some reason, become wary of Belladonna?

'We must go,' Lucian said. As soon as he had seen Belladonna, a terrified look had appeared on his face. I felt warm that he was frightened for me but I wasn't frightened. Not really. Horrified, yes. Disgusted, yes. Scared, no. Not anymore. It was better this way. She wouldn't be able to escape. I'd reveal myself to the Duke in front of her and she would be completely powerless to stop me.

Ignoring Lucian's pleas for us both to leave, I strode up the hall towards the retreating couple.

'Duke Ottakar,' I called, in a ringing voice.

Belladonna turned around at once, twisting her arm away from his like a serpent. I was fiercely happy to see that all the colour had left her face. She had recognised my voice, of course. And for an instant she seemed incapable of speech.

The Duke had turned, too. He looked puzzled as I approached.

'Duke Ottakar,' I repeated, flinging off the cloak and pulling off the glasses I was wearing.

Belladonna went white. The Duke stared at her and then at me, looking even more puzzled.

'Who are you?' he said. 'Your face seems familiar . . .'

I opened my mouth to speak, but at that moment, Belladonna stepped up to me and placed her hand on my arm. At once, I felt as though my throat had closed up. I tried to open my mouth to speak, but no words came out. I tried to move, but could not. I was utterly helpless. My body was frozen, but I could hear and see everything.

'Forgive me,' I heard Belladonna say. 'It was . . . modelled on my poor lost stepdaughter, Lady Bianca. It was meant to be kept shut away. One of my servants must have bungled and brought along the box for this one, too. And it malfunctioned. They do, occasionally.' She shot me a blue glare then that was filled with something I could only describe as a kind of gleeful loathing.

The Duke stared at Belladonna. 'You mean to say this is another of your automata?'

I tried desperately to free myself, but couldn't. I couldn't move. Not a muscle, not a nerve, not a twitch. I was trapped, shouting in my head, but could do nothing while she spun her web of lies. And now I knew the truth. She was much more than a murderer and a liar. She was a witch, and a powerful one, too. She had used magic, some kind of spell that held me bound, that rendered me helpless.

My mind worked to process what I'd just heard. 'Automata', the Duke had said. I could only assume that was the name for those dummies Belladonna had made. But, unlike the mute dummies at the Ladies' Fair show, unlike the stationary dummy twin she kept of herself down in Drago's house of horrors, I had moved, I had spoken – and Belladonna's explanation hadn't baffled the Duke – which meant that she must have been creating more lifelike machines. For what purpose? And what did it have to do with the beggar killings?

'Yes, your grace,' she said. 'It is an automaton, like the one I showed you that was made using my features.'

'Heavens above, my dear Belladonna,' said the Duke, sounding a little uncomfortable. 'That one was startling enough, but this one – it is quite something. It's like seeing a ghost come to life.'

'Oh, your grace,' she said, as her eyes welled with fake tears. 'I am sorry it has disturbed you. It has given me a shock, too – because, you see, my poor stepdaughter – she . . . she modelled for it, in . . . in happier times. But now . . .' The hypocritical tears continued to roll down her cheek. 'Oh, I'm so sorry! How unfeeling you must think me, your grace! I *had* given orders for it to be packed away. I can't imagine why it was brought out!'

'There, there,' said the Duke, awkwardly patting her arm. 'Please don't cry. I certainly don't think badly of you. This ... This automaton – it is a little ... er ... startling – but it is quite a tribute to your talents. And the fact that you didn't want it displayed shows your delicacy of feeling.'

'I'll arrange to have it removed, your grace. It certainly should not be in the exhibition.'

'Oh, I wouldn't say that,' said the Duke.

He walked up to me and touched me on the shoulder. I could feel his touch but was unable to react. I could not even move my eyes. I stared glassily ahead, like a dummy, like a veritable automaton whose clockwork had run down.

'This one is really very lifelike indeed,' he continued. 'It is the summit of your art. It is more amazing, even, than that very clever one you modelled for. It hardly even feels like it's made of wax.'

'You are right. This is our prize specimen, your grace. And we have perfected the flesh tones this time, using the highest-quality wax.' She pinched my cheek.

It hurt, and although I could not react, in my heart, volcanoes of anger and hate and fear rumbled. Anger against Belladonna, but against myself, too. Why hadn't I listened to Lucian?

Lucian! Where was he? I could not turn around to see if he was here but I did not need to. If he were here, he'd have tried, somehow, to help me. Where was he? Where had he gone? *Why* had he gone? I could feel tears at the back of my eyes but I knew they would not fall.

'Yes, I definitely think you should show it,' said the Duke. 'If you think you can bear it that is, my dear.'

'I will do what you think is best, your grace,' murmured Belladonna, sweetly. She clapped her hands. 'Take it away and get it ready!'

And so it was that I was carried away by the servants, like a block of wood, like a lifeless dummy, in fact, and packed into a crate filled with straw. As they prepared to slam down the lid of the crate, I tried once again to scream, to shout, but it was impossible; I could not even utter a whisper, not a sound. Nothing. Darkness rushed in at me as the lid came down.

After what seemed like an eternity of jolting and bumping, the lid of the crate was finally flung open. Dazed, I stared up into bright light. I still could not blink. The spell held fast, and I was powerless to move or speak. But as I was hauled out of the crate, I saw that I was in a long, large room, something like an exhibition hall in a museum. The hall was filled with rows of big glass boxes the size and shapes of coffins, with a panel opening at the top. The bottom of each glass box was lined with a long velvet cushion. A few were empty except for the cushion. In most, however, a lifelike dummy rested on the velvet.

The sight of these made terror run like melted ice in my veins. Were those stiff figures lying in the glass coffins actually dummies, or living people like me, trapped in a hideous spell? Only one of them did I recognise, and that was the Belladonna dummy, the one she must have removed from Drago's dungeon. All the others bore the faces of strangers. At least there was no Lucian there, which was a relief.

I tried to summon up every reserve of strength I had to struggle free. But I could not make a single flicker of movement.

And then I heard her voice, commanding her servants.

'Put it in that one, in the middle . . . Yes, the one on that low curtained platform. And be careful with it. It's the prize specimen, after all. The day after tomorrow is the public exhibition. I want them all to be in perfect condition for that.' Her voice was sharp, cold, impersonal, just as though she were indeed talking about a lifeless thing, not a person. I knew there would be no mercy from her. And with Lucian gone, there was no-one to save me, now. No-one to take pity. There was no escape. Until she chose to break the spell, I was completely in her power.

'It's strange, this one feels somehow different to the others,' I heard one of the servants whisper as they hoisted me onto a trolley and opened the top panel of the glass box. His colleague said nothing in return, but only cast a wary glance over his shoulder to see if Lady Dalmatin had heard.

Please, I thought, desperately. Please, let the man be curious enough to come back later to investigate, to see why this automaton feels different to the others . . . But it was a very slender chance to pin any hopes on.

They lifted me in and settled me into the box, on the velvet cushion, then closed the glass panel. I was imprisoned, on display like an exhibit in a museum. The prize specimen . . . To all eyes, I must look like a perfect waxwork, so lifelike it was incredible, but an automaton only, a thing which only simulated life, whose innards concealed only wires and mechanisms and gears, not the roiling mix of terror and rage that boiled in my poor human belly like the most virulent poison. I was to die here in plain sight, die slowly as the oxygen in the glass coffin slowly diminished, die under the eyes of the hundreds or even thousands who would file past the glass coffins and marvel at the workmanship that they would be told had been used to create me.

When the servants finished setting out the remaining few of the dummies, Belladonna sent them out of the hall and locked the door behind them. She came up the low step that led to the platform and opened the panel at the top of the box. She smiled in at me. That smile was the most terrible thing, for there was joy in it, pleasure, but of the cruel sort that chills the blood.

'Well, you heard the Duke, my dear. You're to be the prize exhibit. I rather think you will be the talk of the town. Such artistry! Such a beautiful tribute to my poor dear stepdaughter so tragically lost! A little macabre, though, mind, but that is what makes you even more effective. Now, let's put you through your paces.'

She reached in a hand and touched me on the shoulder. I felt the touch like a jolt of lightning. She touched me again and I jerked up.

'Out,' she said, and I found myself stiffly climbing out of the glass box and walking down the step onto the floor, as she beckoned me forward. I was unable to do anything but advance, unable still to speak, to make any movement of my own accord.

Belladonna kept talking, in a soft, gentle voice, her eyes fixed on my face.

'Good. Very good. They will be astonished. They will come from far and wide to see such a lifelike doll. My dear, I hope it feels good to know that you will be the catalyst for the most extraordinary revolution in our land, even though you won't live long enough to see it. You see, these automata are not like the usual clockwork dolls, for their inner workings are powered by real human essence. Yet, unlike humans, they are infinitely controllable. I do not need to spellbind them by touch, as I did with you. They will do what they are ordered to, every time. I am creating the perfect helpers, the perfect servants. Soon, everyone will want one or two or three at home. The military will want them in the field. The industrialists in their factories. The merchants in their homes.

'But the real catch? Each of them will be bound to me, for it is I who hold the secret of their manufacture. In time, I will have an army on which to call, an army which will obey me without question, for all the automata will be programmed to follow my commands, and mine only, when the time comes. Even the Duke will be powerless to stop me.' She put her head on one side and considered me. 'I suppose you must wonder at that – my plans for the Duke. I'm sure you must see that I plan to marry him – but marrying him is only part of my strategy. He is an arrogant, foolish bully, but he has what I need for the moment: riches and resources, so that I can continue creating my automata. In time, he will have a regrettable fatal accident, and I will be sole ruler. As to Lady Helena, she has taken an annoying dislike to me – but no matter. I will deal with her in my own time. Perhaps in the same way as I dealt with you. That would be amusing, no?'

She is mad, I thought. Quite, quite mad. And treacherous. Vile treachery was what she was planning, against the country that had welcomed her, against the society that had welcomed her.

'You, of course, my dear, I will retire gracefully. I will say my grief has made the simulation of you too painful to bear. I will remove you from display and release you, so that I can harvest your life-essence. It's taken me a long time to perfect the process, but I have invented a magical tool that can extract in useful form the life-essence of a person, that thing foolish people call a soul. That life-essence is the most powerful thing there is, for it makes inanimate things like my automata come to life. And I'm sure your life-essence will fuel one very powerful automaton indeed! You are strong, you are persistent, you are imaginative, bold and clever. You have many uncommon traits, my dear Bianca. So . . . I guess that I will not kill Drago for his disobedience. He did me quite a favour, letting you live, for your dead heart would not have been half as useful as your life-essence will be.'

Too late, I had discovered what Belladonna had been doing with those poor beggars, and understood what I'd seen Drago doing, down in the basement prison. That fluid he'd been extracting, which had vanished like quicksilver – that was Simeon's life-essence. Despair filled me. Helpless, speechless, I wished now only that I might fall asleep in that glass box and never wake up – for I did not want to live in a world ruled by a ruthless Belladonna and her army of automata, powered by the stolen life-essence of the poor, the outcast and the betrayed.

'And another thing,' she said. She was smiling. 'Don't think that anyone can help you now. All those who helped you will die, but not before I've harvested their life-essence. I already have the tailor, that Master Kinberg – we snatched him from his home this very morning.'

My body was paralysed but the stunning shock of her words almost jolted my frozen muscles into reacting. Almost – but then Belladonna put her hand on me and said some words I did not understand and my body locked down again. I could only listen helplessly as she went on.

'He'll talk, under torture, not a doubt of it. He'll reveal where all your friends are hiding. Your friends – they will all be smoked out, hunted down. All of them will die. Except the one you call the Prince of Outlaws. For him, I will reserve a special fate. Like you, my dear, I can sense that his life-essence must be a truly powerful one. I have informers everywhere, Bianca. Did you really think you could defy me?'

My heart was heavy. She would kill everyone who had ever helped me. And it would be my fault. My commitment to exposing Belladonna for who she really was, my commitment to revenge, had endangered them all.

At that moment, there was a knock on the door.

'I told you all that I was not to be disturbed!' Belladonna called out.

'I'm sorry, my lady, but it is most urgent,' came Drago's voice.

'Wait,' she called back. She clicked her fingers and I found myself forced to walk stiffly back the way I'd come, up the steps, jerkily climbing back into the box and lying down. Before she slid the glass panel shut, she looked into my eyes and I looked into hers, and for an instant I had the sensation that I was looking into a blue abyss, an empty depth, a hungry absence that shocked me even in the midst of my despair. It was as though there was nothing there behind those eyes.

That was only for the tiny flicker of an instant. In the next, she had turned away from me. I heard her walk down the stairs and across the hall, open the door, and lock it behind her.

I was alone.

Twenty-Six

Alone, and yet not, for all around me, in their glass coffins, the automata waited for an order from their mistress Belladonna, which would bring them to some sort of life. They were all waiting for an order to wake and walk in a simulation of life, waiting patiently and obediently to do her bidding, waiting to become the army she dreamed of, the army that would in time take over our country and make it her fiefdom.

Lying immured in that glass prison, unable to move or speak, I could still think. I turned over and over in my mind everything I knew about Belladonna. Everything I'd learnt. She was an orphan of uncertain parentage, brought up by her adoptive grandmother in Aurisola. She had contrived to murder that poor old lady, thinking to gain from it, but had not. She had then moved elsewhere, eventually become a Fairest Lady candidate, murdered a rival, stolen my father's heart, come to live in Noricia, then contrived to murder my father and tried to murder me.

What other crimes had she committed throughout her life? She was behind the beggar killings, I knew that. And she was planning something much bigger – a revolution, she'd called it.

But none of these facts struck me as much as this: just how powerful she was. At first I had thought she was a witch. But the powers she had shown – the strength and cruelty of the spell I was under, and complexity of her magic in creating the automata and the uncanny tool that extracted human life-essence – didn't this extend beyond those that a human witch would possess? What if Belladonna was a feya?

I thought back to what I knew of Belladonna's past. She was an orphan – that could be a good cover story for many things. What if Belladonna's adoptive grandmother had taken into her home not a lonely human child but something completely different? A strange child, a feya child. If Belladonna was a feya, she was a twisted one. A dark, perverse one, damaged beyond redemption by something or someone – or perhaps she was simply bad, right from the start. That sort existed. They were rare, very rare, but their existence was not unheard of. Their nature was demonic, and though they could be thwarted by humans, they could not be finally defeated and destroyed by one of us. Their downfall could only be brought about by someone like them. Someone, in fact, like that one Olga called Lady Grandmother. But only if she knew. Only if she was told. Ever since I had escaped from Drago in the forest, I had tried plan after plan to expose Belladonna. If I ever did somehow escape from this glass coffin, if I was somehow released from my own unresponsive body, I would find the feya Lady Grandmother. She was now my only hope.

Just then, I heard the door open again, and voices. For an instant, I thought my prayers had been answered, that Olga and Andel and the old woman had somehow learnt what had happened and come to my rescue. Of course it was nothing of the kind, just Belladonna, accompanied, it seemed from the voices, by the Duke and a crowd of chattering people who were apparently about to be given a private viewing of the automata. Through the thin curtain around my box, I could glimpse silhouettes, but not much else.

The Duke made some kind of speech that I only half-heard, something about how the technology was such an incredible breakthrough, how extraordinary Belladonna was, and how pleased he was to have the opportunity of showing these people around. I heard the sound of boxes being opened, and the somewhat heavy movement of automata as they moved around jerkily to Belladonna's brisk commands. I could not, of course, see the crowd, but I could hear their gasps of astonishment mingled with a kind of nervous amusement.

How had she kept her true nature, her true plans, hidden from us all? Neither my father nor I had had the slightest idea. Apart from Drago and perhaps one or two of her most trusted servants, no-one had had the slightest idea. Only that dummy at the fashion show had been a hint of what she'd been doing, and who could have known the full extent of what lay behind it?

But before I could run off with my thoughts once again, the curtain around the box I was in was drawn and

I was revealed to the crowd for the first time. Now I could see them, their mouths hanging open in amazement – and something else, too. Horror. But there was dead silence as Belladonna ascended the step, opened the glass panel, and tapped me on the shoulder. As I sat up, stiffly, the crowd fell back a fraction, and at that moment I caught sight of a face I recognised. Emilia – flanked by her mother and another woman. Our eyes met, above the heads of the crowd. She went completely white. Opened her mouth. And screamed.

'Oh my God! Mother! Aunt! It's Bianca! It's Bianca!' She turned to Belladonna. 'What have you done to her? What have you done?'

'Emilia!' Her mother and aunt vainly tried to calm her as she struggled within their grasp, sobbing, now, her eyes wild in her chalk-white face. Belladonna had hesitated, but only for a moment. She tapped me on the shoulder again so that I had to sit stock-still, helpless as a machine whose clockwork has run down, then she calmly went back down the step towards Emilia.

'We're so sorry, my lady,' Emilia's mother and aunt kept repeating. 'We don't know what's come over her, she's not usually like this . . .'

'I understand,' said Belladonna, gently. She looked at Emilia, gave her a smile, and touched her on the shoulder. My guts twisted inside me. She was going to do the same thing to Emilia as she had done to me . . . In front of all these people?

But she didn't freeze Emilia. She withdrew her hand and said, 'I'm sorry it's given you such a shock. I wasn't thinking. You were her friend, of course. And these things . . .' She waved a hand at me, at the automata. '. . . They can look so real, can't they?'

Emilia looked at her, the horror still in her face. Then slowly, she nodded. It was as though she was doing it automatically, not of her own will. As though Belladonna had put a spell on her . . .

'I hesitated about showing this one,' continued Belladonna. 'My poor stepdaughter modelled for it. But his grace the Duke – he persuaded me it would be a fitting tribute to a girl who was much loved. That it might help us to bear her tragic end, and that of her poor father, my dearest husband.' Her voice trembled with fake emotion and inside me, the fear and despair was ebbing away as rage rose. She might be powerful – she might even be an immortal – but even if I were to die in the attempt, I would do everything I could to try to defeat her.

Emilia was led away. She was still sobbing a little, but calmer now. Her mother and aunt went with her. The crowd, disturbed at first by the little scene, gradually relaxed again, as Belladonna's soothing voice explained how I – a supposed automaton – had been made. Of course, she mentioned nothing about stolen life-essences, she just spoke technical talk about wires and levers and cogs and amazing synthetic materials that could be made to look just like skin. The crowd oohed and aahed while I was made to parade before them, and one or two of the bravest came up to feel my hand or poke at my side. It was unbearable but I had to bear it because there was nothing I could do to stop it. As to the Duke, he was gazing proudly at Belladonna, all the while perorating about how creating the automata was going to make Noricia wealthy and famous beyond any dreams.

'We will be the powerhouse of the future,' he proclaimed. 'We will show every other country the way forward. And it will be all thanks to the genius of Lady Belladonna Dalmatin!'

'Well, I think it is an outrage!' came a loud voice from across the hall. Everyone turned. It was Lady Helena, the Duke's sister, storming across the hall. She was in full sail, red in the face, her eyes sparking, striding purposefully towards her brother.

She gave me a glance. Something flickered in her eyes. Turning to Belladonna, she snapped.

'This is shameful. The poor girl went to a miserable death and here you are parading what seems to be some kind of simulation of her.'

'Helena . . .' began the Duke, but she brushed him aside.

'It is outrageous,' she said, biting each word off, 'that a widow whose husband is hardly cold in his grave should be leading a crowd of gawkers to a ridiculous and repellent spectacle of giant dolls – one of whom was modelled on her poor late stepdaughter who has been dead only a week.' She surveyed Belladonna with great disfavour. 'I do not like this at all. Something unpleasant is afoot.'

Belladonna was quite still. Her ivory skin had not flushed, but her eyes were bright and hard as she said, softly, 'I am sorry you feel that way. But I am sure you understand that grief takes us in different ways, my Lady Helena. I have found that my work helps to soften the pain. And his grace is kind enough to take an interest in my project, and help me through these difficult times.'

Lady Helena snorted, but before she could say another word, the Duke spoke. He was as red in the face as his sister, and his eyes were equally angry. He said, sharply, 'That is quite enough, Helena. The lady you address so discourteously is a person of the finest feelings I have ever known. Her sensitivity is second only to her intelligence and beauty. You think to insult her? Well, know this. In doing so, you are insulting me. And I do not speak as your brother.' His tone became commanding. 'I speak as your duke.'

Everyone in the crowd held their breath as Lady Helena looked at him – her brother, her Duke. She gave a strange, sad, little smile. 'I see,' she said, after a moment. 'Very well, then. Clearly there is nothing I can do here.' And without another word, she turned on her heel and strode out of the room as abruptly as she'd come in.

'Good heavens,' said the Duke after a moment. 'What a to-do! Let's all forget about it, shall we?' His words were light, but his tone was not. As he looked around the crowd, people tittered nervously, nodding like fairground clowns. Of course they wouldn't forget it, but there had been a definite warning in his tone. There would be no-one here who would dare repeat such gossip.

'Get that thing put back in its box, will you? And the others, too,' he said, gesturing to the servants, who hurried over to do his bidding. As I was settled back down in the box, the panel shut above me and the curtain drawn, I thought of what had just happened. First Emilia, then Lady Helena. Both of them had looked at me with eyes that just for a tiny instant saw something other than what Belladonna wanted them to see. But I had no hope that they guessed the terrible truth. How could they?

As the hours wore on, I fell into greater despondency, my mind beginning to feel as trapped as my unmoving body. The shadows lengthened in the room and night fell and still I lay there surrounded by the hollow, lifeless figures of the automata I so closely resembled. My thoughts turned to the Prince, to Lucian. Why had he abandoned me at the Duke's palace? I hoped against hope that he had somehow – I couldn't think how – realised that the beggars and other outcasts had been discovered, that they were in danger. I hoped that he had gone after them, gone to make sure they were safe. Belladonna's words stuck in my mind: she would reserve a special fate for the Prince of Outlaws . . . No! I thought. He will save his people; he will save himself. She will not destroy them. She will not!

The night marched on. I fell into a light, unrefreshing, open-eyed doze from which I woke suddenly: there was someone in the room with me. No, not someone, I saw, as a ray of moonlight fell onto the newcomer. *Something.*

Eyes. Hazel eyes, with a yellow light to them. Bright, pitiless eyes. Glowing at me through the glass, set in the face of a wolf with jet-black fur that was touched with a strange shimmer. Its face bore a scar, just under one eye.

The wolf gazed at me through the glass without blinking. Unable to tear my own gaze away, I stared into its eyes. I knew that hazel glare. I had stared into it before. At the station. The masked policeman. It was he, and he was a wolf – or, rather, he was a werewolf, like Lucian.

Only, unlike Lucian, he was not a friend. This was a dangerous creature, a creature of dark and shadows.

Lucian had said that some of the police were in Belladonna's pay. This was clearly one of Belladonna's creatures. Just as he'd been sent to find me at the station, he'd been sent to watch me here, to make sure that I didn't escape once again.

For a while, the wolf prowled around the room. Trapped as I was, I could not follow his movements. Presently, he came back, and nosed at the glass panel. Terrified, I thought my last hour had come. But, quite suddenly and without my knowing how it happened, the wolf was gone. It was as if he had disappeared into thin air. And I was alone again. Only this time, my mind no longer felt frozen. It was skittering like a little animal, trying to make sense of what I'd seen. But I could not.

The night spun on. Daylight came. The morning light sparkled on the rows of glass coffins. Nobody and nothing else came into the room after the wolf except for the cleaners. When they came in, I had to submit to their dusters and polish as if I were an automaton. The smell of the polishes filled my nose but I could not sneeze or cough, and nor could I protest in any way when they used a wire brush to untangle my hair and flicked the dusters over my face. I heard what they said as they dealt with me and the other automata. They found us creepy. But, just like Emilia and Lady Helena, although they found us uncanny, they did not think beyond that. The cleaners could only see giant dolls, cold machines with the pretence of humanity. They found the automata half-fascinating, half-disgusting. I wasn't surprised. I found myself disgusting, too. If I had been able to weep, tears would have fallen in floods.

Time passed. The cleaners left. Other servants came in and out. Preparations were being made for the public exhibition tomorrow. From where I lay I could see the bustle. Tables were being set up, banners were being hung. Again, I fell into thought about Lucian and the outlaws. Would they be safe?

I must have fallen into a doze again for suddenly it seemed that the evening was beginning to draw in; darkness was pressing in at the windows. And then, just as night really fell, but before the moon rose, the lights came on, and in walked three servants who were wheeling in a crate.

The servants put the crate down and one of them pulled a piece of paper from his pocket. I heard him say something but didn't hear the words clearly. But they all looked over at me. One of them said something, and the first one shrugged, then nodded. What was going on?

I soon found out. Opening the top panel, they leaned in and pushed me a little up, so that my head touched one end of the box. Then they opened the crate and lifted out another still figure, which they plonked unceremoniously at my feet. It was when they lifted it from the crate that I saw that it wasn't a human figure, but . . .

A wolf!

Not the hazel-eyed, sinister black wolf of last night, but a small white wolf, with sharp pointed incisors and eyes that glowed green. Eyes that sparkled with friendly life. And I knew in that moment two things: the outcasts were safe, and the Prince had not abandoned me. For he had sent Verakina to save me.

Twenty-Seven

'Funny kind of idea, if you ask me,' said one of the servants, 'but the note clearly says it has to go in with this one. Look.'

The other servant looked at the dispatch note. 'Yes. It's a stuffed husky dog, says here. Meant to represent some kind of pet or something. Looks creepy if you ask me, with those bright glass eyes . . . But then the whole place gives me the creeps. Tell you what – I wouldn't like to be here in the dead of night.'

'Me neither. Come on, let's get out of here,' said the first one.

They slammed the lid down and wheeled away the crate. At my feet, the white wolf crouched, unmoving, until they had left the room. There were a few uncertain moments when I began to wonder if I'd imagined what I'd seen, if the wolf was in fact a stuffed husky, intended to be some kind of strange companion for me in tomorrow's show. And then, very faintly at first, I heard a rustle.

Another. I felt a small movement against my feet. Another. And then I felt the animal stretch as she rose to her feet.

She did not speak at all; I only learnt later that in her wolf shape, her human voice left her. But her eyes spoke for her as she carefully stepped up my side and, with a gentle paw, prised my mouth open. Then she opened her own mouth, and out dropped a small vial, which she picked back up with her teeth and struck against the glass. The stopper came free and she poured what was inside into my mouth. It released a cold, cold liquid that shot down my throat like an icy fire.

An agonising pain surged through me, a pain worse than anything I could have imagined. For a horrified instant, I thought that I'd been poisoned and was about to die. Was that how the Prince sought to free me? But I didn't think much more than that because the pain was so intense that I blacked out. Coming to – I do not know how long later – I felt weak as a kitten. But the pain had gone. And so had the paralysis. Instead, I was shivering, shaking like a leaf, every muscle and nerve trembling into life again, like a massive case of pins and needles after a long numbness. The wolf watched me calmly, her eyes fixed on my face. As the pins and needles subsided, I found my voice again – a thread of sound, a whisper, my throat sore as though I'd been ill – but still, it was my voice.

'Oh, Verakina,' I whispered, 'I am so very glad to see you.'

The wolf Verakina bared her teeth in what was clearly meant to be a smile, and I tried not to look at those sharp rows of teeth.

'Did the Prince send you?'

She nodded her head up and down.

'What do we do now?' I started to panic. Although I could now move, I was still trapped in the glass coffin.

Verakina pushed up against me with her head. Her eyes glowed.

'I don't understand,' I said.

She put a paw up to her throat and tapped it. Puzzled, I was about to repeat that I didn't understand when I suddenly got it. Reaching in under the thick white fur at her neck, I discovered a thin chain and, hanging from it, a thin instrument that must be . . .

'A lock pick!' I exclaimed.

Carefully, I detached the instrument from the chain and inserted it into the panel lock. It took me a couple of goes but to my delight I soon heard a click as the lock sprang open. Verakina lithely jumped out of the glass box and stood waiting for me to follow.

My own exit from the glass prison was less supple, but I was soon out and standing on my rather wobbly legs. It was the most indescribable feeling to be free, but I didn't waste time savouring it, for I knew we needed to leave that place straightaway. The trouble was that the only exit that I could see was the door through which the servants had come and gone. It was a risk – we might bump into someone – but there was no help for it; we had to go that way.

Tiptoeing to the door with Verakina at my heels, I carefully eased it open and looked out. There were no guards. They clearly thought that dummies in glass boxes were not prime candidates for escape.

We crept out of the hall, closing the door softly behind us. Verakina, nose to the ground, took the lead, and we slipped along a corridor, then another. Though I did not recognise the place, judging by the portraits on the wall I felt sure we were in one of the Duke's residences. We came to some stairs and Verakina nosed down them, with me following her. The stairs led to a rabbit warren of kitchens, sculleries and cellars and, keeping well out of the way of the noisy areas in which servants were busy working, we discovered at last a door that led to a kitchen garden. In the garden, we could at first see no exit. And then we spotted it, half-hidden under greenery: a door, stiff because of its old rusted hinges. It took me a few tries but at last I was able to wrench it open, and we were outside.

'I think we might be on the western side of the city,' I said, looking around. 'I know the Duke has a residence in that area.' I looked at Verakina. 'We have to find a safe place to hide in the city. But Lu—' I broke off, remembering that Verakina had only ever called him 'the Prince', and went on smoothly with, '— the Prince's safe house is finished. Has he told you where we should go now?'

Verakina shook her wolfish head from side to side.

'Oh. Well, then, we'll have to see if we can —' I stopped suddenly, remembering something that had come to me, back in that terrible hall. 'Verakina,' I said, 'we don't need to hide, we need an ally. And I know just where one is to be found — and they're on this side of the city!'

The Wheat Sheaf Inn is one of the oldest hotels in the city. Its main claim to fame is that one of our greatest poets, Franz Keren, once had rooms there, a hundred or more years ago. Framed signed copies of some of his poems still hang in the inn's big main room, and starstruck admirers from all over Noricia and beyond still make their way there to gaze at the master's actual handwriting. But aside from that, it is hardly what you would call an elegant hotel, being modestly appointed – though it's not without a certain quaint charm.

Here it was, I knew, that Olga, Andel, little Frans-Ivan and the old feya they called Lady Grandmother, had set up temporary residence. It wasn't a bad place for them to be, for among the motley and colourful mix of literary folk, students and travellers, they wouldn't stand out much.

'They're not here,' the girl at the reception counter told me, when I asked after the party of Ruvenyans.

'I mean,' she added, seeing my crestfallen expression, 'they're out. They'll be back. Somebody called in to see them this morning and they went out shortly after.'

Quickly I thought of what we should do next.

'Who came to see them?' I asked her. 'You see,' I added, thinking of a lie to tell, so that I might be able to find out where they'd gone, 'a mutual friend was to call on them and I wonder if they've gone off together.'

'Wait a moment,' she said, consulting the visitors' register. 'Ah yes. It was a "Dr Nord".'

For a moment I was baffled by the familiar-sounding name. Then it came to me. Dr Nord was the gentleman I'd met on the coach. But what was his connection to the others?

'Was that your friend?' the receptionist asked me suspiciously.

I nodded, trying to contain my surprise at what was surely not a coincidence. 'Did they say where they were going?'

'No. But I did overhear their visitor mentioning his lodgings. They might have gone there, wherever that is.'

'Thank you,' I said. 'You've been most helpful.'

'It's no trouble.' She looked at me with a little puzzled frown, as if something about me had triggered a recollection in her. I didn't wait for the receptionist to begin to remember the newspaper photographs of the tragic drowned Dalmatin heiress, but left.

'We'll have to try Dr Nord's hotel,' I told Verakina once I was outside, 'but if they're not there, we'll have to think of something else. Do you really have no idea where the Prince is?'

She shook her head, mutely and mournfully. I looked at her. She had waited for me outside, while I had gone into the Wheat Sheaf Inn, and I saw that while she waited she must have rolled in the dust, for her fur looked greyish rather than white now, making her look more like a stray dog than a werewolf. It gave me an idea.

'I've seen beggars with their dogs outside those smart hotels before now,' I said. 'We're going to play that part, you and I.'

So I rubbed my own face with dirt, ruffled my hair so it looked tangled, and scuffed my shoes till they looked utterly disreputable. In a nearby bin I found a ragged old shawl someone had thrown out. Holding my nose – it smelt somewhat of fish – I pulled it over my head to help with my disguise. Verakina looked at me with a glint in her eye.

'I know what you're thinking,' I said to her. 'No-one will ever let me into the front door of that hotel. Well, you'll see.'

It was strange. I was in grave danger. Once Belladonna found out I was gone, she'd set the hunters on me. If they caught me this time, I'd be dead. I had no illusions about that. And yet there was a lightness and brightness in me that I could hardly explain. Perhaps it was because I'd been so close to death that every moment seemed like a miracle. Or perhaps it was because I knew Lucian had not abandoned me. With the Prince – and Verakina – helping me, I was no longer alone. Hope no longer seemed like a crazy dream.

We reached the environs of Dr Nord's hotel without challenge. The Villa Valverd is situated on one of the biggest, finest squares of Lepmest and is one of a string of smart hotels lining the square. As I'd thought, nobody gave a second glance to the beggar girl and her skinny grey dog. But though I'd told Verakina so confidently that I would easily get into the hotel itself, in reality I knew that it would be difficult to inveigle the doorman into letting me in. We had to trick him, but not with words. It had to be a distraction – and I wasn't at all sure my plan would work.

Crouching in a little alley just off the square, near the hotel, I explained my plan in a whisper to Verakina. 'So are you clear on it?' I asked, when I'd finished.

She shot me a look. Do you take me for a fool? her look said, as sharply as though she'd spoken the words.

I smiled. 'Forgive me, Verakina. I'm just nervous.'

Verakina barrelled out of our hiding place and headed straight for the Villa Valverd and the doorman standing on guard in his tail coat at the front steps. I watched her sprint up the steps and saw the doorman fall back for an instant, then try to shoo her away. I watched in growing delight as, with snarls and yowls, Verakina went for his tail coat and yanked on it, while he flapped and squawked and tried to make her let go. As a crowd began to gather, I sidled out of the hiding place, after rubbing my face with the shawl, which I then ditched, with some relief. Verakina yanked hard on the tail coat and the doorman was pulled down the steps. He was furious now, bright red in the face, yelling that he'd chop the mongrel dog into little pieces if she didn't let go of his coat at once.

As I scuttled unseen up the steps, blocked from his view by the crowd, I heard a rending noise as the cloth tore and, completely forgetting his duty or even caution, the doorman threw himself at Verakina, who nimbly side-stepped him, baring her teeth in a grin.

'I'll get you, you evil mutt!' the man was yelling as I slipped in through the unguarded door.

In the foyer, the commotion outside had not passed unnoticed, and I knew I would not either. So I chose the boldest approach. Marching up to the reception desk, I announced, 'Urgent telegram for Dr Nord, to be delivered into his own hands.'

'Give it to me, girl,' said the receptionist.

'No. I cannot, sir. I have strict instructions. It's to be delivered into Dr Nord's hands, and his hands only.'

The receptionist looked at me. For a moment, I thought he was going to have me thrown out. Then his expression changed. He shrugged. 'Very well. Room twenty-three. Second floor.'

As I went past the counter to the lifts, I noticed that in a rack nearby was a row of today's newspapers. One of them was the *Ladies' Journal*. I picked it up. Sure enough, there in the middle of the paper was the next instalment of my story. Shoving the paper in my skirt pocket, I hurried to the lift, ignoring the rather disdainful look on the face of the liftboy. Emerging onto the second floor, I followed the arrow pointing to rooms twenty to twenty-three and had just gone around a turn in the corridor when suddenly a door to one of the rooms opened.

I whipped back around the corner, for I had seen that the man standing on the threshold wore the black uniform of the Special Police!

I felt as if my heart might stop beating. Though he wasn't wearing the black balaclava he had been wearing when I first saw him at the station, and though he wasn't in his wolfish shape as he had been the last time I'd seen him, I was certain that this was the same sinister policeman, and when he turned his head a little to the side, I saw that scar running close to one eye, just as it had in his wolf form, and I knew that my instincts were right.

What was he doing here? And why was he talking to Dr Nord? For even though he spoke in a foreign language and I could not understand his words, I could hear that it was Dr Nord speaking. Could I trust Dr Nord, after this? From the tone of his voice I could tell that he wasn't happy, so surely that meant that he was not an ally of the policeman's . . . Still, I was reluctant, now, to take any more chances and reveal myself to him, not unless I had to . . .

I decided to leave.

Backing away, I hid behind a service trolley and waited until I heard the lift open. Peering out, I saw the policeman get in, and as the lift doors closed, I caught another glimpse of his unmasked face. I have seldom seen a harder or crueler face, with its high cheekbones, thin lips, and livid scar. I could not see his eyes, for he wore tinted glasses, but I shrank from their imagined glare. He was tall, broad-shouldered, and his closely-cropped hair was jet black. And he was younger than I had imagined. Perhaps Lucian's age, perhaps a little older. He carried such an aura of danger and threat that I could all but smell it.

The lift doors closed. I stayed behind the trolley for a moment longer, for I did not want to run the risk of running into that creature downstairs. Just as well I did, for very soon Dr Nord came hurrying down the corridor. Instead of going to the lift, however, he headed for the stairs, close by. Clearly, he, too, did not want to risk running into the policeman again.

An idea seized me. My Ruvenyan friends were clearly not with Dr Nord. I had no way of knowing where they were, but my next-best chance of finding them was to follow Dr Nord. What if he was heading out to meet them?

I had to follow him.

Twenty-Eight

For a gentleman of his age, Dr Nord certainly moved fast. Just as I arrived breathless on the ground floor, he'd already trotted out the front door. I missed seeing which direction he'd gone in and thought I had lost him. Thank heavens for Verakina who, having successfully escaped from the furious doorman, was able to track Dr Nord's scent after I told her which man we were following.

Dr Nord didn't walk for long. Hailing a cab in the next street, he got in. What was I to do now? Could I trust Dr Nord? I made up my mind.

'Verakina, follow us,' I said, and before the driver slammed shut the door of the cab, I jumped in nimbly.

'What on earth . . .!' Dr Nord exclaimed. 'This cab is already taken, you can't just –'

'Please, Dr Nord. It's a matter of life or death. You must help me.'

He stared at me. 'What? Who are –' He broke off with a little gasp. 'You're the girl from the coach.'

'Yes. I am. But that's not really who I am.'

'I beg your pardon?' he said, faintly.

'I'll explain. Please, just tell the driver to go, or we might attract attention.'

He looked at me and nodded, then tapped on the side of the cab. As the vehicle lurched to a start, Dr Nord said, 'Now you must explain.'

Instead of replying, I handed him the newspaper I'd picked up in the hotel, and showed him the middle page.

'What –' he began.

'Have you read it?' I asked.

He looked at me. 'Yes. This morning. Interesting tale. But what –'

'I wrote it,' I said.

He stared. 'But it's signed "Syrena" . . .'

'That's me.'

He shot me a hard glance. 'You mean to say, you have played this little comedy and commandeered this cab just to get an audience with me? I've had some very impertinent approaches from young writers in my time, but this takes the –'

'Dr Nord,' I broke in, cutting him off. 'Do you remember how you said, when I first met you, that a story is never just a story?'

He looked at me warily.

'This is such a story. I am Syrena – but I am also Snow White. In real life.'

There was a stunned silence, in which I thought I'd badly miscalculated my trust of Dr Nord. Why had I chosen this way of telling him? Instinct. But had my instinct been completely wrong?

And then his expression changed. He went pale and gasped. 'Oh my goodness. I saw a portrait, in that department store. That poor girl – that can't be you . . . She is dead . . . And yet you're . . .'

'And yet I'm here,' I said.

'But how . . .? The drowning . . . Your stepmother – Lady Dalmatin . . . It was her?'

'The drowning never happened.' I tapped the newspaper. 'The story I wrote is the truth. Everything else the papers have reported on me is a lie. I need help, Dr Nord. I need you to help me.'

'This is too much,' he said. He was still pale, but there were two spots of red on his cheeks. 'Too much to take in. Too much to believe.'

'Mr Nord, you told me you were an author looking for stories. Here I am, telling you a story. I need you to help me find my frie–'

But Dr Nord interrupted me. 'Tell me what you want. If I can do it, I will.'

I said, slowly, 'This morning you went to see some people I know. At the Wheat Sheaf Inn.'

His eyes widened, but all he said was, 'Correct.'

'It is they who can help me.'

'But how . . .? I mean . . . they're just folklore researchers . . .'

'Please. Can I ask you how you know them?'

'I don't really know them,' he explained. 'I met them for the first time yesterday. I was at the National Library, looking up certain manuscripts – original manuscripts of ancient tales both from Noricia and other parts of the Faustine Empire, and modern retellings of them. Such things, as I've mentioned before, are useful background for my own work. While I was there, they came in –'

'All of them?'

'The young woman – Olga, is it? And her husband and baby son.'

'Not the old woman?'

'No. I didn't know there *was* an old woman. Not until this morning, when I went to the Wheat Sheaf Inn. Olga introduced her as her grandmother. She seemed like an odd body . . . Anyway, at the library, Olga and her husband requested the very same manuscript I was consulting. We fell into conversation. Olga told me they were researching a particular folktale – a modern one, about a man who had stolen a shaman's secrets and become a powerful and dangerous sorcerer, with a wolf familiar. He had passed on his secrets to an apprentice, from Noricia. I was able to tell them I had not seen such a tale in the manuscript and I was not familiar with that story, but that it was possible it might be mentioned in other documents held in the library.

'They ended up looking at some other manuscripts, but I don't think they found anything of interest because when they were leaving, Olga asked me if I would be so kind as to let them know if I found anything. Anything, she said, any kind of reference – even a slight one. Well, the story intrigued me, and I was going to spend the rest of the day in the library anyway, so I said yes. I found nothing in the end, but this morning, on waking, I remembered that extraordinary story that chatterbox Tomzin woman told us on the coach – about a witch's curse on a Norician family – and remembered that had something to do with a wolf. It was a tenuous link, but worth mentioning. So I went to see them.'

'And how did they react?'

'They were very kind, but only mildly interested. It was clear that wasn't quite what they'd been looking for. But then, this afternoon . . .' He broke off. 'Wait a moment. You haven't told me. How do *you* know them? And how can they help you?'

'I know they will help me because they have already helped me once. They saved me from the black wolf,' I said, simply.

'The black wolf?' he repeated, staring at me.

'That policeman at your door – '

'Oh, I see! The man from the Special Police. A Norician term for them, I suppose. But I don't understand. Why is he after you?'

'He's working for my enemy. And it's not a Norician term. He really *is* a wolf. A werewolf, that is.'

'A werewolf! Oh my goodness!' His writer's eyes were full of an expression that mixed excitement with fear. 'I've never met a werewolf in the flesh before.'

'I believe you have,' I said. 'Olga. I'm pretty sure she's one of them.'

His eyes bulged. Before he could speak, I added, 'And look out the window. There is another one following us.'

He gave me a startled glance, then looked out the window. Turning back in, he breathed, 'That grey dog trotting alongside us –'

'Is not a dog,' I finished. 'But she is a friend. Unlike the black wolf. And the old woman – she is no ordinary old woman. She's a feya.'

Dr Nord wiped the sweat off his forehead. 'My goodness. I feel as though I've strayed into one of my own stories. Or a dream.'

'This is no dream, Dr Nord. No made-up story, either.'

'No . . . No . . . Of course not . . . I'm . . . I'm sorry.'

'Tell me, please – what did the black wolf want with you?'

'He asked if I knew the whereabouts of a young man named Lucian Montresor.'

'What?' I exclaimed.

'Of course I knew the name. The family with the witch's curse on them.'

I felt a shiver rippling under my skin. 'So he must somehow have learnt you had been talking about it?'

'I don't think he knew who I had been talking to, only that word had reached him that someone had been speaking about the family curse. I explained. Told him that not only had I no way of knowing the man's whereabouts, that I didn't know him from Adam, and had only heard of him in passing. He told me it was much better if it stayed that way. Lucian Montresor was a dangerous spy and a traitor, he said, and anyone who associated with him would soon find themselves in trouble.'

'The swine!' I said, heatedly.

'Anyway, I managed to convince him that I had no intention of trying to track down the Montresor boy. My only involvement had been to hear a story from a chatterbox on the coach and retell it to some foreign researchers.'

'And he believed you?'

'Yes. I think so. I told him my real name, which he recognised.' He gave me a sideways glance. 'My books are not altogether unknown in Noricia, after all.'

'He was not speaking to you in Norician,' I observed, not wanting to be drawn into a diversion about his books.

'No. He spoke in my own language. In Viklandish. He spoke it well, though with a foreign accent. It didn't really surprise me that he knew the language. The Special Police often get training in foreign languages.'

'Is that where you were going now? Were you going to warn our friends about him?'

'Not exactly *warn* them . . . I just wondered if our mutual friends would be interested in hearing about him; they might be more interested in Lucian Montresor and the wolf if they know that he is sought after.'

At that moment, the cab lurched violently as the driver came to a sudden, jarring stop. We were flung against each other, painfully. As we recovered our balance, we heard loud voices outside, booming in the quiet of night. I poked my head out of the window. There was an accident just ahead, blocking the road. It was a bad one by the looks of it. I could see vehicles twisted together, could hear injured horses screaming.

'We're not going to get any further by cab,' I said. 'We'll have to go on foot. Come on, Dr Nord.' I added, because he looked pale and shaky, 'I'll help you get out.'

'Thank you,' he said, but grimaced as I helped him out. 'I think I might have twisted my ankle, though – I don't think I'll get very far on foot.'

I looked around. There was an all-night cafe not far away. 'Why don't you wait there and rest until your ankle is better? I'll go to the Wheat Sheaf Inn. I need to speak to Olga and her family. The feya – she is the only one who can help me.'

'After what you've told me, I hardly think it's safe for you to be out on the streets, especially at night – you don't know who could be hiding, or where,' he said, fretfully. 'What if Lady Dalmatin should find you? Or the black wolf?'

'They won't,' I said grimly. 'I'll take great care that they won't. And if they do – why, I have Verakina. They'll not take me easily.' Verakina had kept pace with us, and bared her teeth just then, as if to highlight what I'd said.

Dr Nord winced a little and looked away from the teeth. 'Of course. Yes. But I am still concerned that –'

'Don't be concerned for me, Dr Nord. I will be very careful. I promise.'

And so saying, I helped him to a seat in the cafe, and left, Verakina at my heels.

Back at the Wheat Sheaf Inn, however, I was disappointed once again.

'I'm sorry, but they're out,' said the receptionist. It was a man, this time – the young woman I'd seen before must have finished her shift. 'No, I don't know where they are.' He had not shown a flicker of recognition of me, which I was grateful for.

'May I leave them a message? It's very important,' I said, and when he conceded that it was indeed possible, I hurriedly scrawled a note passing on Dr Nord's message about the black wolf, and adding my suspicions about Belladonna's true nature. I pleaded for their help in exposing her, in destroying her. I put the letter in an envelope, sealed it, and left it with the receptionist, who promised faithfully that he would give it to them as soon as they came back.

Verakina was clearly tense as we retraced our steps to the cafe where we'd left Dr Nord. Indeed, she had been looking more and more nervous in the last little while, and her fur bristled from time to time as though picking up the scent of danger in the air. As we headed rapidly through the maze of back streets, her nose stayed up, sniffing at smells that were well beyond my feeble human senses.

Just before we reached the cafe, Verakina halted and stood stock-still, her green eyes glowing, her ears pricked, her fur standing on end, as if she had been struck by lightning. Suddenly, she threw back her head and gave an almighty howl that echoed across the square and froze my blood. In the next instant, she sprinted away from me and down the street. What could I do but follow?

The further we ran, the surer I became of our destination. We were heading straight for Moonlight Boulevard, straight for my family home.

Twenty-Nine

Of course I went after her. I didn't even think about it. I knew that if Verakina was reacting like that, it could only mean one thing: that the Prince we both loved, each in our own way, was in the gravest danger. And Verakina's keen nose, so much keener in her animal than her human shape, had smelt where the threat was. Dalmatin Mansion, my family home. Lucian must have been captured, most likely trying to save Master Kinberg, who Belladonna had told me would be tortured.

It didn't matter to me that I, too, was in the gravest danger. It didn't matter that the whole of Lepmest might see a dishevelled girl, with a face that looked strangely familiar, running like a hare not from a wolf, but towards one. The time for hiding and secrecy was over. No more plans. Just action.

We reached Moonlight Boulevard. Our house was half-way down. I ran up the steps and pounded on the door with all my might, while Verakina stayed close by me.

The door opened. And there stood Drago. Our eyes met. He went white, as white as the bandage around his head, as white as the pillars at the door.

'Yes, it is me, returned from the dead, from the two deaths your mistress sought for me,' I said, bitterly, pushing past him, as he seemed incapable of movement or speech. 'You will take me to where they have Lucian. Now.'

He was still staring at me, not moving.

'I'm not afraid of her anymore. I have powerful allies now. Verakina!'

She growled, deep in her throat, her eyes glowing like emeralds. Her fur was on end, and she looked somehow bigger than she had only minutes before. Drago took an involuntary step backwards.

'She will rip you to shreds in an instant,' I warned. 'I only have to say one word.' I did not know if Verakina would really do that but she looked mightily impressive and Drago clearly did not look as if he was about to question what I had claimed. There was something different about him, I thought, something shrunken, something that I might have said was fear. I guessed that Belladonna would not have forgiven his betrayal, but may have continued using him because it suited her. He must know that he was living on borrowed time.

'If you bring me in, think how grateful she'll be,' I added.

He gave me a strange look then. Was it pity? Or relief? I did not know. 'As you wish,' he said, tonelessly. 'Follow me.'

How strange it was, to be back in my own home, yet to feel as though I was in enemy territory! But I did not waste much time on these feelings, for all I could think of was how I was going to save Lucian. It was all very well to declare that I wasn't afraid of Belladonna. But that wasn't the same as knowing what to do.

We came to the room that had once been my father's study. The door was closed, but now that we were closer, I could hear confused noises going on behind it. A murmur of eager voices and a low snarl of pain. Drago looked at me.

'Take me in. At once.'

He shrugged. Knocked. No answer. He knocked again.

'What is it?' Belladonna called angrily. 'I said we were not to be disturbed!'

'My lady,' Drago began, 'this is urgent. Most urgent . . .'

'Tell her,' I hissed. 'Tell her it's me!'

'Lady . . . Your stepdaughter, my lady. She is here. With a . . . with a creature.'

The door was flung open. Belladonna stood there. I could not help recoiling, for she looked terrifying, her beautiful face twisted into a mask of fury and, dear God, a splash of blood on her cheek and a thin-bladed dagger in her hands.

'Why, it really *is* you. You little fool,' she said, and smiled. She looked down at Verakina. 'And I see you've brought a little friend,' she added. 'Quite a party. Do come in and join us.' When Drago made as if to leave, she hissed, 'And you too, my dear loyal servant. You come in, too.' She stepped aside, ushering us in, and then closed the door behind us.

For an instant, I could see hardly anything. The heavy curtains were drawn and the room was very dark, except for a faint light burning in a corner. I could just make out vague shapes – including the only one that mattered to me, the twisted shape of a man lying very still, huddled on the floor, face down. Beside me, Verakina howled, and tried to make straight for him; but Belladonna moved swiftly, touching her just briefly, and Verakina froze, turning as still as a statue. I knew that if I made one step towards the Prince, Belladonna would do the same to me. And I knew already what that meant. So instead, I stayed by the door.

Trying to keep my voice steady, I said, 'Let him go.'

'How touching,' said Belladonna. 'A life for a life, is that it? Let him go and I can have your life instead? The classic bargain. Always works in stories. You think that this is just a story? Is that what you think?'

'I'm not here to duel in words,' I said, 'and I'm not offering you my life, either. I'm offering you *yours*. I'm offering this to you, once and once only: leave this room, leave this house, leave this city, right now, and never return. That is the only way you can save yourself.'

I heard an indrawn breath. Drago's? But it might as well have been mine, for I'd stunned myself as well – I had no idea where these rash words had come from.

Belladonna was silent for a heartbeat, then she laughed softly and said, 'Well, you have courage, I'll give you that. And if I don't accept this bargain of yours?'

'Then you will die,' I said.

'Really? Is that so?' She came closer to me, and I smelt the strange, sweetish odour of her breath. The smell of cruel magic. It came off her in waves, and I felt as though it were seeking me out, curling into my mind, my body, my whole being like tendrils of evil smoke.

'It is,' I said, trying to stay calm. 'Let Lucian go. Leave this place and never return, or you will die.'

She laughed again. 'Poor little fool,' she whispered. 'I think it's time to end this charade.' And then, quite suddenly, she turned up the lamp, so that soon the room was bright as day.

For a moment I was too dazzled to take anything in. Then, as my vision returned, my attention was drawn away from the huddled shape lying on the ground and to across the room, when I saw a man fling his arms up to shield his face against the bright light. It made no sense, no sense at all . . .

'Lucian,' I whispered. 'Lucian, I don't understand. Why are you . . .'

But I could not finish. I looked from the handsome face of Lucian Montresor to the unconscious man huddled on the floor, and the dreadful beginning of knowledge plonked down in my belly like a stone. I had been wrong. So wrong. So terribly, stupidly, horribly wrong, and the pain of it seared through me.

'Surprised, Bianca?' said Belladonna. 'I thought you might be. You are such a trusting fool. A handsome face, a sad story, and you fall for it hook, line and sinker. Lucian's been working for me for quite some time now. Even before the ball. How would he have been able to come to the ball, when it was the time of hunter's moon, if someone had not given him a powerful spell to suppress his wolf side?'

With a shock, I remembered seeing Belladonna talking to Lucian the night of the ball. In my innocence, I'd thought she'd been warning him off. Instead, she'd been briefing her spy . . .

'I had no choice,' he burst out, his eyes not on her but on me. 'No choice! You must understand.'

'Oh, she won't, Lucian,' said my stepmother, with a mocking smile. 'That kind never does.'

'I was forced to do it, Bianca,' he burst out. 'I tried to warn you. I didn't want you to be hurt. I tried to tell you to leave Lepmest, but you wouldn't listen . . .'

'Touching. But I don't think her heart will be touched, Lucian. Because she doesn't care what you say. The scales have dropped from her eyes.'

She was right. Oh, so right. I saw him for what he was, now. A coward, an informer. It was Lucian who had warned Belladonna that her underground house of horrors had been discovered. Lucian who had told her who Master Kinberg was. Lucian who had betrayed me at every step. And worse: for he had most likely actively participated in Belladonna's crimes, I thought, remembering the beggars' tale of the brown-haired, brown-eyed man who had lured them into the trap. Once again I had been fooled. Once again I had thought I had loved someone – only to turn back around and realise that the person I loved had never been there.

He whispered, 'If you only knew what it's like – being cursed . . . Living with that thing gnawing inside you . . . When somebody offers you a cure – when you learn that it is possible and that you can be made whole again – then you will do anything – *anything* – to keep that blessed state safe. You would. Anyone would.'

So that was how she'd done it. That was how she'd bound him to her. A cure. The curse lifted. He had paid for his cure with the lives of others. He would always be in her debt, because he would always want to stay human, always want to keep the curse at bay. And he would be her most faithful servant, because he wanted what only she could give him. It was pitiful. It was disgusting.

'It must have been very annoying for you that I didn't do as I was told,' I said. 'That I didn't stay put, that you had to chase me all over town.' The voice that left me sounded strong and spiteful, but inside my heart was breaking at having found that my trust was once again misplaced.

He went red. 'No! You don't understand! I hoped that you might . . . that you might become properly afraid. That you might run. Far away. Yes, I was working for Lady Dalmatin, but I tried to keep you out of danger! I came to the station because I heard the City Police had spotted you! I told them about Master Kinberg but not about the safe house! And at my apartment . . . Don't you remember? I told you to leave, but you wouldn't! I couldn't understand why you wouldn't!'

'Because she's got what you've never had, my dear Lucian,' said Belladonna. 'She has courage. Not that it will do her any good, of course.'

I turned away from them. I did not care anymore what either of them said. I had trusted them both, once. And they had both betrayed me. But the worst of it was that it was I who had been the real traitor. The real destroyer. The stupid fool whose selfish arrogance and prejudice had blinded her to the truth. The truth about my real protector, the real Prince, who had paid the ultimate price for my blind folly.

Dropping to my knees beside the still figure on the floor, I touched his shoulder, gently, through the thick black serge of his Secret Police uniform. He did not move. I whispered, 'I'm sorry . . . I'm so sorry . . .' The stone in my belly was turning to molten lead now, but my head was spinning so much I thought I might faint. 'Oh, Prince of Outlaws, I'm so sorry . . .'

Belladonna sneered. 'Prince of Outlaws, indeed! Did your so-called Prince ever tell you the truth? He has been one of the Special Police's most zealous hunters, an obedient, unquestioning, ruthless servant of the State, delivering scores of people to their deaths – even one or two who later turned out to be innocent.' She saw my expression, and smiled. 'No, I didn't think so. He wouldn't tell you that. He'd want you to think he was a shining hero when all along, that ridiculous crusade to save the dregs of society was just a feeble attempt to salve his pathetic conscience.'

At the haven, when I'd asked him how he'd found those documents, he'd told me that he knew how to find things. And he'd said that if I ever knew the truth about him, I would recoil from him. I'd imagined his secret to be something quite other than this, but now I knew what it was, I could not stop the feeling that I'd had since the moment I met him in the haven. I realised with sharp relief that I had never loved Lucian. At the ball, I had *wanted* to love Lucian; I had liked the idea of being in love. When I saw him back in Lepmest, I had never felt love for him. It had been the Prince who I had loved. He was kind. He was courageous. I didn't care about what he had done in another life. I loved the man he had become.

'It doesn't matter,' I said, very softly, those words only for him. 'It doesn't alter what I feel.' My heart clenched with the terrible pain of knowing it was all too late. 'You might have served the State,' I whispered, 'but you never sold your soul. Never.'

Belladonna laughed. 'A soul! What is it but a shield for the weak. A miserable consolation for the defeated. A thing that can be used and twisted at will.'

'Of course you would think that,' I said to her. 'Mock as you will, but I know the truth. I know about the crimes you have committed and the people you have murdered. I know about your boundless corruption and your treasonous plans to overthrow the Duke.' I saw Lucian's face clench in shock at those last words, but Drago's stayed expressionless. He knew all those things; Lucian must have only blindly followed. 'And I also know that you are not even human, but –'

'You are tiresome, and this has gone on quite long enough,' said Belladonna, and she touched me on the shoulder. At once I felt my throat begin to seize up and my limbs clench, but this time I knew what was to come, and I pitted all the desperate strength of my mind, all the fury of my grief and determination, against the force of her magic. I fought hard but was losing the fight – when all at once I saw the Prince's right hand fluttering, very slightly. Reaching over, I clasped his hand, and this time I *felt* the movement, slight, but there, most definitely there. He was still alive! An astonishing feeling flooded through my whole being, rushing through my veins, my heart and my mind, dissolving Belladonna's paralysing spell like the sun's rays on ice.

I knelt there, triumphant that I had the strength to fight Belladonna's spell, but my triumph was short-lived for a moment later, something hard and heavy came down on the back of my neck.

A shattering pain exploded in my skull and I fell into darkness.

Thirty

I came to with a groan. The back of my head throbbed, my tongue felt thick in my mouth, an unpleasantly musty smell filled my nostrils and my eyes hurt when I tried to focus in the semi-darkness. I had no idea where I was at first, only that the solitary light shone in from under an iron door. The floor was of beaten earth, and the walls of stone. I was probably in some kind of cellar. Or dungeon. I knew such a place did not exist in my childhood home – we must have been moved to someplace else.

I wasn't alone. As my eyes got used to the grey light, I saw Verakina, no longer in her wolf-shape, bareheaded and dressed in ragged clothes. She was crouched protectively over something – no, someone – and as she heard me move and she looked up, I saw the pain etched like the cuts of a knife in her face.

'Is he . . .' I could not finish, the words scratching my throat.

She shook her head, but I could see from her face that though he was not dead – not yet – she did not hold much hope that he would survive.

'Verakina,' I murmured, 'I am so sorry . . .'

She shook her head again and looked away, but not before I saw a tear roll down her cheek.

'I know you must blame me,' I said. I swallowed. 'And you are right. It is my fault he is here. My fault you are here. My fault that everything he built – everything that you and the others have made – will be destroyed. They know where the haven is now . . .'

'Hush,' she said. 'Hush, child. It doesn't matter if they know. The others will be safe. They have gone from the old haven, and they have taken the new people with them. Our Prince arranged that, just as he arranged for me to rescue you from the glass coffin. And he gave himself up to the witch so she might be distracted from watching over you. It is not your fault. It was his choice, and mine. Freely made.' She looked up at me, her eyes shining with tears, and beckoned me to her side.

I could not help a gasp of distress when I saw him up close. They'd beaten him severely. There were gashes and bruises on his face and hands, and the scar I'd seen when I'd glimpsed him in the lift had been reopened with Belladonna's knife, so that it was crusted over with dried blood. His eyes were closed, the long dark lashes lying on his bruised cheeks, and his close-cropped black hair was sticky with dirt and sweat.

When I'd glimpsed his strong-featured face back when I had been searching for Dr Nord, I'd thought it hard and cruel. But now I saw only nobility and suffering.

The Prince was breathing, but only just. I could hardly see the rise and fall of his chest.

Verakina had tried to make him comfortable, with her headscarf balled up under his head, to make a pillow, and her shabby coat covering him. But it was clear that the hope that had flared in me when I'd felt his hand move against mine was just a brief burst of light. Now he had gone back into the darkness, and the pain of his most likely mortal injury knifed into me so that I thought I would scream with the horror of it.

But I did not scream. And I pushed the horror away. It was long past time for that.

'Come, sit by his side, too,' said Verakina, gently, and I did as I was bid. 'Take his right hand. I'll take his left.'

Verakina was far wiser than me. She did not try to offer false hope, or lose time in futile regret. She knew that all we could do now was give our Prince a few small comforts to ease his passing. Nothing else really mattered but the warm touch of loving friends.

So I sat next to him and took his right hand. Verakina took the other. His hand was cool. Very cool. Fighting back the panic and grief that threatened to rise into my belly, I held on gently but tightly, willing my own warmth into him, praying silently with all my might, begging for a miracle. But his hand stayed unmoving and grew no warmer than before.

Suddenly, there was a rattle of keys and a thumping, and the next moment, the iron door crashed open. Drago stood on the threshold. He was carrying a tray on which reposed a plate of sandwiches.

He looked at us, but did not speak. Placing the tray just inside the door, he turned to go. Perhaps it was the knowledge that we had nothing more to lose or perhaps it was the last ember of hope, but I found myself saying, 'Supper for the condemned, is it?'

He looked at me and shrugged.

'What is to be our fate?'

He shrugged again.

'We deserve at least to know, Drago.' I could feel Verakina's surprised stillness even without looking at her.

'You are to be tried,' he said at last. 'Tomorrow morning.'

'Tried? By who? For what?'

'By the Duke himself.' He saw my expression. 'You have all been charged with high treason, murder and black magic. The tailor would have been too, if he'd survived interrogation. Not that he gave any useful information.' Poor Master Kinberg, I thought, sadly. He'd paid a high price for his loyalty. 'And because this is such an unusual and extreme case,' Drago went on, 'there will be no jury. Only the Duke, acting as Grand Judge. The evidence is strong against you all.'

'Ah,' I said. 'Of course.' Of course Belladonna would know what lies to spin; she'd had practice enough for that. A pause. 'And of course we know what the outcome will be.'

He said nothing, only turned to leave.

'Drago,' I said. 'Please – just one more thing. I have always wondered. You have done many terrible things in the service of your lady. Yet this one thing you did not do: you did not kill me in the forest, as she told you to do. Why?'

He looked at me, briefly, then lowered his eyes. He did not reply.

'I'll answer, then,' I said. 'You did not kill me in the forest because you were uneasy about what you'd been asked to do . . . And that is also why you are here, right now, bringing us supper. I can't believe your mistress would have asked you to do that.'

He shot me a quick glance.

'You are uneasy about this too. About the trial.'

At first I thought he would not answer. Then he said, 'Perhaps. But don't imagine my uneasiness is for your sake.'

'I don't,' I said. 'In the forest, it wasn't just pity that stayed your hand. It was also that you thought my death would serve nothing useful, and you had an instinct that it might, in fact, bring great danger. You are a hunter for a reason. You can sense when things aren't right. Belladonna knew that once, too, but the scent of blood has gone to her head. The arrogance of power. She is over-reaching herself and you know it. We both know she is on the edge of the precipice. One wrong move and she will fall off. And you with her.'

I saw him swallow.

'You still have an instinct about me,' I went on, pressing my point home. 'You tried to stop me going into my father's study because of that. And you feel – no, you know – that this trial is too great a risk.' I took a deep breath. 'Indeed, you know that if it goes ahead, it will end in your death. And hers. But there is a way out of it. Go to the Villa Valverd hotel. Ask for a man called Dr Nord. Tell him to contact our mutual friends at once. He will know what you mean.'

Our eyes met. His expression was hard as stone. Unreadable.

'You are quite mad,' he said. Then he turned and flung himself out of the door, slamming it shut behind him. The key rattled in the lock, and we heard his footsteps moving away before silence fell again.

'Angels in heaven,' whispered Verakina, 'what was that about?'

I shook my head. 'I don't know. It just . . . It just came out.'

I felt numb, yet oddly calm. Verakina didn't say any more. She didn't have to. I could see the expression in her eyes. I had tried a desperate ploy and it hadn't worked. Of course it hadn't. Drago was not a slave, not bound like Lucian. His ties to Belladonna were those of true loyalty, and his hands were almost as bloodstained as hers. I'd been right about his unease. But I'd been wrong to think that he would act on it a second time.

'That's a little tight.' It was a thread of sound, hardly even a whisper, and yet it made my pulse race, for it wasn't Verakina's voice . . .

I looked down at the Prince of Outlaws. His eyes were open. Hazel eyes with golden lights in them, still shadowed by pain but alive, most definitely alive.

Vaguely, I heard Verakina's gasp of delight, but could make not a sound myself. My eyes were riveted on his, my body tense as a bowstring, my heart thumping so hard it seemed as though it might jump out of my chest.

'Bianca . . .'

He had spoken my name and still I couldn't speak. How could I let myself be taken by the sudden flood of happiness that flowed through me, the sudden rebirth of hope?

The Prince struggled to sit up. Turning his glance away from me and towards Verakina, he whispered, 'I am sorry, dear Verakina. I am so sorry I dragged you into this.'

'Why?' said Verakina. Her voice was hoarse with a mix of tears and joy. 'I was honoured to help. I only wish I could have been more –'

'You are the bravest of the brave,' he said. 'I know how the transformation frightens you, yet you never flinched from the task of turning when you didn't have to.' He saw my puzzlement. 'Hunter's moonlight aids transformation, makes it almost impossible to stop – but a true werewolf can change any time they choose.'

'Yes. And I will tell you the truth,' she said. 'Listen. Please. I must say this. What use would I have been, in getting the others to safety? I know neither how to fight nor how to find hidden paths. I could only be useful to Bianca, and only in my wolf form. But I have learnt much from my recent experiences. I had been repressing my wolf-instinct for too long. Letting myself roam as a wolf had many benefits I had not considered. I learnt that I can pass as a dog and sneak unnoticed into places that no person – indeed, no wolf – can enter. But more importantly, I learnt that being afraid of what you are serves the purposes only of those who would turn you into a slave. For the first time in my life, I am not afraid – either of others or of myself. And that is down to you. To both of you.'

'No,' I croaked, finding my voice at last. 'I had nothing to do with it ... And without me, you would not be here – neither of you would be . . .' I choked and turned my head away so that they would not see my tears. 'I have been such a fool, and because of it I have caused so much suffering . . .'

'Bianca.' His voice was getting stronger. 'Please, look at me. Tell me if you know me. *Really* know me.'

I knew him – he was the true Prince of Outlaws. What could he mean? Swallowing, I turned my head slowly and looked at him. And for the first time I saw something in those eyes, something in that expression that prompted a memory, of a time long ago, of a laughing young boy who looked . . . But it wasn't possible. It couldn't be. That boy was dead, he had died in the same house fire that had turned my beautiful friend Margy into a shadow of what she had once been . . . And *his* eyes had been brown – the Prince's were hazel, almost green . . . No, it could not be . . . And yet . . .

My breath was tight in my chest, my heart no longer pounding but instead seemingly clenched in an iron grip. I whispered, the words dragged out of me, 'No, it can't be . . . It can't be . . . Oh, Rafiel! They said you were dead . . .'

'And so I thought I was,' said the young man who had once been my dear childhood friend and confidant. 'I know Tollie told you about the house fire. I did not know that Margy had escaped. I was told that all my family had been burned to death, and that I had been pulled out of the rubble, burned from the heat and sick from the smoke. I thought that I would die, too . . .'

I could hardly believe it. How could the Prince of Outlaws be the same man as my friend, my old playmate,

Rafiel? And how could he also be the creature I'd called the black wolf? I was certain that had been him . . . Those eyes . . .

'You've changed,' I said, helplessly. 'Your face – it has changed. So much . . .'

'And even more, now,' he said, and all at once, an extraordinary smile lightened his poor bruised features. 'I must look a hideous sight indeed.'

'Stop it, Rafiel,' I murmured, a sweet lightness bubbling in me like champagne as I spoke his name. 'You always did like teasing me, I remember.'

'And I remember, too,' he said, quietly. Our eyes met again and I felt a little thrill ripple up my spine. To cover it, I said, 'Margy . . . Where . . .?'

'She will be all right,' he said, and smiled again. 'Thanks to you.'

'And the others?'

'All safe. They are in the mountains now. Nobody will ever find them.' His gaze darkened. 'All except for poor Master Kinberg.'

But I hardly heard, too taken up with the wonder of finding him again. 'Rafiel, in all that time . . . That day I met you in the haven . . . Why didn't you tell me?'

He looked at me and said, softly, 'It was night when I first saw you again, Bianca . . .'

Suddenly an image came into my mind, an image I'd half-forgotten. A night when I'd awoken to find a gentle, healing hand hovering over my wounded ankle. I'd thought it had been my father's ghost.

'So that was you,' I breathed. 'Why . . . Oh, why didn't you tell me?'

'I was afraid,' he said, simply.

'But what were you afraid of? I would . . . I would have been so glad to know it was you. So glad. I . . .' I bit my lip. 'I missed you so much, Rafiel. You – and Margy. You were my friends. I was so young . . . I didn't understand why you'd had to go. If only . . . If only I had done something to stop Belladonna, to stop her from forcing you to leave. I could have done it somehow . . .'

'How could you? What could you have done?' he said, gently. 'You were a child. Just as Margy was. Me? I was fifteen. I was no longer really a child, and I knew your stepmother did not want us around you. We were not good enough to associate with a Dalmatin. And I knew that eventually you'd think so, too. That is the way of the world.'

'No!' I stammered. 'That would never have happened . . .'

'You ask me why I was afraid to tell you,' he went on. 'After I recovered from the injuries from the fire, I left Noricia. I could not bear to be here – I had lost all the people I cared about – my friends, my family. I did not come back for some time. But when I did come back, I made sure to look for news of you, to make sure you were safe. Occasionally I did hear news – saw a photograph of you and your father and stepmother in the papers. I wondered what you'd do, if I came to see you. But I did not do it, because I knew those childhood days were over. We could not be friends. So seeing you again that night – especially after Verakina and the others had told me what had been done to your father, what had been done to you – it was more than I could bear. I had put my old life behind me, had hardened my heart against all the memories . . .

'I had made a new life for myself. Two lives, if you like. I see, now, that in neither of those was I truly Rafiel. Each was only a role, a cipher, a shadow. A zealous policeman. A hooded protector. I'd told myself that one was redeeming the other. But when I saw you, I knew that everything was hollow. A sham. I'd lost myself, long ago. I knew that you'd see that, if I told you. And I knew it would break my heart – the little I had left.'

'Oh, Rafiel,' I said, and took his hand once again. It was warm now. Almost as warm as mine. 'Do not say such things . . . Do not. You have a greater heart than anyone in this world.'

'And so you have!' said Verakina, vigorously. 'Where would we be, if it weren't for you? Without the haven, I'd be dead – and so would Grim and Lisbet and Rasmus, Carlo, Mattias, Tofer and all the outcasts you have sheltered!'

'And if there'd been no haven, I would have wandered in the forest till I died from hunger and exhaustion, or wild beasts killed me. Tell me, Rafiel,' I said, determined to know everything, 'when I was in that glass box – before Verakina came – you came to that room. I saw your eyes – in the face of a black wolf. A . . . A black werewolf . . .'

Verakina burst out, 'You think the Prince is a werewolf? Like me? Oh no. No, no. You are quite wrong. The Prince is no shapeshifter.'

'You're going to have to stop calling me "the Prince", Verakina,' said Rafiel, with a small smile.

She shrugged. 'I am old enough to call you what I like, young man.'

'There, that's better already,' said Rafiel, lightly.

I could feel the life rising in him now, stronger than ever, and rejoiced in it even as I wondered at the strangeness of what I'd learnt. But there was much more to learn, and I had to know it.

'No, Bianca, not a werewolf,' continued Rafiel. 'Verakina is right. I am no shapeshifter. Not in the usual meaning of the term. It's true I was there in that room and yet at the same time I was not – and that is why I could not help you myself, why I had to send Verakina. I wasn't the wolf – I had sent my spirit-wolf.'

I stared at him. 'I don't understand.'

Verakina clicked her tongue. 'Have you never heard, then, of the Northern shamans and how they can travel in the shape of spirit-beasts?'

I'd heard vague tales of such things but had never imagined them to be true. I remembered the look of that black wolf, how his fur had shimmered unnaturally, how he had somehow seemed to disappear from the hall, and could not help a little shiver.

Rafiel saw it and smiled a little sadly. 'I can see why you might recoil. A werewolf is one thing to grasp, but a spirit-wolf – that is altogether different.' He paused. 'You said before that my face had changed. You meant my eyes.'

'Yes,' I said, swallowing.

'The change of colour – it is a side effect of spirit-travel. Temporary, I had read. But it proved not to be.'

'But who . . . How . . .' My mind was whirling, imagining Rafiel in the frozen Northern wastes, crouched at the feet of some ancient shaman with tangled hair and feather-and-claw necklaces around his neck.

'The liquid that Verakina brought for me, that broke the spell,' I asked. 'What was it?'

'It was water from Nellia's Spring, up in the mountains near our old haven. And flowers of plants harvested at hunter's moon. And a few other things . . .'

'But how did you learn to make it? How did you learn to create a spirit-wolf?'

'I have learnt many things,' he said.

I looked at him and my heart pounded. He didn't seem to want to say any more, at this moment anyway. 'I owe you my life,' I said. 'More than once now.'

'You owe me nothing. There is no debt between us,' he said, softly.

At that moment, we heard the rattle of keys in the door and the sound of voices. One was Drago's, the other one was another servant's.

'Lie down and close your eyes,' I whispered to Rafiel, obeying an instinct I could not explain.

He shot me a glance but did as I asked. Grabbing the scarf from where it lay bunched on the ground, I placed it gently over his face. Verakina gave me a startled look, then nodded as I gestured for her to crouch by Rafiel, next to me. With my head in my hands, I keened softly, my heart racing.

Thirty-One

The door opened with a clang. I heard heavy footsteps. Two sets. A voice – Drago's – said, 'What the blazes is going on?'

We kept up our keening.

'Stop that noise,' hissed Drago. In the next instant I was yanked up, painfully. He looked at my red, contorted face, then at Rafiel, lying as still as death, the scarf over his face.

'What the devil . . .' Drago pulled the scarf off and looked at Rafiel's face. He put a finger to his neck to feel the pulse. I held my breath. He would know, now, that we were faking.

Drago straightened. He looked at me and said, 'When did this happen?'

'Only a few minutes ago,' I said, quavering.

'Yes. He's still warm, so he can't have been dead long,' said Drago, tonelessly. I did not dare to say anything, or to look at Verakina.

Drago turned to the man who was with him, who was dressed in the uniform of the Duke's guard. 'Go and get a stretcher from the stockroom. Now.'

'But if he's dead, there's no need. We can just –'

'Do as you are told. Or do you want me to tell his grace the Duke that you are less than willing to do your job?'

That's where we are, I thought. The Duke's palace.

'No, of course not. My apologies, sir.' The man scuttled out and for a moment no-one moved.

Drago got up and half-closed the door. 'You have precisely two minutes before he comes back,' he said. 'How bad is he, really?'

'Not dead,' said Rafiel, sitting up, 'and not as injured as your mistress thought. You know how to blunt the blows.'

The two men's eyes met. 'I don't know what you mean,' said Drago, as expressionless as ever. 'Now, instead of jawing, get out. Take the steps leading down, not up. There's a grate. Beyond that, there are steps to the river. Your friends will be waiting there. Go. I'm going to pretend you knocked me out. Lock the door behind you. Throw the key in the river. That'll buy you a little extra time.'

I stared at him.

'I'm not doing it for you, girl. You know that. Now go, before I change my mind!' he snapped.

We took him at his word. I helped Rafiel to his feet. He was a little unsteady at first, but it was remarkable how quickly he seemed to recover as we slipped out of the room, closed and locked the door behind us, and hurried away, down the steps and along a short passage. All the time, we were expecting to hear running footsteps or shouts of alarm. But no-one came after us.

We arrived at the grate Drago had told us of. We stopped. I could hear the lapping of water, below. We looked at each other. Had Drago lied? Was there an ambush waiting for us? Had Belladonna changed her mind about a trial and decided to just be rid of us straightaway? Was our escape to end in a watery death?

'We have no choice but to trust him,' said Rafiel.

He was right: we could not go back.

It took a few seconds to shift the grate but then we were through, and entered into another passage that led to some steps, going down into darkness.

We started down the steps – carefully, for they were slippery. We were halfway down when we heard the soft clapping of oars against water, and in the next instant, a voice, whispering, 'I'm just bringing it alongside.'

'It's all right,' I told the others, relief surging through me as I recognised the voice of Olga's husband. 'It's Andel. He's a friend.'

The rowboat drew up alongside us and Andel helped us get in. The water sparkled in the early-morning light.

'Oh, Andel,' I said, 'I am so very glad to see you.'

'And I you,' said Andel. 'When Dr Nord came post-haste to tell us that a stranger had informed him you were being kept prisoner, we knew at once that we had to act quickly. Sorry the boat's not exactly big, but it's the best I could do at such short notice.'

'It is the best boat in the world,' I said warmly.

'Here,' he said to Rafiel, when we were all settled, 'put this over that uniform of yours.' He threw a coat at Rafiel. It was a heavy old tweed coat and rather shabby, but it was full length, and it covered the telltale black serge well.

'Thank you for thinking of that,' said Rafiel.

'Couldn't have you attracting more attention than we have to – those bruises on your face are bad enough,' Andel said, pulling away from the steps with sure strokes of the oar. 'I'm taking you to the quay near the Wheat Sheaf Inn. Olga will meet us there. She's arranging travel for you.'

'You're all taking a great risk for us strangers,' said Rafiel.

'What is life if not a risk?' said Andel. 'And strangers are only people who have not yet become friends.' He looked at Rafiel and Verakina. 'It is good to meet you, friends. I am Andel.'

They introduced themselves and then, as he rowed, we told him briefly what had happened. Andel nodded, listening intently but also watching the currents of the river carefully.

The river had been diverted into this underground passage for quite a stretch under the Duke's palace. But eventually we reached the end of it, and emerged into a quiet section of water not far from the Swan Gardens, one of the most beautiful gardens in Lepmest. At this time, in the early morning, they were deserted, and the park looked enchanted.

As we passed the bend in the Swan Gardens and drew away swiftly eastwards, I remembered three things that I had been told, and suddenly they came together in my mind. Olga had told me they were looking for a sorcerer's apprentice. Dr Nord had mentioned that it was rumoured that the sorcerer had a wolf familiar. And Rafiel somehow knew how to cast spells and create magical potions . . .

I had to warn Rafiel. I did not care if he was the man they were hunting. I did not care to know why. All I cared about was that he was safe.

'We'll need to halt here for a moment, Andel,' I said, hoping my voice didn't sound too shaky.

'There's no time,' said Andel. 'Every moment we delay means –'

'It will be very quick,' I said. 'Something I hid over there,' and I pointed in the direction of a bed of rushes. 'It's very important.'

I could feel Verakina's and Rafiel's surprise, but hoped they might trust me enough to understand I must have a reason for this. Or even that they might believe I really had hidden something important. Whatever the case, they did not argue, so with some reluctance, Andel steered the boat in the direction I had pointed.

'Three pairs of eyes are better than one,' I said to Verakina and Rafiel, as we drew closer to the rushes. 'Will you help me look?'

'Of course,' said Rafiel, calmly.

'You'll have to hurry,' said Andel rather fretfully, as we got out of the boat and splashed towards the reeds.

I nodded. 'No more than a minute or two, I promise.' And I headed in a determined way into the thickest part of the rushes, where I knew he wouldn't be able to see us from his boat. The others followed without a word, Rafiel still limping a little.

As soon as we were deep in the rushes, I crouched down, as if I were looking for something. Rafiel and Verakina followed suit.

'What are you doing?' Rafiel whispered.

'You have to know,' I said, and quickly explained.

It was Verakina who spoke first, when I had finished.

'Bianca! You surely can't believe such a thing! Whoever these people are after, it surely cannot be –'

'It is,' interrupted Rafiel. He had gone pale. 'It must be me they are looking for. But they are wrong about this, at least: I was never the sorcerer's apprentice. I never knew he *was* a sorcerer. I knew him as Messir Durant, the great explorer and adventurer.'

'But how?' I asked.

'You remember that I told you that after I recovered from my injuries in the fire, I left Noricia? Well, I ended up in Palume, and got work in the household of Messir Durant. It was there I heard about his trips to the Northern lands. I heard about the shamans, and how they could travel in spirit in the form of a beast. Something in me came alive at the whole notion, and so I took to reading a good deal about it, borrowing books from the public library about the Northern lands and the custom of the Northerners. My own spirit was so heavy in me. I longed for peace, but even at night I could not escape terrible dreams. I thought that maybe if my spirit could break from its human shackles to roam free, then perhaps . . .' He paused, and in the expression in his eyes I read all the pain and loneliness he had suffered, and my heart was wrung with sorrow and love.

Timidly, I touched him on the arm. 'You don't need to go on, Rafiel. I know that nothing you have done can have been wrong. I just wanted to warn you –'

'Oh, but that is not true,' he said. 'There is so much you do not know about me, Bianca. So much! You see,

I soon discovered I had the gift, like the shamans. It came naturally. I could send my spirit out as a ghostly wolf. And I found that in my wolf-shape I could track others. When I left Palume, I had already decided what I would do. I would become a hunter. I would hunt down those who did evil to others, like the arsonist who had burned down our house because he wanted the property and our landlord hadn't wanted to sell it to him.'

I gasped.

'Yes, that was what had happened,' he continued. 'That man was the first one I brought to justice, after I joined the Special Police. But not the last.' He gave a crooked smile. 'So that's what I did. I used my spirit-wolf in the service of the Special Police. I thought that bringing the evil to justice would help to heal my torn heart.

'But the day came when I discovered that one of the criminals I'd helped send to the gallows was innocent. And then I worried – had I made the same terrible mistake before? I could no longer trust that I would not be condemning the innocent. I knew it could not go on. I knew I must try to make amends for the harm I had done by helping the outcast, the hunted, the helpless. You see, I thought too that if I'd had such a place to go – a place like the havens – after I'd lost everything, things might have been so very different for me. And I knew that I had to cage the wolf, and never let it out again . . . That night I came to see you was the first time in more than two years that I . . . that I opened the cage.'

Verakina had been listening to this without comment, but now she said to me, 'Then surely our friends will understand. All we have to do is explain.'

'You haven't seen the old woman,' I said. 'She helped me, but . . . but Rafiel – how can I trust her? I have been wrong when I have trusted so many times – with Belladonna, with Lucian . . . She is a feya, not human. There is no way that we can know what she'll do, if she'll even listen . . .'

I stopped as Rafiel straightened up. Holding his hand up in the air, clasped as though it held something, he called out, loud enough for Andel to hear, 'I've found it, Bianca!'

'No, Rafiel!' I whispered ferociously.

'Yes. I must do this. The feya and her friends have tracked me this far. If I run, it would only be a matter of time before they found me again. I must face her sooner or later, and I choose not to hide anymore. I choose to face her now. But you – Bianca, Verakina – you must go. Please. We are far enough away now, from the Duke's palace for you to have a real chance of escape. Go. Run.'

'The past is gone but the future might still be ours, if you let it be,' I cried fiercely, and, reaching up, I kissed him full on the lips.

His eyes widened but, putting an arm around me, he kissed me right back. It was likely the strangest kiss to ever have been, with the two of us standing soaked in the middle of the rushes, and an audience of an astonished – and slightly embarrassed – werewolf. But it was the sweetest thing, the most beautiful thing, I had ever known.

'We will not be parted, ever again,' I said, rather breathlessly, as we emerged from our kiss. 'Do you understand me, Rafiel?'

'I do,' he said, smiling, 'and it makes me glad. But –'

'No buts,' I said, firmly. 'As you won't run with us, I will go with you, and face whatever it is the feya Lady Grandmother might have in store.'

'And I will come too, of course,' said Verakina, as we marched back to the boat.

Andel looked at us a little curiously as we got into the boat. 'So you found what you were looking for?'

'Yes,' I said. And, as Andel rowed out into deeper waters, steering the craft further east, I thought that I *had* found what I had been looking for: I had found Rafiel, and he had found me. And we would face the feya Lady Grandmother together.

Thirty-Two

Very soon after, we arrived at Wheat Sheaf Quay, where we were met by Olga, alone, wrapped in a shawl against the early-morning chill.

'You have passage on the first ship that leaves for Faustina,' she said, handing us some tickets before we could speak. 'It leaves in an hour. You can go onboard right away.'

The river is wide at Wheat Sheaf Quay, so even fairly big ships can moor, and we could see the ship she meant, just a short distance ahead. It was the kind of cargo vessel that also takes a few passengers. It was not normally the fastest mode of transport, but this one was a steamship, and so it would be a good deal speedier than the older models. We could be far away from here in a short time. For an instant I gazed at it in longing, but I knew we could not back out now.

So I said nothing as Rafiel explained to Olga and Andel that our plans had changed, that we would not be fleeing

Lepmest for a little while yet, and that we must speak with Lady Grandmother. I tried not to look too anxious as Olga and Andel, swapping a questioning glance, agreed that we may see her, and that they would rouse Lady Grandmother at once.

As we followed Olga and Andel back into the maze of streets, Rafiel's hand stole into mine. I clasped it tightly and was glad that it was mine to hold. With his hand in mine, all I was really aware of was his closeness; thoughts of what might happen when the feya Lady Grandmother discovered that it was he she had been searching for floated to the back of my mind.

So much had separated Rafiel and I – especially those long years when we had vanished from each other's sight – and yet now it was as though we had never been parted. We had been friends – good friends – in childhood. I had admired him so much, engrossed by his laughter, his daring, his adventurous spirit.

Now, as I walked with him in the dark morning streets, I knew that it had been more than a little girl's hero-worship. It had been the dawn of love, a love that had lain dormant through all those years, and that was now reawakening, like a flower after a long winter.

What I'd sensed in the veiled eyes of the man they called the Prince had been a trueness of heart that went to the core of who and what he was. That trueness of heart had been there in the boy I'd missed so much. And it was there in the man he was now, the beautiful man by my side. His own suffering had turned him into a hunter, but the suffering of others had transformed him into a protector. It was never easy for a person to see what they had become and to change it, but Rafiel had done it. He had accepted the fault in the path he had chosen without trying to justify his mistakes, and he had sought to do only right from that moment onwards.

We reached the Wheat Sheaf Inn. Olga left us outside with Andel while she went in. We didn't have to wait long. In a few moments Olga came out again. 'She is not here.'

'What?' exclaimed Andel, echoing our own thoughts.

'But I think I know where she is,' added Olga.

'Oh no,' said Andel. 'You don't mean . . .'

'Yes,' said Olga. 'The buffet at the Grand Dome Station. She's gone to raid it. Again.'

Verakina and Rafiel looked astonished. But I wasn't. I remembered the greed on the old feya's face as she circled the glass display case full of cakes.

This comical development should have made me feel better. An old woman who sneaked out to raid cream cakes in a railway buffet could hardly be a fearsome enemy . . . But I knew better by now than to trust such superficial things. I had learnt that people – and feya – could be many things at once, and that it was only a fool who thought danger might not come laughing as much as scowling.

'She's just not used to the city,' said Olga. 'Her senses are disturbed, away from the forest. It makes her do strange things.'

'Stranger than usual, you mean,' grunted Andel.

Olga did not answer. Rafiel and Verakina and I looked at each other. We were all thinking the same thing. If the old feya wasn't as sharp as usual, that was a good thing for us.

As we approached Grand Dome, the station clock struck six. The deep sound felt ominous, and I shivered a little. Rafiel felt it. Taking my hand, he whispered, 'Whatever comes, we face it together.'

'Yes,' I said, 'but . . .' I began, then trailed off, for now we were in the big central hall, which at this early hour was still practically deserted apart from a busy sweeper, a passenger snoring on a bench, and a station attendant or two in the ticket office. The buffet was closed, and there appeared to be nobody there, but I remembered how the old feya had hidden in plain sight when I'd last been here.

'Wait for me there,' said Olga, gesturing to some benches at the other end of the hall. 'She's here all right, but she's not going to like it if we all ambush her.' She loped off, the wolfish grace of her movements clear at this distance.

'She's not afraid of the transformation, your wife,' said Verakina to Andel.

Andel shook his head. 'She's learnt to control the wolf inside her without the need for any spell. But then,' he added proudly, 'she's an Ironheart. A great werewolf family,' he explained, when we looked blank. 'One of their ancestors saved the Emperor of Ruvenya a long time ago, and because of that, Ironhearts and all their ilk are greatly honoured in the land.'

'Werewolves are greatly honoured there?' said Verakina, in some amazement.

'They are indeed. As are all shapeshifters and all kinds of magical folk. Including, of course, feya like Old Bony – er, I mean, Lady Grandmother.'

Olga was circling the buffet now, but carefully, so as not to be noticed by the station attendants and the sweeper. We saw her incline her head once, twice, three times. Then all at once, she disappeared. Vanished. One instant she was there; the next she was gone, as if a hand had reached in and snatched her through an open door.

'She's in,' said Andel. 'Now we can only wait –'

He broke off as we heard the drumming sound of many running footsteps. Suddenly, the City Police in their green uniforms appeared in the station entrance. Police whistles exploded in the air and one of them spotted us and shouted, 'Over there! They're over there!'

'Olga! Lady Grandmother!' yelled Andel, and we sprinted towards the buffet after him, startling the attendants and the sweeper and rousing the sleeping man, who woke up with a yelp.

And then I found that we were behind the spell wall, invisible to the startled policemen, who ran around in complete confusion as the sweeper, the startled-awake man and the station attendants fled in terror. Safe behind the spell wall, we gasped in relief, but it was a short-lived respite. For inside the spell wall there was the woman they call Lady Grandmother, her eyes as hard and shiny as black marbles, calmly wiping cream off the side of her mouth. And then she spoke for the very first time.

'I smell lies,' she said, the words absolutely clear and without accent. She pointed a bony finger at Rafiel. 'Tell me it isn't so, boy.'

'It isn't his fault –' I began, but the old feya waved a hand at me and I fell silent.

'I cannot tell you it isn't so,' said Rafiel, 'because what you say is true.'

'Ah!' She came up to him. Walked round and round him. Sniffed. 'The wolf is in you.'

'Yes,' said Rafiel, without flinching, though he was very pale.

Andel and Olga looked on, shocked. I could read the questions in their faces. This is the evil sorcerer's apprentice? Him, the one we helped to rescue?

Andel said, 'It's not right –' just as Olga said, 'Lady of the forest, please –'

'Silence, both of you!' commanded the old woman. 'Boy,' she went on, peering at Rafiel, 'this wolf of yours – you have used it for ill.'

'And for good!' burst out Verakina. The old woman took no notice.

'Answer, boy!'

'Yes, ma'am,' he said, steadily enough, though I could see his Adam's apple bobbing in his throat.

'The sorcerer from Palume – did you know he also used a wolf for ill?'

'No, ma'am, I did not know,' said Rafiel. He was deathly pale now, but still he held himself proudly, his hazel eyes blazing with golden light. 'I only knew him a short time. And I never learnt from him.'

'Is that so?' She looked at him without moving, her black eyes utterly unreadable as they gazed into his. 'Yet you studied in his books. I can see it in your mind.'

'Yes,' said Rafiel, and now his voice had a definite tremble in it.

I took a step towards him, but the feya held up a hand for me to stop.

'Be patient. Your time will come, girl.' She looked at Rafiel. 'Continue.'

'I read and I studied the ways of the shamans from the Northern lands,' he said. There were beads of sweat on his forehead. 'And I discovered that all along . . . all along it was in me. It was waiting for me to be ready. Waiting for when I needed it.'

'The wolf,' said the old woman.

'The wolf,' echoed Rafiel.

There was a silence. Then the old woman said, 'The sorcerer's eyes never changed. Yours did.'

'Yes,' said Rafiel, startled.

'That is because the wolf is in you,' said the old woman. 'It wasn't in him. He enslaved another creature's spirit. But you – you transformed your own. You are the one we seek. There is no doubt.'

Forcing the words past my tightened throat, I burst out, 'If you try to hurt him –'

'Who said anything about hurting, girl?' snapped the old woman, her black eyes sparking with temper now. 'We seek him, but does that mean it is for ill?'

We all stared at her. 'But, Lady Grandmother, I thought –' began Olga, weakly.

'Fie, girl! Are you as dense as the others? You, an Ironheart? I seek the truth, and now I have it. And I have something else as well. Do you know what it is, boy?'

'No, ma'am,' he said, his face very still.

'News for my friends in the Northern lands,' she said, 'who thought that the old ways were dead, and whose sadness is a burden to me. They will be glad to know the wolf can still walk. Pah! No doubt you had to cage it because you used your spirit-wolf to stalk in a forest of stone and glass and blood in this city and all the dark places where humans plot evil. Such a place is unnatural for its kind, and its senses are disturbed, its truth distorted. Is that so, boy?'

'Yes,' he said, and I saw that there were tears in his eyes.

'When the time is right you will come with me to the Northern lands and my friends will show you how the wolf can walk safely, in its own truth.'

'I will go,' said Rafiel, and now his face was filled with the beginnings of laughter. 'I swear it.'

'Good. And now for you, girl,' she said, turning her hard gaze on me. 'Look at me. And don't try to close yourself off to me – oh yes, I can tell that you are a strong one – or it will be the worse for you.'

Swallowing hard, I did as I was told. I felt her mind in mine, looking at what was there. I felt her probe inside my memories. I felt her cold feya intelligence weighing everything, seeing everything in the blink of an eye. It would have terrified me had Rafiel not been holding one of my hands and Verakina the other, and had I not felt the anxious goodwill that emanated from Andel and Olga.

It was only for a moment, though it seemed like forever. 'Very well,' she said.

'Very well?' I echoed. 'Hardly!' Now that Rafiel was out of harm's way, I thought once again of why I had tried to seek Lady Grandmother thrice in the single night that had just passed. If Belladonna was a feya like her, only Lady Grandmother could defeat her. She must help us!

'Listen to me, girl. This witch is not my concern. No,' she snapped, seeing the expressions on the faces of the others, 'she is not. She is not a feya, so there is no need for me to do what you yourselves might do. I have never done the bidding of others. Ever. I do not propose to start now.'

'Lady Grandmother,' said Rafiel. 'I will try to keep my promise to come with you to the Northern lands. But if you do not help us against the witch and if we are killed, how can I keep my promise to you then?'

The feya snorted. 'She will find a way to beat the witch,' she said, turning her head to look directly at me.

Sharp into my mind came an image of the first time I'd seen Lady Grandmother, in this very place, with the station swarming with police as it was now. It was she who was pushing the image into my mind, I knew that, and I knew she must be doing it for a reason. But . . .

'I do not understand,' I said. 'How does that help?'

'You will know,' she said, her hard black eyes still on me.

And then, quite suddenly, she vanished.

With her went the spell wall and the invisibility that had protected us until that point from the gaze of the policemen who were still there, searching in every corner of the station for us. They didn't see us, at first – our reappearance was too sudden. We were sidling towards the exit when all at once the shout went up and in an instant, they were surging towards us, their leader shouting, 'Take them alive! There's a big reward!'

'Hear that?' Rafiel shouted. 'Let's make them work hard for it, shall we?' And he threw off the heavy coat that would hamper his movements. 'Are you ready?' he asked Andel, Olga, Verakina and me.

'Yes,' spoke Andel. Verakina and I nodded. 'You?'

'Yes,' said Rafiel.

'Then let's get these blighters!' the giant boatman said, and into the horde we plunged, hitting out to the left and right, some of our blows striking home.

The policemen fell back at first, but soon they were advancing again, drawing their clubs. I threw myself at one of the policemen, causing him to lose balance and crash to the ground. Meanwhile, Verakina, with a blood-curdling yell, went after another, scratching at his face with her clawed hands.

The policemen's blood was up now and though we fought hard, we were being forced to retreat, back and back. I heard the crunch of bone as a club came down hard on Andel's foot, watched as another narrowly missed the side of Rafiel's head, and felt another hit me on the back of the legs, so that I staggered and almost fell. Then Verakina did fall, after being whacked behind the knees, and I saw her disappear in a forest of green-clad legs. Yelling incoherently, I threw myself at them, but was pushed aside by a huge policeman with a face as mean as a rat's.

All at once, a howl filled the air, and a grey wolf raced straight into the melee and, faced with the snarling beast, the police instantly fell back. I saw the wolf's eyes only for an instant as she dashed past me, but I knew instantly that it was Olga, transformed into her wolf-shape. And then her snarl was answered by another as a small white wolf rose from the ground where Verakina had fallen. Clearly she had now learnt how to transform at will, like Olga. She leaped for the throat of the rat-faced man, who screamed and scrambled away from her, fleeing for his life.

He wasn't the only one to run. The leader might blow his whistle all he liked but the men had not bargained for wolves and had no intention of staying to have their throats ripped out. One after another, they took to their heels until only the leader was left and then, taking one look at Andel advancing on him with a captured truncheon in each hand, a gleam in his eye, and a grey wolf at his heels, he too decided discretion was the better part of valour, and fled. Verakina and Olga went after him, making sure he'd not turn back, and then they returned instants later, no longer in wolf-shape but human once more.

Panting, breathless, we looked at each other, exhausted but exultant. We'd done it! The five of us had won against at least six times as many policemen!

But there was no time to linger on our victory.

'If the police were here, it is because our escape has already been discovered,' said Rafiel, voicing our thoughts.

'Yes, but how did they know we were here?' Olga asked, frowning.

'I doubt they did. I think that there would have been men sent to each exit from the city and every way of escape: the port, the railway stations, the coach stops. That is what I would do if I were in charge of recapturing escaped prisoners,' said Rafiel, grimly.

'So wherever we run, they'll be waiting,' Andel said.

'Yes.'

'We're trapped, then!' cried Verakina.

'No. There is a way other than running,' said Rafiel.

'Yes. You will have to stay in the city and hide,' said Olga.

'No,' said Rafiel. 'They would find us sooner or later.' His eyes met mine, and I saw what was in his mind. I nodded. It was time.

'You have been the kindest of friends,' I said, looking at Andel and Olga. 'But it is time we stopped running, stopped hiding, and faced Belladonna.'

'What?' burst out Olga. 'The witch will kill you at once!'

'Olga's right. This is madness,' said Andel.

'I'll go back to Lady Grandmother,' cried Olga. 'I'll beg her to help –'

'It will do no good,' I said. 'You know that, Olga.'

'Then we will come with you,' said Andel.

'No. You and Olga have done more than enough for us,' said Rafiel. 'And you have a child to think of, waiting for you back at the inn. This is not your fight.'

'We will not abandon you –' began Olga.

'And you won't be,' I said, 'if you do something very important for us.' A sudden thought had come to mind – of Lady Helena, convinced that something was not quite right with the automata, but unable to prove it. I hadn't even considered it before – but could we convince her to help us? 'And that is to go to Lady Helena – the Duke's sister – and tell her everything. She sees through Belladonna, I am sure of it, and she can sense that there is something not quite right with the automata. She fears Belladonna's influence on the Duke.'

Rafiel nodded, his expression lightening. 'Lady Helena has her own detachment of soldiers who are completely loyal to her. If she can be persuaded to move against the witch, then we may have a chance.'

'If that is what you want, then we will do it,' said Olga.

And after clasping our hands, briefly, she and Andel hurried off.

Thirty-Three

'We have to give them time to reach Lady Helena's house,' Rafiel said, 'but we can't wait here – those policemen will soon raise the alarm. There's only one way we can get to where we want without running into a street patrol.'

'What way is that?' I asked.

'The railway tunnels,' he said. 'Come on!'

We hurried through the station, past the turnstiles, down the stairs onto the platform area, and ran to the far end of the platform until the end. Jumping onto the tracks, we headed towards the mouth of the tunnel a short distance away.

'I hope there's no train due yet,' murmured Verakina, at my elbow, as we followed Rafiel. 'If one comes, we have nowhere to go . . .' For the tunnel was dark and narrow and as we went further and further inside, the point of light that was the platform at the far end receded more and more so that soon we were in the pitch dark. Rafiel lit a match, and waited for us to catch up.

'Stay close behind me,' he said to us, 'and don't worry. I know the way. I've tracked men through here before.'

If he had, then other policemen might have too, I thought. Any moment I expected to hear the thump of a policeman's boots or the rumble of an approaching train. But I didn't voice my worries; instead I focused on following the matches he lit, one after the other, as we advanced slowly through the musty tunnel.

Oh, if only I could have forced that old mule of a feya to help us! Truly help us, not merely awaken a useless memory of last time I'd seen her. For what was the point of making me relive that, unless it was to drive home how stupid I'd been, running from Rafiel and rushing towards Lucian?

On the tunnel went, and on we stumbled through it. Suddenly, ahead, I saw a pinprick of light.

'A train coming!' I called.

'No,' said Rafiel, gently, 'it's only the daylight. The tunnel ends there – that is what you are seeing.'

'Then what?' said Verakina.

'We'll be coming out into a cutting and will have to climb out of it. Just a short distance from there is the head-quarters of the Special Police. That's where we're going.'

'What?' I cried. 'Why on earth would we go there, and not to Belladonna's?'

'I've been thinking. The head of the Special Police takes orders directly from the Duke,' he said, calmly, 'and I think the Duke will be there to oversee the search. And if he's there, then she will she be, too. Belladonna has to keep an eye on what the Duke is doing, if she wants to be sure nothing goes wrong this time. Remember, it was from the Duke's prison that we escaped, not from hers, and it was the Duke's guard who gave us the chance to attack Drago and escape.'

'That is, if she believed that's what happened,' I objected.

'It doesn't matter if she did or not,' he said, as we emerged blinking from the tunnel. 'We were going to be tried, remember. She had already convinced the Duke that we were dangerous criminals. Our escape would prove that to him. Even if she had her doubts about what happened, she'd know that there would be no way she could convince him *not* to launch a full-scale search – and a full-scale search is exactly what's going to make it difficult for her to try to find us in secret, and arrange more of her lies. No, I think Belladonna is there, making sure she knows exactly how the search is going, so that she can think quickly when we are brought in. But we can use that to our advantage. It will be good for us if she's there, because it means it that she will see us – the Duke will see us – in public. She cannot dare risk using that paralysis spell again, not there. Even the Duke cannot believe you are an escaped automaton the second time.'

'Rafiel?' I said.

He turned and smiled at me. 'Yes?'

'I just wanted to say that I . . . that I am glad we found each other again,' I said.

'And I am glad too,' he said. And though we used no endearments and did not kiss or touch each other, our eyes spoke thrilling promises and what flowed between us was like a shield of strength against anything that would come between us.

As we neared the top of the cutting, the first train passed below us in a clatter of iron and a hiss of steam. From the summit, we could see the city spread out below. A childhood memory came to me, of my father hoisting me onto his shoulders and showing me the city panorama from the roof terrace of the Lepmest Ladies' Fair store.

I had hardly thought of him since I had discovered the basement where Drago concocted Belladonna's terrifying life-essence extractions. Yet now I could see him, clear as a bell, with that tender lilt in his voice, whispering, 'I am with you, my darling. I will always be with you.'

Rafiel saw my expression. 'Are you all right?' he asked.

'Yes,' I said. And oddly, I was. Hearing my father's voice had not saddened me, it had given me renewed heart. 'Where are we going?'

'There,' he said, pointing down at a great grey building taking up a whole city block. He looked at me, then at Verakina. 'You have to let me do the talking; don't be surprised by what I say or do.' We nodded.

We understood what he'd meant a short time later, when we arrived in front of the police headquarters. Close up, the building looked even bigger than it had from the hill: big and forbidding, with small windows set into grey stone. Two large, black-uniformed men with big shotguns slung across their chests, stood at the top of the steps by the front door and watched expressionlessly as we approached.

'Sergeant Goran bringing in witnesses for interview over an assault on an officer,' Rafiel said in a calm voice to the men, showing them his badge, as he motioned us up the steps. 'Me, that is,' he said, showing them his bruised face.

Verakina and I exchanged a startled glance. Why didn't the guards recognise us? Wouldn't the men be on alert against us?

Apparently not, for one of them said, in a roughly joshing sort of tone, 'These ladies beat you up, Goran? You're slipping, my friend.'

'They're the *witnesses*,' said Rafiel, in the same tone, 'I told you. But you should see the fellow who did it. If his own mother recognises him, it'll be a fair miracle.'

'Just as well, or your reputation would take a beating, too,' said the man, laughing, and he stepped aside to let us pass.

'How did you know that would work?' I whispered, as we walked into the entrance hall.

'I didn't. I just gambled on the idea that they think we've run and that the last thing we'd do is come here. I doubt that our names have been released even to the search parties. Just descriptions. And not even that to rank-and-file people like the guards and clerks.'

So saying, he approached the end of the lobby where three or four uniformed policewomen were busy at a long desk. 'Sergeant Rafiel Goran, with important witnesses for the Commander,' he said.

The woman looked at him. 'The Commander is in closed conference. He cannot –'

'He'll want to hear these witnesses, I guarantee it,' interrupted Rafiel.

She looked at him. Shrugged. 'Oh, very well,' she said. She reached for the little telegraph machine on the desk and tapped out rapid words. 'There. Now you'll have to wait till they –'

She broke off as suddenly the double doors behind her burst open and the lobby filled with black-uniformed men, their weapons trained at our hearts as they surrounded us.

'Get down on your knees! Now!' came the shout from the leading officer.

We obeyed. We had no other option. As three men approached and handcuffed us where we knelt, I glimpsed the shocked, horrified expressions on the faces of the women at the desk, and knew that we were at the point of no return.

We were dragged up and marched off, each of us surrounded by five or six men. They were not taking any chances that we'd escape again. Through the double doors we went, down a long corridor, until we reached some stairs. Up we were shepherded, one after the other, and then marched to the end of another long corridor, and to another set of double doors. A knock, and then we were dragged in, Rafiel first, then Verakina, then me, half-hidden at the back.

We had been taken to a large conference room. And there they were, sitting at a table. The Duke, backed by six impassive men in the uniform of his personal guard; a man whose uniform and insignia of rank clearly indicated he must be Commander of the Special Police; another man, standing, whose uniform and insignia showed he was from the City Police and whose crestfallen expression clearly showed he'd just received a severe dressing down for the debacle at the Grand Dome Station; Lucian, sitting alone at one end of the table, huddled in on himself, and looking as though he'd aged ten years; Drago, standing pale and impassive; and Belladonna.

The duke was first to speak. 'So, you're giving yourself up, are you?' he boomed, addressing Rafiel. 'You think that will get you some clemency, I suppose.'

'No, your grace. We are not giving ourselves up,' said Rafiel steadily. 'We might have been miles away by now, and not one of you could have stopped us.'

'How dare you speak thus! Vermin! Traitor!' shouted the Commander of the Special Police.

'How dare you, you traitorous vermin!' echoed the Commander of the City Police, not to be outdone.

'Quiet, both of you,' said the Duke in an irritated voice, and they subsided. He looked at Rafiel, his curiosity sparked. 'So *why* didn't you run?'

'Because, your grace,' I said, moving from behind the ranks of police, 'you have to know the truth, or we can never be safe – none of us, and no-one in Noricia.'

For an instant, everyone stared at me in stunned astonishment, except Belladonna, though I saw her eyes flicker, as though in shock. Hidden at the back of the group of policemen, she hadn't known I was there. Her shock heartened me a little.

A policeman moved to haul me back but Belladonna held up a hand. 'No, let her be,' she said, quietly.

She leaned towards the Duke and spoke into his ear. He listened. Nodded.

'Get out, you,' he ordered, waving at the policemen. 'Yes, you too,' he added, glaring at the two commanders.

'But your grace,' squeaked the Commander of the Special Police, 'these are dangerous crimi–'

'I said to get out!' he repeated, in an exasperated tone. 'Drago and my guardsmen will do the job well enough. Now do as I say.'

They obeyed, filing out in rather bad grace.

'Good,' said the Duke. 'Now lock the door, Drago. We don't want to be disturbed.' Turning to Belladonna, he said, 'You are quite right, my dear Belladonna. Too much fuss with those fools around. Now, where were we?'

'I care little if I am thought to be a traitor,' said Rafiel, before I could speak, 'but Lady Bianca Dalmatin who stands before you is an innocent victim of –'

'Do you think I am a fool?' roared the Duke, making everyone start. 'This is not Bianca Dalmatin! This is an impostor, and you know it!'

Of all the things we might have expected, this was not it. For an instant, all we could do was stare at him with our mouths open.

'Ha!' he said, triumphantly. 'You didn't think we knew, did you?'

'But your grace,' I stammered, finding my voice at last, 'how can you possibly believe that I am both an automaton and an impostor?'

'Eh?' he replied. 'What are you talking about?'

He is a stupid man, I thought. 'Last time you saw me,' I hurried on, 'you were led to believe that the figure you saw wasn't real, that it wasn't really me, that it was an automaton –'

'You are mad as well as wicked, girl,' interrupted the Duke, 'if you think that you can pull the wool over my eyes! There is an automaton that looks just like Lady Bianca Dalmatin, I agree. I saw it with my own eyes. But it is a mere machine. An invention of my Lady Belladonna's.'

'If that's so,' burst out Verakina, 'if it really is just a machine, it should still be in the exhibition room. Ask her to show it to you and prove it is an automaton. Ask her.'

'Drago, perhaps we should bring the policemen back in here, and lock them up before they spin any more lies. There's no need to check the hall,' said Belladonna, hastily, the tension showing in her hands clenched on the table. 'No need to disturb yourself, no need at all –'

'Belladonna,' said the Duke, in a bewildered tone, 'is this true?'

'It is, your grace,' she said, quietly. 'The machine that you saw – it is no longer there.' Her voice shook as she went on. 'The truth is that I . . . I decided that I could not bear it to be on public display. It brought back too many memories.'

'So . . . where is it?' asked the Duke. There was a guarded expression in his eyes now. Were we at last shaking his belief in Belladonna?

'I had it destroyed,' she said, quietly, her eyes on him. Bright eyes. So bright, so blue, so intense. She reached over to touch his hand, and . . .

I opened my mouth to shout a warning, but I was too late. The Duke's glance had gone hazy.

He murmured in a voice quite unlike his own, 'I am sorry you destroyed it. Such a clever piece! But I understand why you felt you had to. A woman's scruples. My own sister – she did not like it.'

'Lady Helena was right, of course,' said Belladonna. She dabbed at her eyes with a handkerchief. 'My poor stepdaughter is dead, and I have to learn to accept that, as I have to learn to accept the fact of my poor husband's murder. But what makes it doubly hard is the notion that people like these might try to use these tragedies for their own twisted ends.'

My heart was racing, my belly twisting with rage. 'Your grace,' I said, ignoring Belladonna and looking straight at the Duke. 'Listen to me. I am Bianca Dalmatin, and this woman, my stepmother, has stolen everything from me. My father. My home. My trust. My very life she has tried to take not once, but several times. Please, your grace, you must listen. You must –'

'Enough!' The Duke shouted, banging his fist on the table. 'Whatever motive you and your accomplices have for inventing these monstrous and absurd accusations, you cannot hide from the real truth. Lucian Montresor, stand up,' he bellowed, 'and recount again what you told us. Stand up, I say!' he repeated, when Lucian was slow to obey him.

Lucian scrambled to his feet. He stammered, 'Your grace?'

'You heard me, Montresor,' said the Duke. 'Tell them what you told us.'

With bent head, Lucian muttered, 'I . . . I was in need of money, your grace . . . My . . . My family's fortune has diminished considerably, and I . . . I have had bad luck at cards . . . and owed some dangerous people money. I was desperate, your grace, and so when the . . .' He flicked a wild sideways glance at Rafiel, who did not react. 'When the renegade policeman came to me and told me he could arrange to have my debts wiped . . . I found I could not refuse. It was then he introduced me to the impostor. She . . . She looked a good deal like the vanished daughter of the late Sir Anton Dalmatin. The resemblance was, in fact, quite . . . astonishing . . .'

My skin crawled. How could I have been so wrong about this pathetic excuse of a man? Glancing at

Belladonna, I saw the same contempt in her face. She might use this man, she might have created for herself the most loyal servant she had ever had, but she utterly despised him. At that moment, our eyes met. She gave a little smile. You have lost, it said. You have lost because you don't know how to use people. You don't understand how to use their secret hopes, their darkest fears. And so you will lose. People like you always lose. And people like me always win.

'Go on,' said the Duke, impatiently. 'You haven't told it all, yet. What did the impostor and the renegade want you to do?'

Before Lucian could answer, Rafiel said, in a hard voice, 'Take care, Montresor.'

'Threatening the witness,' growled the Duke, 'condemns you out of your own mouth. Be quiet. Now, continue.'

Lucian mumbled: 'They . . . They wanted me to come in with them on a plot to . . . to fool the world into thinking that Lady Bianca had been abducted by bandits in the pay of . . . of Lady Dalmatin. I was to . . . to say that I had discovered the place where the bandits had been keeping her, in the mountains near my home. And I was to confirm that this was the real Bianca Dalmatin – I had met her at the Presentation Ball and would know her again when I saw her.'

'And what was this all for?'

Lucian licked his lips and looked away. 'They did not say, but I suppose it was . . . well, your grace, the Dalmatin fortune is large . . .'

Belladonna spoke up, in a sombre voice. 'And if I were tried and found guilty of such a terrible crime, then at the very least I would be exiled and stripped of all my poor husband had left me, not executed.'

'My dear, that would never have happened,' said the Duke fervently. 'I would never have allowed it! How could anyone believe such a dreadful thing of such a good and beautiful woman?'

'Thank you, your grace,' murmured Belladonna, 'you are very kind. But "mud sticks", as they say, even if it is false information. My reputation would have been ruined. And in any case, villains like these would know that even the threat of such an accusation might be enough to be able to bleed their victim dry. Blackmail can be the most effective weapon for villains,' she said, and sighed, shaking her head.

But she should not have said that. For her words awoke in me a memory of that image Lady Grandmother had left me with. And this time I did not see a station full of police. I did not see me, running from Rafiel and towards Lucian. I saw Lucian's face. I saw the haunted fear, written in his eyes. And I knew, finally, what weapon I had to use.

'You will never be free of the curse, Lucian,' I said, looking right at him. 'Never. And you know it, in your deepest heart. '

He was very pale, and his eyes had a feverish gleam. I could tell that he was trying to ignore my words but that something inside him would not let him.

'No. That is not so!' he cried.

'What?' said the duke, frowning. 'What is this talk of curses?'

'Nothing, your grace,' said Belladonna. 'Just the ravings of –'

'Quiet, my lady,' he said, crossly, earning himself a black look from Belladonna. 'Montresor! What is this about?'

'Just . . . Just a silly story, your grace,' he whispered, wiping sweat off his forehead, with a fearful glance at Belladonna. 'A . . . A myth they tell about my family.'

'Oh, but it's no myth, Lucian,' I said. 'It is reality, and you have lived with it all your life. You thought you were free. There was a price to pay, but you had accepted that. It was a price you were willing to pay for the magic that would bring you your freedom. But now . . . now you have realised that you are not free. That you never were. That any time she wants, she can bring the curse back. Any time she has a use for you, or any time she thinks you are weakening, that you are trying to get back on the right path, she can threaten you with it. As she has done today. And so many other days.'

There was a silence. Lucian's lip trembled. He looked at me, his gaze anguished and wild. 'You must understand! It takes everything from me! It turns me into a monster, thirsting for blood. It watches and waits for me in the shadows, slavering, ready to devour my humanity forever . . .'

'I know,' I said, gently. 'I understand. But she has not driven the wolf away. Far from it. She feeds it – as do you – with evil acts. And in your deepest heart, you know that.'

Lucian held my gaze for a heartbeat. Then he turned to the Duke with an unexpected air of determination and spoke. 'Your grace, I have something important to say.'

The Duke, who had been listening in stupefied silence until this moment, burst out now with, 'I'll say you have! If I am right in understanding this, you, only child of the

Montresors, are a werewolf! And a dangerous one at that, going by what you say. I do not want such a . . . such an unpredictable person in my court! I hereby declare that you are exiled until further notice.'

'I will gladly obey, your grace,' said Lucian, and his eyes had a hectic shine. 'Gladly. But that is not what I wanted to say.' He straightened. And he said, with a voice that tried hard to be steady, 'I want to retract everything I said. It was lies. All lies. This girl is no impostor, but the real Bianca Dal–'

Belladonna reared up, like a snake striking. She threw herself at Lucian, and screamed words in a language I had never heard before. Lucian shook, writhed, twisted in on himself, his skin stretching, his form changing. His jaw lengthened and narrowed, his ears grew, his teeth sharpened, his hands shrank, his legs shortened and thickened, his clothes were replaced by a hairy pelt. All this in the blink of an eye, in one heartbeat, one frozen moment.

Where Lucian had stood was a huge golden wolf with unblinking amber eyes.

We fell back in shock, but the wolf took no notice of us. Instead, he advanced on the Duke, who retreated in terror, yelling for his guardsmen. They did not move a muscle, but stayed eyes ahead, gaze fixed. As though they were spellbound. As though they were not human.

As though they were automata.

The door handle rattled as someone tried to enter the room. But it had been locked. There was a tumult of voices beyond the door, with one rising above them all, commanding, 'Open the door at once, or we'll have it broken down!' I recognised those imperious female tones.

Olga and Andel must have fulfilled their mission, and Lady Helena had come at last!

But Belladonna laughed, a great peal of laughter that resounded in the room. Her eyes were as bright as the most brilliant sapphires. She gestured rapidly and barked an order, and the six mechanical guardsmen instantly turned and marched to the door, barring the way.

'Go, Montresor!' she hissed to the wolf. 'Give in to the wolf! Devour Ottakar the Usurper! Claim your family's rightful place back at last!'

The wolf snarled, deep in its throat. His eyes were like twin suns, full of rage and hate. He advanced another step towards the Duke, who tried to scramble away but tripped and fell.

'Devour!' shouted Belladonna, again.

Rafiel and Verakina and I raced to the Duke's side, trying to shield him. The wolf's burning glance raked over us, and then in one rapid, fluid movement, he turned and leaped.

Not on the duke.

On Belladonna.

She screamed and fell, and instantly the wolf was on her, ripping at her throat, his ferocious claws deep in the flesh of her arms. Drago moved like lightning, throwing himself on the wolf, a long knife in his hand. The wolf snarled and growled but did not lose his grip, even when Drago stabbed him again and again.

It was over in moments. Moments I will never forget, for as long as I live.

And when it was over, the wolf who had once been Lucian Montresor, and the witch who had once been my beloved stepmother, both lay dead on the floor in a pool of blood, while a wounded Drago wept silently over the body of the woman he had served so loyally all his life.

The Duke got up, shakily. His face was grey, his eyes full of shadows. He looked at us. 'You . . . You tried to save me,' he croaked. 'After all I –' He broke off, then said, more strongly, 'I will never forget what you did, Sergeant Goran. Or your friend,' he added, looking at Verakina. But . . .' He swallowed. Looked me right in the eyes. '. . . But especially you, Lady Bianca, whom I have so bitterly wronged. I am so very, very sorry. I hope you will forgive me. Things will be different now, I promise you that.'

I could find no words to answer, for my throat was choked by my heart. So I nodded, while Rafiel put a tender arm around me, and Verakina gave me a watery smile. And then we turned away from that place of death and followed the Duke to the door, where the automata, deprived of the guiding hand of their creator, presented no resistance to us at all.

Epilogue

It has been a year, now, since the events of that day. Just as the Duke promised, things have been different. My home has been restored to me, along with my inheritance. The automata were destroyed and the human life-essence that had powered them was allowed to escape into the gentle ether, as it should after death, while the magical tool she had created was burned to ashes. Belladonna's lies have been swept away, and the truth about my father's murder and the beggar killings exposed. However, to spare the Montresor family, and to acknowledge Lucian's last-minute attempt to make amends, there was no public mention of the part Lucian had played in Belladonna's conspiracy, or in the manner of Belladonna's death. It was reported instead that she had been shot dead while making an attempt on the life of the Duke, and Drago's trial was a closed one, with the verdict only – life imprisonment – publicly revealed.

Even so, the revelations caused a sensation, and not one that I relished, even though I knew it was necessary that not everything be kept secret. But I did not have to face the half-horrified, half-fascinated curiosity of the press and the public, for on Lady Helena's advice, I was far away in Ruvenya at the time, taking refuge with Rafiel in Olga and Andel's summer home, and from thence we visited the Northern lands and the strange world of the shamans, as we'd promised the feya 'Lady Grandmother'.

When we returned, most of the hue and cry had died down, and though occasionally there is a mention in the press of it, I am glad that most of the attention centres not on the terrifying ordeal I went through but on my plans to build on my father's legacy in Ladies' Fair. For something dear to my heart and Rafiel's is a charitable foundation, partly funded by profits from Ladies' Fair, which will help to sponsor the building of more outcast havens, not only in Noricia but well beyond. We hope to help change people's attitudes towards outcasts.

The idea had come about after I had offered a home in my own house to Verakina and her friends. They had refused, gently but firmly.

'You understand,' had explained Verakina. 'We have a home already in the haven, and one in which we feel most ourselves. And all we could wish for is that those like ourselves might too know the same comfort.'

It is Rafiel, discharged with honours from the Special Police, who directs the Haven Foundation, with help from Verakina and his sister Margy, who has now fully recovered from her terrible ordeal. And it is Rafiel whose reputation has also made donations flood in from all over the country and beyond, so that already work is well underway for the construction of several new havens. For the legend of the Prince of Outlaws lives ever more brightly in the minds of the people, and the memory of those shining deeds will endure much longer than the horror and darkness that was Belladonna's only legacy. For that I am glad. For that, and for the slow and beautiful way in which Rafiel's and my love is growing hour by hour, day by day, as the years that separated us give way to the discovery of each other as we are now, and as we will be.

My renewed friendships with Margy and Emilia also give me great joy. As to Olga and Andel and little Frans-Ivan, they will always be in my heart, and that ferocious feya Lady Grandmother – she who, in her own way, helped me discover a strength in myself I didn't know I had – will always have my thanks, as will that famous Viklandish writer who goes under the name of Dr Nord.

But there are times when I am haunted by the images of the past. Times when I miss my father so much that it is like a physical pain tearing at me. Times when remembering the evil of what Belladonna did in her search for power and control almost overwhelms me. What makes people become like that?

We have learnt more about her background: that she was abandoned as a baby, sent to an orphanage, then adopted by Signora Gandelfiri, who treated her more like a servant than a child. Maybe there is something in that to explain her. And maybe not. I do not know. But somewhere, sometime, there must have been some good in her, however hidden, however neglected. For I could see that when Belladonna died, Drago truly grieved. He had been with her from childhood, and I can think of no other reason that he would have been so loyal, other than that he saw some good in her, too. And if there had not been good somewhere inside her, she would not have spared him, after he twice crossed her. Yes, there must have been some good in her, or otherwise, how could I ever have loved her at all? It is a painful thing to think about, and I try not to. But occasionally it comes, as do images of Lucian Montresor and his terrible fate, and then I am torn between horror and sorrow. It saddens me that his life was lived in fear. That he never realised – until the last moments of his life – that the curse from which he suffered was not that he was a werewolf, but that he allowed fear of the wolf to distort and twist him.

The other day, Rafiel and I went to visit Drago in prison. It was the first time since the trial that we had seen him, and the first time that we actually spoke to him since that terrible morning in the police headquarters. It was he who had asked for the meeting.

He sat across the table from us in the prison visiting room, his powerful frame a little hunched, looking older, thinner, more gaunt. But his tread was firm and his expression gave as little away as ever. He did not speak for quite some minutes, just sat there with his hands folded together and his eyes lowered. But suddenly he lifted his gaze and looked right at me.

'I have never asked for your forgiveness, Lady Bianca,' he said.

I felt a clenching in my chest. 'No,' I said. I wanted to say more, but couldn't.

Rafiel took my hand and held it, tight, under the table.

'And I will not,' Drago went on, as though I hadn't spoken, 'because I have no right. Because enough has been taken from you.' In his eyes now was an expression of such bleak sorrow that it caught at my throat. 'And I would not take that from you as well,' he added. 'I wanted you to know that. That is all I want to say.'

I could not speak.

'Look after her, Sergeant Goran,' he said, to Rafiel.

'I will,' said Rafiel, quietly.

'If things had been different . . .' Drago began, then broke off. Standing up, he motioned to be taken out of the room again. Soon we heard his heavy footsteps moving away.

But Rafiel and I sat in silence together for a few moments more, hand in hand, our hearts filled with the same strange mixture of sadness and gladness. And when we left that bleak place, when the prison doors closed behind us and we stepped out into the bright light of a summer morning, I felt light, as though a weight had been lifted from me. The past would still have its hold on us, for otherwise we would not be human. But it would never drag our future down. Not ever. Human life is made of light and of shadows. And the best thing any of us can ever do is to face that without fear, so that the darkness does not blot out the light.

The Crystal Heart

Sophie Masson

A girl in a tower. An underground kingdom. A crystal heart split in two, symbolising true love lost . . .

When Kasper joins the elite guard watching over a dangerous prisoner in a tower, he believes he is protecting his country from a powerful witch.

Until one day he discovers the prisoner is a beautiful princess – Izolda of Night– who is condemned by a prophecy to die on her eighteenth birthday. Kasper decides to help her escape. But their hiding place won't remain secret forever.

Will they find their happily ever after?

Available at all good retailers

Scarlet in the Snow

Sophie Masson

When Natasha is forced to shelter from a blizzard, she is
lucky to see a mansion looming out of the snow. Inside,
it is beautiful – except, instead of paintings, there are
empty frames on every wall. In the snowy garden, she finds
one perfect red rose in bloom. Dreamily she reaches
out a hand . . .

Only to have the terrifying master of the house appear, and
demand vengeance on her for taking his rose.

So begins an extraordinary adventure that will see Natasha
plunged deep into the heart of a mystery, as she realises she has
stumbled upon a powerful sorcerer's spell of revenge.

But even if she can break the spell, the Beast she has come
to love will be snatched from her. Natasha will have a long
journey ahead before there can be a happy ending.

'Utterly enchanting!
A wondrous mix of magic, adventure and romance.'
Kate Forsyth, author of *The Puzzle Ring*

Available at all good retailers

Moonlight & Ashes

Sophie Masson

The story of Cinderella as you've never heard it before . . .

A girl whose fortunes have plummeted from wealthy
aristocrat to servant-girl.
A magic hazel twig. A prince.
A desperate escape from danger.

This is not the story of a girl whose fairy godmother
arranges her future for her. This is the story of Selena,
who will take charge of her own destiny, and learn that
her magic is not to be feared but celebrated.

Available at all good retailers